Praise for Lindsay Starck's

Monsters We Have Made

"A riveting journey into the bright and terrifying landscape between what is real and what is imagined. In *Monsters We Have Made*, Lindsay Starck conjures an exquisitely suspenseful story of a nightmare crime and a family's hard-won love and forgiveness that can conquer even the most dangerous acts of the mind. Fast-paced and vivid, a book that will transport you to the edge of the familiar world and draw you back."

—Ariel Djanikian, author of *The Prospectors*

"For a parent, there is no greater fear than something happening to your child. In *Monsters We Have Made*, Lindsay Starck jams a knife right into this nerve. She—truly—scared the hell out of this reader, as I breathlessly followed these characters through years of love and heartbreak, mystery and paranoia and paralyzing horror. Beware the Kingman—and beware Lindsay Starck, who swallows you whole with her masterful storytelling."

—Benjamin Percy, author of *The Ninth Metal*

Lindsay Starck

Monsters We Have Made

Lindsay Starck was born in Wisconsin and raised in the Milwaukee Public Library. She is the author of the novel *Noah's Wife*, and her short fiction has appeared widely. She lives in Minneapolis with her husband and her cattle dog.

Monsters We Have Made

Monsters We Have Made

Lindsay Starck

Vintage Books
A Division of Penguin Random House LLC
New York

A VINTAGE BOOKS ORIGINAL, 2024

Library of Congress Cataloging-in-Publication Data
Names: Starck, Lindsay, author.
Title: Monsters we have made / Lindsay Starck.
Description: New York : Vintage Books, a division of
    Penguin Random House LLC, 2024.
Identifiers: LCCN 2023020428
Subjects: LCGFT: Fantasy fiction. | Novels.
Classification: LCC PS3619.T37335 M66 2024 |
    DDC 813/.6—dc23/eng/2020508
LC record available at https://lccn.loc.gov/2023020428

Vintage Books Trade Paperback ISBN: 978-0-593-47103-6
eBook ISBN: 978-0-593-47104-3

Book design by Steven Walker

vintagebooks.com

Printed in the United States of America
10 9 8 7 6 5 4 3 2 1

"Real isn't how you are made," said the Skin Horse.
"It's a thing that happens to you."

—Margery Williams, *The Velveteen Rabbit*

PART I

The Girls

Transcript: Emergency Dispatcher

April 13, 2008

—Nine one one. What is your emergency?

—Hey, yes, hello, I need—I need—

—Sir, what is the address of your emergency?

—It's not for me, it's—it's for—we found her on the side of the road, but I don't know who she is, I don't know her, oh God, her face is covered in—

—Your address, sir? I need the address of your emergency.

—It's—the woods along the Eno. The state park? I'm calling from the phone—that pay phone near the entrance. Can you—is there someone on the way?

—Yes, an ambulance should be there momentarily. Is this person conscious?

—She is, she says—wait—she says she's been—

—She's been what?

—Stabbed.

—[Static.]

—Hello? Hello?

—You're talking to her now, sir? She's breathing?

—She's breathing—but it's shallow, she's groaning. I'm worried— I'm worried that she's going to—I'm not trained, neither is my brother, I don't know—how to—how to do anything—we wouldn't know how to—

—Sir. Please stay calm, and stay on the line. How old is she?

—How old? I don't know! Fifteen? Sixteen? Is it important? How can—I don't—don't have any children, so—

—Sir, the paramedics are already on their way. Can you stay with her until they arrive?

—But if they don't get here in time, oh God, what the hell am I supposed to—

—Is she still conscious?

—[Static.]

—Sir? Are you still there?

—She says—she says she was stabbed and left here. We were out for a hike—we were maybe two miles in—and then I thought I saw someone, I saw something out of the corner of my eye, standing on the side of the trail, but when I turned my head there was nobody there, nothing but branches and leaves—

—Sir—

—But I slowed down, and five seconds later I saw her, I saw—oh God—

—Sir, the ambulance will be arriving any moment. Please stay calm, and listen for the sirens. Do you hear them yet?

—She said something about girls. [Static.] I can't understand her! Are there other girls out here somewhere? Do they need an ambulance, too? I don't know what to do, it's impossible to understand her—

—What about now? Can you hear the sirens?

—No, there's nothing else, no one else on the path but me and my brother and her, nothing out here but trees—and I'm just—I'm scared of—

—Sir. I need you to stay with me. Now listen again. Can you hear the sirens?

Sylvia

I grew up in a house of disappearing children. I want you to know this. I need you to see how the infants spun through my world like carousel horses, fretful and untamed. For thirteen days they would squall in their cradles and coo in my mother's arms, and on the fourteenth day the caseworker would click through the front door on her scuffed black pumps, sling the baby across the padded shoulder of her blazer, and crunch back down the crushed-shell driveway to her car. My mother and I would watch from behind the screened windows of the porch, the sea breeze ribboning through our limp hair, our elbows hoisted in a paltry imitation of a wave. The gulls pinwheeled overhead, and I imagined that I heard in their high-pitched, anguished cries an echo of the emotions that I did not yet have the words to express. The next month, a new infant would be swaddled and delivered to our door, and the carousel would careen around again.

I've tried to remember how the situation was first explained to me. Was it my sister who described the sterile hallways of a distant hospital, the nurses scuttling around a woman who was writhing on a white bed, straining to bring a baby into that fluorescent-lit room? While I didn't know what it meant to be in labor, somehow I came to understand that the infants who flitted through our lives possessed not one mother but two. In addition to the woman on the white bed, there was another shadow-figure, lingering somewhere nearby, waiting to spirit that child away.

It would be a long time before I learned about adoption laws, the transferal of parental rights, and the revocation of consent. Back then, between the ages of six and nine, all I knew was that I adored those strangers' babies. I spent hundreds of hours combing their bald heads and humming fragments of invented lullabies and, when I ran out of those, rattling off the names of all the seashells I could recall. *Coquinas, augers, olives, whelks.* I celebrated whenever a new infant arrived and I sobbed each time one of them left us, and I swore that when I was finally old enough to have a baby of my own, I'd never ever let her go.

Do you see what I mean? To figure out where I went wrong, I must tunnel back to the source. When I turned eighteen, I left the Carolina coast and drove three hours inland, through woods so lush that the emerald arms of branches wrapped around the highway. My second year in college, at a redbrick state university that towered over a town of bungalows and barbecues, I declared myself an English major. I made friends out of novels, and I wrote long-winded essays in a corner booth of the café near my dorm. I analyzed centuries-old poems with the furious patience of a detective assigned to a cold case, scanning line after line while patrons nearby clinked their pint glasses together or dipped their sweet potato fries into bowls of lightly garlicked mayo.

It was during my final year, in a course on the history of the English language, that I became hooked on etymologies. How thrilling to trace a word back to its source, to shovel down through generations until you strike a root! You cannot understand a thing until you've memorized its nuances and transformations, until you've tracked it back to the beginning. The word *origin* is from the Latin *originem*: a commencement, a rise, a lineage, a birth. The stem *oriri*: to appear above the horizon, to become visible. In other words, if you can uncover an origin, the world brightens. You see more clearly. Something that was once invisible is revealed to you, and as you drift through the corridor after class, the colored flyers fluttering on their pushpins as you pass, your head feels so heavy with knowledge and significance that your neck strains beneath its weight.

You see now why it is so important to understand about the babies. I want you to ache with my yearning for them; I want you to feel in your open palms, your empty arms, my hunger for a child of my own, and my fear—even then!—that if I loved her too much, she would be taken from me. Years later, when I was pregnant with Faye, I would hear in my dreams the clip of the caseworker's heels and the slam of her car door and the roar of that ancient engine, the sound ebbing as the distance expanded between us and another infant was carried away. I'd hug my swollen belly and sidle closer to Jack, who could somehow sense my distress even in his sleep. He'd roll onto his side and fling an arm across my bare shoulders and tug me toward his rib cage. "There, there," he'd murmur drowsily, his breath warm and unexpectedly sweet. "Everything will be all right."

When the doorbell rang last September—insistent, dismayed—my book tumbled from my hands to the floor. I jolted up and away from my armchair, but when I reached the front hall, I hesitated. The shadow on the other side of the textured glass door shifted its weight, cleared its throat, rang the bell again and then again. Through the window: the warnings of a red-winged blackbird.

I was remembering the first time the bell rang that way, thirteen years earlier. That morning, too, as I tugged my bathrobe over my shoulders and hurried to the door, I feared what waited on the other side.

Back then, it had been the police on my doorstep. Later, the investigators. After that, the reporters, the lawyers, the psychiatrists, the social workers. Years later, when I believed the furor had died down, I opened the door one afternoon to find a video camera shoved into my face. Three young men in black T-shirts and sunglasses took advantage of my surprise, wedging themselves between the door and its frame, and while I struggled to shut it again, they told me that they were making a documentary about the Kingman, and they needed to ask me a few questions.

That name—*the Kingman*—fueled my fear and my anger, calling the adrenaline to my arms and legs. I slammed the door against them and jammed the deadbolt back into place.

The Kingman. Even now, I can't say those words without shivering. My hand trembles if I write them. *The Kingman.* Look! Can you see how the letters blur and wobble on the page?

On the day that the Kingman entered our lives, Jack and I spent the morning in bed together. The plastic blinds were thumping against the windowsill, blown forward by a damp spring breeze. It's odd, isn't it, the things one remembers. It was early April, and the scent of spring was so powerful that I had not been able to resist the urge to throw the windows open. We'd fallen asleep in front of the blue glow of our crime shows the night before, and that morning Faye had gone to the woods with her best friend and her babysitter. It had become increasingly difficult to find time to be together like this—and so here we were in bed, making the most of Faye's absence, bars of light pinning us against the sheets.

I've returned to that moment a thousand times and more over the years that followed. It was the last time Jack and I would touch each other like that. Every other memory from that day, that month, that year, is perilous: toothy and bitter. But those minutes with Jack just before the doorbell rang—the loamy air whispering through open windows, the blankets tangled at our feet, the taste of cinnamon and Earl Grey on his tongue—well, those minutes took on the incredible, ethereal quality of a dream. It is a gift for me to remember them.

———

By the time I was ten, the steady flow of infants through the house had stopped. My mother, pulling double shifts at the hospital, returned home with her face haggard and her gaze unfocused. An early stroke had bound my father to his chair; my sister, nine years older than I was, had already left for school. Alone along the shore-line, I lobbed clamshells back into the waves and stalked among flocks of royal terns and pelicans.

When I found a great blue heron chick chirruping in the ditch that ran behind our mailbox, I built a nest from a box of T-shirt scraps and chopped up chunks of fish that my mother didn't see me sneaking from the freezer. For weeks, the yellow-eyed fledgling followed me through the tall grass of our backyard, cocking his head to the left when I read aloud to him from fairy tales and chapter books. By the time the heron had reached his full four-foot height, my father had grown sicker, and my mother was brittle and pale. When the bird finally tilted his tufted head toward the impassive sky, leaned into his pewter-blue wings, and relinquished me, the pain in my chest was so searing that for a moment I believed that my heart would tear through my torso in pursuit of him.

I remained earthbound. Still: whenever a feathered shadow crossed the sun, whenever I caught a glimpse of a familiar silhouette skimming over the reeds, I wondered if he was mine. Even now, hundreds of miles from the coast and decades away from that bird, I find my steps slowing and my pulse singing every time I approach a flock of birds on my walks around this snowcapped city.

I know that it's foolish. But this is what I'm trying to tell you. No matter how old we grow or how far we travel, we can never escape our childhood.

You can see the way a story proliferates, can't you, like a set of monstrous limbs? One scene lurches toward and seizes another, then another, and another, until the past is knotted with the present and it's difficult for even the storyteller to distinguish between what was real and what was imagined.

What I'm trying to say is that when the doorbell rang last September, it contained within it the sound of the bell ringing thirteen years earlier. Maybe that's why I dragged my feet down the hallway. Maybe that's why I took so long to open the door to the police officer waiting there with a gray-eyed child on her hip. Maybe it's because I was transported to the handful of minutes, sweet and aching, before I found myself alone again. Before Jack folded into himself like a paper plane. Before our friends and family fell away from us. Before the silence filled up that empty house like sunlight.

Interview with Lillian Pine, Former Durham Police Officer
Recorded on June 28, 2018

As soon as we got the call about the stabbing, the chief directed me
to find those other girls. The victim had told paramedics that two kids
were out there. She was breathing heavily. She'd lost some blood. She
seemed confused. But we didn't want to take any chances. What I mean
is, whoever stabbed her was still at large. We wanted to get to him
before he caught up with her friends and stabbed them, too. Some of us
scoured the state park: the woods, the river, the restrooms, everything.
The rest of us went out to the roads. We'd been patrolling the highways
for about an hour when we got a call from a driver who'd been listening
to the news. He said he'd seen two little white girls walking up I-85. He
pulled over, and they looked terrified. When he tried to tell them that he
wasn't going to do anything but take them home, they bolted. They ran
like fawns, the guy said.

I pictured it: the two of them taking off with the kind of grace that
girls lose when they get older. In my fifth-grade health class I'd learned
that when my hips got wider, I wouldn't be able to beat the boys in the
mile anymore. I remember thinking it wasn't fair, the way my body was
about to turn against me. When we headed back up the highway to find
those girls, I was remembering that age. You're not a teenager yet, but
you're close enough to know that in another couple years something
will be coming for you. When we finally caught sight of them trekking
through tall grass on the far side of the highway, ratty backpacks slung
across their bony shoulders, all I could think was: *Thank God they're
safe.* Ten years later, I still feel the heat of that relief. *Jesus Christ*, I said.
Thank God.

Of course back then we had no idea that this was only the beginning.
We couldn't know that when we got them in the squad car and secured
them in the precinct, they'd brought their monster with them, too.

Sylvia

I waited for the ghostly shape of the squad car to dissolve into the sycamore trees at the end of the road. Then I called Jack. As the phone rang and rang and rang, I imagined the cabin that I'd never seen: a pinewood porch with a single rocking chair behind the screen; a hand-carved stool beneath the kitchen counter; a plaid comforter pulled square across the bed; shelves and night-stand spare and dusted, devoid of knickknacks, picture frames. Through the window: the haze of blue-gray mountains hanging over the horizon.

"Yes?" Jack grunted when he finally lifted the receiver.

I tried to sound as though picking up the phone and dialing his number a few seconds earlier had not made my fingers tremble. "It's me," I said.

From his end of the line: the creak and slam of a porch door and the four-note trill of a Carolina chickadee. I pictured him leaning against a porch railing, the muscles of his shoulders hard beneath his flannel. Perhaps his gaze was fixed on the ridges in the distance, crowned with spruces and firs. When he took a shaky breath, I could almost taste the woodsmoke and pine on my tongue.

"What's going on?" he asked.

The words skidded out of me. "The police were just here," I said. "With Amelia."

The nature of Jack's silence changed. I knew his face so well that even in that moment, a lifetime away from him, I could see

the worry crinkling in the corners of his eyes, could feel the dread
stiffening his limbs. I knew that within seconds, he would be shoving his hand through his untamed hair. It felt like a betrayal, an
invasion, that I could still sense his thoughts and fears so piercingly.
Is it always this way with people who once loved each other?

I had been engaged to someone else when I met Jack. It had been
my fiancé who insisted that I make an appointment with an eye
doctor. For months, peculiar shapes had been slinking through my
peripheral vision. On one of our Saturday morning hikes, I'd out-
stripped him on the trail, plunging deeper into the woods, fighting
knotted roots and stumbling over rotting trunks, following a flickering silhouette that hovered just beyond my line of sight. When
I paused for breath, I realized I was lost. By the time I'd made my
way back to the parking lot, several hours had passed, and my
fiancé was placing panicked calls to park rangers. Once we were
home, he made me promise that I'd see a doctor.

The doctor turned out to be Jack, his white coat crisp and his
beard cropped close. I don't believe in love at first sight, but Jack
does. He'd walked into the room and seen me leaning back in the
chair with a mystery novel flipped open on my lap, my hair long
and my gaze steady. He'd noticed and dismissed as irrelevant the
glint of my engagement ring. He told me later that although he
knew we'd never met before, he'd recognized me as if from a vision
or a dream.

Once, he told me that the same feeling, that warm tide of recognition, had crashed over him years later in the delivery room when
the nurses had placed Faye in his trembling arms. The labor had
lasted for thirty hours, and by the time she emerged, her skin glistening faintly blue beneath the hospital lights, Jack was so numbed
with terror and exhaustion that he feared he wouldn't have the
strength to hold her. But then: *I know you*, he had thought, gaping at
her wrinkled face in the seconds before she began to wail. *I've seen
you before.*

Recognize. From the Old French *reconoistre*: to identify from a previous experience or former encounter; to acknowledge as true. In thirteenth-century British sources: to investigate by jury; to find guilty.

The eye appointment was supposed to last for fifteen minutes, but Jack kept me in that examination room for over an hour. By the time I stepped out, my fiancé was pacing between the rows of plastic and wire frames, twisting his fingers together, his body coiled with tension. He sprang forward at the sight of me. Jack watched us from a few yards away, reclining against the doorframe as if melded to it, his gaze hooded and his posture deliberately lazy. I glanced back at him on my way out, trying not to imagine what it would be like to press him up against that door, to feel his skillful fingers sliding underneath my skirt. He caught my gaze and held it until I was forced to turn away.

On the way home, my fiancé asked what Jack had said about the ghost shapes in my line of sight. "He said not to worry," I replied absently. "With time and rest, they'll disappear."

I didn't tell my fiancé that Jack had spent most of the hour tilting toward me with his fist on his chin, his gaze keen and searching, the light twinkling along the burnished frames of his glasses. He'd asked about my hobbies, my family, my job. When I told him about my bookstore, he showered me with questions about it. He made so thorough a list of my favorite titles that I almost believed he needed the information for my file. When the hour was nearing its end and his assistant was sighing loudly outside his door, he jolted to his feet and announced that he'd definitely need to see me again.

"There's one more test I'd like to run," he said. When I asked him what it was, I could see him thinking quickly. "Color blindness," he replied, and grinned. The sudden illumination of his face was as blinding as a camera flash. I blinked into the light and smiled back.

A few weeks later, he called to say he had a batch of eye drops that he wanted me to try. He persuaded me to order a new pair of glasses and then informed me, unapologetically, that the shipment was delayed. I made three trips before they were in my hands. Right there in the optical shop, in full view of his staff and his other patients, he adjusted the glasses around the curve of my face and slid his fingers gently into my hair.

"I've run out of reasons to get you here," he murmured, his face inches from mine. By then, I'd memorized it. I knew the angle of his arched eyebrow, the white scar that trailed like a comet along his jaw. The throaty hum of his voice spun through the whorls of my ear for hours after I'd left him. I assumed I'd eventually shake off the crush. Instead, something inside me shifted when I gazed at him through those new glasses. The shop crystallized, and I saw in his bearing, in his eyes and his chin and the pale twist of his lips, a vision of my future child.

From behind us came the sound of my fiancé clearing his throat. I rose to my feet and went home with him. But not too long after, I came back for Jack.

After everything happened, after our love curdled and our family turned sour, I found myself obsessing over that afternoon in the optical shop. I worried over the memory like a tongue over a rotting tooth. Was that the moment where I went wrong? Jack was my doctor, after all, and I'd promised to marry a different man. Were we being punished because we'd broken rules and hearts? Was our relationship, at its core, too selfish to remain intact?

One day, after Jack had left, I'd typed my former fiancé's name into a search engine. The page had filled up with images of his wife and children, and I'd hunched over the screen to scrutinize their faces. I was looking for shadows, I realized; for worry lines, for signs of tension or despair. But no matter how long I scanned the photographs, the faces of that family stayed radiant and blissful. Their eyes shone and their teeth gleamed in pearly, obedient rows.

It's easy to spot happiness when you're not feeling it. It's natural to envy those who possess it and to curse yourself for losing it.

On the phone, Jack's first question was the most obvious one. "Where's Faye?"

Fingers tapped against the kitchen window: the branches of the black cherry tree bumping along the glass. Sunlight slid through its leaves and cast emerald rays into the sink. Outside, a royal-blue sky draped over the rose garden and the wishing pool and, beyond the fence, the tangled woods of the park. I could tell, from the swaying treetops, that the wind was picking up.

"They couldn't find her," I replied. "They asked if I knew where she was."

I heard his thoughts ticking through a multitude of possibilities. I'd forgotten how long it took for him to arrive at a solution; he needed to work through every alternative before making a choice.

"What did you tell them?"

A firework exploded in my chest. "I told them the truth, Jack. I said that I haven't seen her in years."

"Sylvia," he said quietly, warningly. He'd heard the dizzying surge of my voice. He knew what I was thinking, understood the words I'd left unspoken. His instinct was to say something consoling, but what was there to say?

I'm a terrible mother, I'd wanted to confess to the police. *I don't know where my daughter is.*

One after another, everyone we knew produced children. Former classmates, roommates, neighbors, and colleagues. They all toppled as easily, as predictably, into parenthood as a line of dominoes.

Once, at a backyard ceremony that Jack's friends had arranged to announce the name of their forthcoming son, I retreated to the kitchen. I stood at the sink, pretending to rinse out my glass of champagne, and watched Jack through the window. He stood at the edge of the golden yard, among a clump of dogwood trees, with his face turned toward the sky, shielding his eyes with his hand. A bunch of balloons that had slipped from its decorative mooring was rising higher and higher. After a few minutes, the rest of the party strolled back to the picnic table to help themselves to slices of cake. But Jack stayed where he was. He didn't move until long after the balloons had vanished, blue on blue, into the wash of autumn sky.

I dried my glass and filled it again. Then I carried it out to the yard and crossed the lawn. Although he smiled when I drew near, his gaze was distant and his expression was opaque. I sipped my drink and slanted against him while he twined his fingers through the ends of my hair. As I felt the warmth of his skin seep through my blouse, I remembered, as I often did in those days, the phantom child I'd glimpsed in his face many years earlier. She'd been as clear to me then as sunshine, as water. I tightened my grip around my glass, willing it to shatter against my palm. Why was it so hard to conjure her into existence?

Jack, of course, never wavered. He never complained about the expanding stable of doctors. He was willing to spend our savings on fertility treatments. His commitment to parenthood didn't falter until the morning he found me in the bathroom with my head in my hands and my elbows on my knees, shuddering so hard that I couldn't breathe.

"Hey, Syl," he said. "Hey, what's wrong?"

He knew what was wrong. He could see the pregnancy test propped against the cracked porcelain bowl of the sink. He held me while I cried, rocking back and forth with me on the bath mat. When I'd stopped, he announced that something had to change.

Two days later he marched into the house with tickets to New York, slapped them on the kitchen counter, and told me that we were leaving in two weeks.

"We need a break from this," he said.

I didn't see how a weekend away would change anything, but I went along with it to make him happy. The skies were slate gray, wet. The East River bucked at its banks while we strolled over bridges and tossed hunks of our sandwiches toward the gulls. The rain was cold and clean, and at night the yellow light from streetlamps pooled in the streets. When I went out on our hotel balcony, Jack followed me with my raincoat and a warm café au lait he'd requested at the counter downstairs. I lifted the drink to my wind-chapped lips and tried to do the only thing he'd asked of me: I tried not to think about children.

The following morning, he led me to a tiny corner café he'd read about in his guidebook. The few walls that weren't windowed were covered in mirrors and floating shelves of fake flowers. Our little table was bathed in silver light, and the pastries were too beautiful to eat.

"Listen," he said. He took my hands in his. "I don't want to do this anymore. I don't like what it's doing to you. To us."

I gazed out the window. Clouds of black umbrellas. The splash of yellow taxis through wide, open puddles. "We don't have a choice," I said.

At this, he squeezed my hands more tightly. "We *do*, though, Syl. We *do*. We could stop trying." He saw my expression but barreled forward. "We could say—screw it. We could fill our lives in other ways. Travel. Friends. Don't you think?"

"I *think*—" I began, but he heard my tone and cut me off.

"Hold on. Lots of people choose not to have kids. I know you loved all those babies when you were young—"

"*Yes*, and—"

"But you were just a kid yourself. Don't you think it's possible that now, as an adult, you might be able to love something else? Why do we have to go through this heartache *every single god-damn month?*" He slammed his fist on the table, and the silverware jumped. The server glanced our way, flicked her braid over her shoulder, and then, when she tired of watching us glare at each other, returned to her glossy magazine at the coffee bar.

I was angry at Jack for asking those questions. Most people who had babies didn't have to come up with reasons why they should.

Because I love you, I didn't say. *Because we don't know how much time we'll have together. Because if something ever happened to you, I'd want a part of you to keep.*

Now the silence between us was swelling through the phone line.

"Wait a minute," Jack finally said to me. "You said that the police had Amelia with them."

"They did." I could have described how the three-year-old clung to the officer's torso, her solemn gaze a mirror of her mother's at that age. But I was afraid to admit how I'd shuddered at the sight of her.

"Where is she now?"

I craned my neck and peered over my shoulder at the shadow huddled over a bowl of dry cereal on the living room couch.

"They left her here with me."

"They *left*—"

"That's why I'm calling, Jack," I said. "I don't know what to do."

When Jack and I stopped trying for a child, we filled our days in other ways. We tallied up our vacation days and tore through our savings. That winter we drove west, winding our way through the arches of Moab, the peaks of Zion, the hoodoos of Bryce. For six weeks we caught sunsets in orange canyons and we drank red wine in rented cabins and we built fires in woodstoves and we hiked for miles and miles and miles through the parks, our breath crisp and our limbs burning, hoping that somewhere along those icy, lonely trails, we'd be able to lose our longing for a child. We had sex when we felt like it, beneath the raw-pine beams of our bedroom ceilings, the snow drifting in fat white flakes outside the window. I didn't chart anything, time anything. I simply inhaled the scent of Jack's aftershave, gouged my fingertips into the muscles between his shoulder blades, relished the weight of his body on mine.

When our savings had dwindled and our six weeks were up, we pulled back into our driveway. I stowed our suitcases in the basement and returned to the bookstore. I started running again, training for a marathon: early morning sprints on the treadmill before work and long jogs along the creek on the weekend.

Months passed. When my dreams were troubled, I ignored them. When lights and shadows appeared in my peripheral vision again, I ignored them, too. I laced up my jogging shoes, stretched my hamstrings, stepped out into the street, and took several deep, rattling breaths. Every day that I ran, I beat my time from the day before. By the time I was a mile in, my breath was coming sharp and even and my heartbeat was thrumming in time with my sneakers.

Yet on the morning of my first marathon, I woke feeling drained. It was October; the sky was soft and gray. I dragged myself out of bed and got dressed and stumbled down to the kitchen, where Jack was already preparing coffee and whistling along with the radio. He handed me a mug and kissed me long and hard and told me he was proud of me.

When the gun exploded at the starting line, the other runners surged forward in a thundering wave of colored jerseys. Though I forced my legs to keep up, I was running through water. I had trouble breathing; every step was a struggle.

On the side of the road, throngs of spectators brandished glittering signs and cheered. When they saw me, some of them cheered more fiercely and some of them grew silent. "Hey!" one or two yelled. "Number four hundred and thirteen! Are you all right?"

I dragged myself forward, willing the adrenaline to kick in. At the first water station, I took a sip and felt nauseated. At the second, I pulled up short and staggered, my feet as useless as cotton. When a volunteer handed me my paper cup, I saw that his face was not a face at all: it was flat and featureless as a wooden board. I toppled backward. Two jagged branches jerked out of nowhere to snag me, and I twisted to avoid them. It was with relief that I felt the slap of my cheek against cool, damp pavement.

By the time I was lucid enough to tell a volunteer where to find Jack, he'd been waiting for me for an hour. On the way to the doctor's office, he propelled the car through red lights. His face had lost its color; his jaw was set. I leaned back in the passenger seat with my eyes closed and my head aching.

When the doctor informed us of the test results, we were stunned into silence. We didn't celebrate with balloons or sparkling cider. We didn't shout, or cheer. Jack simply tightened his grip on my hand and took me home and put me to bed. Soon we would have a baby, he murmured, his breath warm. The words sang in my ear like a prophecy or a spell.

That was the memory that surfaced as I waited for him to say something back to me, the side of my face hot against the phone. I was thinking about how he used to fold his body around mine. I was remembering the tickle of his beard at the nape of my neck and the sweep of his dry fingertips across my skin. He used to know exactly what I needed.

I glanced through the kitchen doorway to the living room, where the little girl cowered on the corner of the sofa. The pale blue light from the television washed out her narrow face, and she hugged her knees to her chest. She was pretending not to listen.

"Jack," I murmured. I strained to hear something, anything. "Please. I need you to come help me with this. You know I wouldn't ask—"

His voice cleaved through my request. A cloud obscured the late afternoon sun, and the whole house dimmed. "I'm on my way," he said. "Stay right where you are."

Exhibit A: Objects Recovered from Backpacks

- four juice packs (Capri Sun)
- two boxes of granola bars (oatmeal raisin)
- three apples
- one bag of chips (classic potato)
- one spiral-bound notebook + pens
- five photo frames with images of family members
- six books (Susan Cooper's *The Boggart*; collected fairy tales of the Brothers Grimm; Peter S. Beagle's *The Last Unicorn*; Jean Craighead George's *My Side of the Mountain*; J. M. Barrie's *Peter Pan*; *The Complete Book of Drawing*)
- assorted clothing: pants, T-shirts, sweatshirts, underwear, socks
- two toothbrushes, one tube of toothpaste
- one fleece blanket
- one flashlight
- two stuffed animals (one kangaroo, one bear)
- one hand-drawn map of the shores of Lake Superior (not to scale)
- one artist's knife (still stained)

Jack

Jack approached his former life like a homing pigeon: thoughtless, by instinct, the path straight and true. The truck hurtled down from the Blue Ridge Mountains and careened through stands of beeches and hemlocks. He skittered into the valley and through the Piedmont, going eighty or more. The sun was setting at his back. The sky glowed blood orange.

He cranked down the windows and turned up the folk songs. If he worked at it, he was able to hold Sylvia somewhere outside himself. Over the past thirteen years, he'd become skilled at not thinking about her. He couldn't think about her. So on most days, he simply didn't.

Most people who have a kid like to see themselves in her. The color of her eyes, her hair. The way she moves. Her love of hiking, blueberries, birdsong. Jack did that, too. Looked for signs of himself in Faye. That's why people procreate, right? To replicate themselves?

Then came the crime. That made him look harder. Like Faye, he could be impulsive. He could get lost in stories. He could get irritated by unfairness. That's one reason why he didn't go to the hearing: because he knew he'd blow up, cause a scene, and say what he'd been thinking. *We read the books. We took the classes.* He could hear the words jetting out of his mouth. *There are thousands of parents who don't know what the hell they're doing, who actively fuck everything up.* He could picture Sylvia sitting straight-backed on the hard bench beside him with her face drained of color and her heart cleft in two. *So why'd this have to happen to* us?

When the phone jangled through the silent cabin, something popped inside him. He hadn't realized he'd been tense. Expectant. But as soon as he heard her voice, he knew that he'd been waiting for this call. She'd always been able to knock the breath out of him with the way she said his name. *Jack.* Like an ax slicing through silk. *Jack.*

There'd been a slew of new crimes in the past year, after the documentary was released. In Tennessee, a ten-year-old girl donned a white mask. She yanked a kitchen knife from the butcher block on the counter and crouched in the dark until her neighbor walked in. In Wisconsin, two sisters tried to feed their teacher poisonous mushrooms. Other children chose baseball bats or homemade explosives. One poured gasoline around the foundation of his coach's house; then he lit the place on fire.

They all failed in their efforts. The adults survived, horrified. When interrogated, the kids blamed the Kingman. Said he spoke to them. Read their minds. Visited them in dreams. Said that if they didn't do what he instructed, their families' fates would be far worse.

Jack didn't mention these kids to Sylvia when she called. He doubted she was aware. For all he knew, she was still refusing to read the news. In any case, the stories hadn't appeared in major outlets. The articles had been tiny local pieces published in small-town papers. He'd learned of them only because he'd programmed the search engine to alert him when news included the word *Kingman.* That's how he knew that the documentary came out a year before. Following that, these copycat crimes.

The point is that the Kingman had been quiet for years. Until recent months, the monster had lain low. Now the violence was rising and Faye had gone missing. It didn't take an expert to hypothesize a connection: his daughter was up to something.

He was out of the cabin before Sylvia had finished filling him in. He was in the truck, scrambling down the gravel road, his heart hammering against his ribs. It was still hammering four hours later when he reached the front door and found her on the other side, slender as a switchblade, her hair flaming against the hall light behind her. He pulled her close before he could stop himself. He knew better. He felt her muscles tense. But he held her for five, six seconds anyway, before they walked inside to find the girl. He inhaled, exhaled. Breathed her in.

Interview with Lillian Pine, Former Durham Police Officer
Recorded on June 28, 2018

I was young when it happened. About your age, probably. Twenty-four, twenty-five? Eyes so clear you can see straight through to your future. Bones so strong you can't believe you'll ever die.

Still, I wasn't as young as they were. Nine. Filthy and scared. And of what? We had to tug the story out of them, word by word. Even then, we couldn't make sense of it. When they described someone who watched for them and called to them, we pictured your average pervert skulking around in the shrubbery. The chief sent guys out looking for somebody like that. They searched for him all day. When they came back, they said they'd gotten close. They'd heard a crashing through the trees. They'd felt somebody's gaze. They'd caught a glimpse of a guy in a sunlit clearing, but he'd taken off by the time they reached it.

Meanwhile I'd been left with the girls. Their faces were muddy and scratched. One of them shrank against the cinder-block wall with her knees pulled to her chest and her head buried in her arms. The other one stared at me. I'd learned her name was Faye.

"You'll never catch him," she said. Her voice was raw.

I asked her why not.

"Because he's not like everybody else," she said. "He walks without footprints. He talks without a mouth. He can wait a long time in the woods without eating or sleeping. He never gets too hot or too cold. And if he doesn't want to be seen, the trees swallow him up."

I looked at her: hair knotted in a ponytail, T-shirt torn and stained with blood. The skin prickled on the back of my neck.

"Sounds like make-believe," I said.

"That's the idea," she said.

Suddenly I was feeling light-headed. "You seem to know a lot about him," I said. Maybe she'd give me some information that I could report back to the chief. Help along the search. "Who is this guy?"

That's when the other one lifted her tearstained face from her knees and shot Faye a look that Faye pretended not to see.

"You must have heard of him," she continued.

"How would I have heard of him?" I said.

"Because the Kingman has been around forever," she said. "Because the Kingman is very, very old." Then something occurred to her. Her focus sharpened.

"Do you have kids?" she asked.

"No," I said.

She nodded firmly, like everything was clearer now. "No wonder you don't know him, then. He's not interested in you."

Sylvia

My heart stalled at the sight of Jack on the front porch. Then he hugged me and I breathed again. He was thinner than I remembered him: more delicate, with half-moons beneath his black gaze and patches of silver in his beard. My pulse thundered in my ears, and I had to pull back to hear his greeting. As soon as I leaned away, his arms dropped to his sides and dangled there, limp and useless. The stars eyed us from above the tree line.

"Where is she?" he asked.

I led him through the living room and into the kitchen, where a pendant lamp floated above the dining table. In the pool of white light sat the little girl, a plate of cooling casserole in front of her. Her fork rested exactly where I'd arranged it, and her hands were clasped in her lap. At our approach she glanced up with an expression of surprise so like her mother's that both Jack and I froze. Her gaze was ash gray and opaque, her skin flushed. Her hair, as black and glossy as mine once was, had been flattened to her scalp by the knit cap she'd been wearing when she arrived. The effect accentuated her moon-shaped face, her knobby nose and ears like arrows.

Jack cleared his throat and tried to say her name. The girl's focus flicked from me to him. He tried again and succeeded, though the words were ragged. "Amelia, I'm—Jack. Grandpa Jack."

She didn't respond. For an eternity, the three of us held our collective breath. Even the house, usually groaning in the evening breeze, was still. The girl angled her head.

When Jack spoke again, his voice was more controlled, his tone resolute. "Can you tell us where your mother is?"

We'd tried to see Amelia once, almost four years ago, right after she'd been born. I'd received a call from the hospital to let me know that Faye was in labor. When I relayed the message to Jack, he drove straight down from the mountains. I hadn't expected him to show up at the hospital; I'd called only because he had a right to know.

But we couldn't find them there. Jack and I wandered the hospital hallways for a while, poking our heads into white rooms, both hoping and dreading to stumble upon them. Finally we found ourselves outside the nursery, staring at all those babies lined up in neat rows. We were standing a few feet apart, but Jack extended his arm and gripped my hand. I remember that—I remember the distance between us, and the sizzle of his touch. I remember how, for days afterward, my palm felt scorched and raw. By that point, we hadn't touched each other in years. Not like that, anyway. Not with tenderness, or hunger, or kindness.

I must have been crying. Why else would he have reached for my hand? When I stood in that hallway, gazing at those babies, I recalled standing there nineteen years earlier, overcome by the sight of my daughter. How dazzling she'd been; how flawless, how miraculous. I don't know how long I swayed there, staring at her, trembling on weak legs, one palm pressed to the wall to hold myself upright. I don't know if it was a nurse or if it was Jack who finally pulled me away and guided me back to bed. Someone tucked me in and held a glass of water to my cracked lips.

I remember the doctor's irritation when I was discovered outside the nursery window again, in the middle of the night, my forehead smashed up against the glass in order to better discern my daughter's outline in the darkness. I didn't know how to explain my wild need to watch over her, my certainty that if I were not with her, I could lose her.

"What do you think will happen?" the doctor demanded.

We were alone in the hallway. I heard the click of long-ago heels and the rippling of feathered wings preparing for flight.

"I don't know," I said.

I was embarrassed to tell her that my head was crammed with fears and superstitions, that I'd been dreaming of the old folktales even before my labor pains began. In those stories, infants are consumed or replaced by fairies or spirits. *Wechselkind*, the Grimm brothers called these false children. In other cultures: sprites, changelings. Mothers who suspect that their babies are not their own are instructed to hold the infants over a fire or float them on the water.

But I couldn't tell the amber-eyed doctor, with her clipboard and her medical degree, that I feared my daughter could be stolen away. I was bone-tired from giving birth; I was sleep deprived and dream walking. That's why I let her lead me back to my room, and I pretended to believe her when she assured me that I would feel better in the morning.

In former times, when people recognized something ominous in a child, they tried to drive that darkness out. But in the hospital nursery, those tiny faces are scrubbed until they shine. Those little bodies are tucked snug into clean blankets and lined up in rows as even as scales. It's impossible to tell them apart. And so I found myself wondering, as I drifted to sleep on an unfamiliar pillow, how a modern mother could ever recognize the darkness in a place that blinds her with light.

I could hear Jack roaming through the rooms downstairs while I bathed Amelia and put her to bed. Did he, too, feel like a ghost in this house? After he'd left, our home had become strange to me. How many hours did I spend looking for can openers, for cooking utensils, for linens and rain gear and matches? Years later, even after I'd grown accustomed to his absence, there were still days when I'd find myself running my hands over the furniture and brushing every object on the coffee table, countertops, book-shelves. In the kitchen, I'd swing open all the cabinet doors and I'd touch everything there, too: piece by piece, drawer by drawer. Serving fork, corkscrew, garlic press, spoon. I couldn't say what I was looking for. Solace, probably. Sustenance. Perhaps I was also looking for Jack.

And now here he was, waiting for me downstairs, pacing from end to end of the screened porch while brittle leaves rattled in the woods beyond us. He halted when I appeared at the door. It was too dark for me to read his expression. I moved to the porch swing and eased myself into it. The splintered slats creaked but bore me.

"How is she?" he asked.

I'd left her sleeping on the sofa bed in the spare bedroom, her tiny form engulfed in the softest cotton shirt I could find, her head sinking into an oversize pillow. A night-light glimmered in the corner. I'd lingered in the doorway for several minutes, watching the rise and fall of the blankets while my own breath cycloned through my chest.

"She's tired."

"Has she said anything?"

"Not a word."

He twisted around to consider the house, yellow beams spilling out into the night. I stole a glance at his expression, suddenly illuminated. His face was craggier than it had been, roughened by the fiercer wind and sun of high altitudes. He'd given up his practice when he moved to the mountains, living off the proceeds of the optical shop. How did he spend his days?

"Is it normal?" he asked. "For a kid her age not to speak?"

I shrugged, fearing that he'd see the way my body strained to reach him. "I don't know."

Before Faye was born, I'd studied every parenting book we had stocked in the bookshop. I pored over chapters between customers and took notes in a softcover sketchbook. I remember calling my mother from the register to read aloud passages and ask her for her advice; I remember the way she laughed at me.

"You can't study your way into motherhood, my dear," she said. But I was pretty sure I could.

It was not the first time, there on the porch swing, that I wondered what Faye had read and whom she had called whenever she had questions about Amelia. Had she ever wanted to talk to me?

Jack was pacing and the pine boards were protesting. I slid across the swing to make room for him. While he eyed the empty space, I told him about how Amelia had been discovered in Faye's car. The keys were dangling from the ignition; the registration papers, stained with dirty water and juice-box spills, were crammed into the glove box. The permanent address on the papers was this one. That was why they had brought the car and the child to me.

Jack heaved a sigh and collapsed next to me. The wooden slats groaned again, and my skin tingled where he brushed against me. After a few minutes of silence, he said: "What the fuck are we supposed to do now?"

I found that it wasn't too difficult to dismiss my fears and superstitions once we'd returned home from the hospital with Faye. She turned out to be an easy baby to love, with her silky black hair and her saucer eyes. Her skin was sprinkled with tiny white bumps that rolled over her cheeks like ocean spray. Sometimes I'd trace my fingers over her face as if I could read her future in it.

We spent hundreds of nights together in her room, rocking back and forth near the window while the rest of the world slept. During the most arduous weeks of her infancy, her gaze flitted through the dark, never settling. By three months, she began to focus on my face. She stared at my features as if she were trying to place me; as if she'd known my name once and was struggling to recall it. At six months, she strained toward the window. As a toddler, she liked to rest her chin on the ledge and turn her face toward the hazy mass of trees beyond the garden. I'd join her there, my gaze beaming across the silent yard like a searchlight, roving over the flagstones and the rosebushes, straining to see whatever it was that drew her again and again to the glass.

Like other parents, I read aloud to my child: stories about velveteen rabbits and wandering ducks and hungry caterpillars. But it was the fairy tales that she liked best. Her eyes grew wide when she heard about wolves in grandmothers' nightgowns or princes cursed into swans. She liked bears and dragons, trolls and fairies. For her sixth birthday I special-ordered a Brothers Grimm collection, a weighty tome with gold-stamped lettering and woodcut illustrations that Faye traced so frequently with the tip of her finger that I half expected the ink to wear away from the snow-white pages.

"Do you believe in magic, Mama?" she asked me once, a few weeks later, as I was bending down to flip on the night-light beside her bed. By the time she turned seven, she would insist on sleeping in absolute darkness.

I remember looking up at her radiant face above me and thinking about how long I had waited for her and how impossible a dream she had once seemed. That is why I answered: "Yes, my little sparrow. I do."

As she grew up, I found myself admiring the way that she moved through the world: the fluidity with which she poured the milk on her cereal, the waltz of her steps toward the mailbox, the perfect arc of her arm as she hurled pine cones and acorns in the garden. Sometimes I could hear myself in her voice or see Jack in the turn of her head. There was magic in this, too.

If there were moments when the light shifted and her face became unfamiliar to me, or times when her silent appearance in a room sent a tingle down my spine, I ignored them. There were groceries to be purchased, books to be ordered, shrubs to be pruned. My life was too full for mystery.

———

Here is the scene that the police officers described to me: The little Ford Escort idling in a handicapped space in the grocery store parking lot. The headlights blinding; the radio blaring. The stranger who came over to knock on the window, to see what was going on, and who found the child fast asleep in her car seat. He opened the door and lifted her to his shoulder, cradled her head in his hand, carried her inside, and asked the manager to call for her mother over the intercom. Later he told the officers that he wanted to remind this mother of the dangers of leaving a child unattended in a parking lot. People were all kinds of crazy, he was going to tell her. Did she have any idea how many shifty characters were lurking out there, looking for an opportunity to commit their dark crimes? Didn't she know that parents could not let down their guard for a minute?

As I relayed the scene to Jack, I saw the halos of yellow lights in the parking lot; I heard the purr of the idling engine. I squeezed my eyelids shut and tried to imagine what Faye might have glimpsed through the early morning fog. I couldn't believe that she had walked away on her own two legs, of her own free will. What if she had been forcibly removed from her daughter? What if there had been someone, something, waiting to snatch her away?

The moon was swinging over the house like a pendulum. I'd brought out two mugs of tea, and the porch was cloaked in chamomile. "What now?" Jack asked again.

I'd been circling the same question all afternoon. "Now we have to find Faye."

Jack snorted. "The police have to find Faye."

I told him that I'd declined to file a missing-person report. Although I could feel the weight of his gaze in the dark, I kept my chin turned pointedly forward. "Do you really want to deal with the police again?" I asked. "The reporters? The—"

"Of course not." His words were sharp. He had not forgotten the clamor of newscasters or the camera flashes through gaps in window curtains. When he spoke again, his tone was milder. "But where would we even start?"

I'd anticipated this question, too. "Her key ring includes the keys to her apartment," I said. "That seems as logical a place as any."

Another silence settled between us. A twig cracked beneath the porch, reminding me of the kitten Jack had found there years ago. He'd scrabbled among the dry brush and firewood and emerged filthy and beaming, a lump of matted fur drawn to his chest. A pair of green eyes glinted from between his sleeves. She was cream colored after her bath in the kitchen sink, skittish and skeletal. I remember Jack's patience with her, the soothing croon of his voice when he had to coax her out from underneath the couch. Faye must have been Amelia's age then, or a little younger. When she woke from her nap and caught sight of the kitten curled in a flimsy cardboard garment box, she squealed with pleasure. She spent hours cuddling that kitten on her lap and dragging yarn across the kitchen floor. Her laughter in those days: as silver as sleigh bells.

"Have you ever been there before?" Jack asked. "To her apartment?"

I nearly laughed aloud at the thought. The idea of Faye inviting me over, making me dinner, topping my glass with water or wine—impossible. But the bubble of amusement died away before it reached my lips.

"No."

"You know where it is?"

"Windy Cove sent me a notice when she moved out," I told him. "With her new address. Didn't they send it to you, too?"

He nodded and raised his mug, but he didn't drink. He could see what was coming. "And you want me to stay here with Amelia?"

"That's what I was hoping."

His gaze probed my face, and heat rose to my cheeks. How did I look to him? After he'd left, I'd dragged out that book of illustrated fairy tales and recognized myself in their pages: the old witch with parched skin and hollow cheeks. My hair turned silver almost instantly, as if by magic. I had waited for the woods to surge beyond the fence and overtake the house. I'd imagined vines creeping up the bricks, swallowing the shingles. At least then, the house would not have been visible to the tourists who cruised down the road in rental cars, who'd read about the crime and wanted to see where the infamous Faye Vogel had grown up and gone wrong.

Now the house was pulsing with new life, breathing in a way it hadn't breathed in years. I wanted to rise, to go check on the girl sleeping upstairs. But I also wanted to stay where I was, rocking on the porch swing, six inches away from Jack.

"What if I went with you?" he asked.

In our former life, Jack had always wanted to come with me. I remembered trips to the grocery store when I would turn away from a pyramid of plastic strawberry containers to find him folded over the handlebar of the shopping cart, nudging it back and forth with a sneakered foot, watching me with concentrated pleasure. He joined me in the waiting room for oil changes or dentist appointments, flipping through the women's fashion magazines to show me dresses that he thought I'd like. He became such a weekend fixture at the bookstore that I finally put him to work as the reader for our Saturday morning children's book circle. They rushed to his chair after his performance and clung to his knees when their parents called for them to leave.

I shook my head, even though he couldn't see the motion in the dark. "No," I said. "We can't drag Amelia all over town in search of her mother. We don't know what she's been through. You'll be able to keep her company. Keep her calm."

It was three in the morning by then, and he was too exhausted to argue. We carried the mugs inside, and a few minutes later he was sprawled across the sofa, snoring. I shuffled upstairs, looked in on Amelia, and then lay down on my bed without bothering to undress. I watched the moonlight swing across the ceiling and I thought about my daughter.

I wanted to track her down and embrace her. I wanted to peer into the shadows of her face and promise her that everything would be okay. And after that I wanted to scold her, to grab her hand and drag her home to be with her child.

You can't just give up on people, I'd tell her. *Once a mother, always a mother.*

I could already see the way that she'd look at me. I could feel the judgment, swift and searing. Here's what she would be thinking: *Who the hell do you think you are?*

Stabbing Victim in Stable Condition
April 15, 2008

WASHINGTON (AP)—Doctors at Duke University Hospital in Durham, North Carolina, stated today that Brittany Sawyer, 16, is in stable condition after two days of surgeries following a brutal stabbing.

Officials say that she had been called Sunday morning by a family she often worked for to accompany their nine-year-old daughter and her friend to the state park. The two girls allegedly brought their sitter out into the woods and attacked her with knives they had stolen from the art room at their school. After they left, the victim crawled through the trees to the side of a road, where she was discovered by a pair of hikers.

The attackers were located shortly afterward and taken into custody. Both are currently awaiting a hearing in juvenile court.

Sylvia

The apartment complex sprawled across acres of clipped dry grass, man-made ponds, and asphalt parking lots. The roads wound around squat wooden buildings and looped through groves of adolescent maple trees whose leaves were limp in the September heat. It had taken me only half an hour to reach the complex, but it took me a half hour more to find Faye's apartment once I was there.

When I'd left the house, Jack had been flipping pancakes on the griddle while Amelia silently supervised him from her position at the dining table. Against the tall wooden back of the chair she'd chosen, still enveloped in my shirt, she looked even smaller than she had the night before. Her attention was so glued to Jack that she didn't notice when I entered the room, and she startled when I rested my fingertips unthinkingly on her shoulder. I removed them. The batter sizzled on the stovetop, and the microwave hummed as it spun its pitcher of syrup.

"Will you eat with us?" Jack asked.

I shook my head. "I'm not hungry."

He opened the cabinet above the microwave and pulled out two plates. When he lined up the silverware beside them on the table, eye level with Amelia, she lifted her fork obediently.

"She won't be home," he said.

"I know."

"So what are you looking for?"

A forwarding address, maybe? A receipt showing the purchase of a bus ticket, hotel room? A threatening message still blinking on her answering machine? *Leave your daughter at the corner of Main and Broad Street, then walk fifty paces to the right.*

"I'll know when I find it," I said.

The sunlight flared on the polished wood table. A shadow slid across the windowpane and my gaze flashed toward it, sharp and wild. I moved to the sink to scan the backyard, and Jack, after flipping a pancake onto Amelia's plate, followed me to the window.

"There's no one out there, Syl," he murmured, resting his forearm on a high cabinet. "Remember? It's just a trick of the eye."

I glanced up at him then, the familiar contours of his arm etched in blue light, his eyes as warm as embers. The blood flooded my cheeks.

"I should go," I said stupidly.

"We'll be waiting," he said. Then he grinned, and it took every ounce of grit I had to spin around and march toward the front door instead of throwing down my bag and walking straight into his arms. What would he have done then? He would have tensed against the shock of it, probably. He would have drawn politely or bitterly away.

"He *left* you," I reminded myself as I rattled down the highway. My tone was grim, and my heart cooled down. "He left you, and you wanted him gone."

The inside of Faye's apartment was dim and spare. It squatted on the second story, with a view of the parking lot and, beyond that, a swampy duck pond. The light that managed to worm through grimy, rain-streaked windows illuminated a neatly swept linoleum floor, a collection of scrubbed dishes in the drying rack, a heap of folded laundry on the coffee table. Short stacks of library books concealed the glossy surface of a dining table. In the bedroom, I stumbled over two mattresses—one large, one small—each with sheets tucked to the floor and blankets pulled up to the pillows. The air was thick and stale.

As I rummaged through drawers and tugged open cabinets, it was impossible not to think about the officers who'd arrived to comb the house for evidence on the afternoon of Faye's arrest. Once their boots had clomped up the stairs and down the hallway to her room, Jack had jolted to his feet, mumbled something indecipherable, and skulked out the back door. I'd teetered at the bottom of the staircase, dredging up some courage. Finally I took a breath and climbed up.

"Ma'am," a ponytailed officer said gruffly, stopping me on the landing. "You can't be here right now."

I peered past her into Faye's bedroom. Dresser drawers hung open like mouths; papers snowed across the floor. One man knelt before Faye's bookshelf, jotting down the titles in a palm-sized notebook. Another, wielding a baton, prodded at the skirts and jackets hanging in the closet. When he stepped away, the empty sleeves swung forward as if trying to pull him back.

I tried to elbow past the officer, but she blocked me without effort.

"Ma'am," she said again, more gently, gripping my forearm and drawing me back. "I told you already. You can't be here right now."

I squinted at the name on her vest. "Can you tell me what you're looking for, Officer Pine? This is—it's—" With a sweep of my arm, I indicated the hills of stuffed animals, the backyard-birds calendar, the dried daisy chain draped over the silver neck of the lamp. "It's *private*."

She blinked at me. Something tightened in her bearing, and I sensed a change in strategy. "Tell me, Mrs. Vogel," she said. I was still using my married name then. "What do you know about the Kingman?"

————

No one believes me when I say that I knew nothing of the monster until the day of the crime. But I wasn't on the message boards. I hadn't seen the photographs or watched the homemade videos with those shaky, handheld cameras. I had no idea that in the year before the crime, the Kingman's online popularity had soared to staggering heights.

During the hearing, I saw some of the papers that Pine and her colleagues had retrieved from Faye's bedroom. Someone rolled a projection screen into the courtroom on squeaky wheels, and the lawyers clicked through PowerPoint slides with photographs of colored-pencil drawings. I could remember the fresh box of colored pencils open on the edge of Faye's desk; I'd purchased them for her at the beginning of the school year because she'd worn her old ones down. When I'd asked to see some of her drawings, she'd shown me sketches of the cat, or the house, or the pond. I'd never seen the ones projected over the judge's head in the courtroom: lush forests filled with hundreds of jade leaves; heavy lines of yellow sunlight slashing through clearings; textured branches dripping with multicolored birds. My breath hooked in my throat. The images were painstaking, vibrant, beautiful. Faye had breathed life into those woods.

It wasn't until the prosecutor pointed out the figure that I saw him: a midnight-colored smudge in the distance. I could make out limbs, though it was hard to tell which belonged to the figure and which belonged to the tree. An amber crown spiked above his head, but the space where his face should have been was expressionless, featureless, blank as the paper beneath him.

Although that was my first glimpse of the Kingman, a cold recognition shook me. Was it just my memory playing tricks on me, or had I once seen the same nebulous silhouette, the same sharp glimmer of gold, just across the borders of my vision?

That night, after arguments had ended for the day, I went home to hunt down the Kingman. I crawled deep into the thicket of the

Internet, digging through forums and chat rooms and blogs for stories, photographs, explanations.

I learned that the Kingman was a creature of the forest; that he
could be found among any stand of trees, no matter how young
or how thin, but that he preferred the primeval perfume of black
spruce and balsam fir. He wore a light-colored crown and a black
cloak that was sometimes, when he appeared in colder climates,
rimmed with the fur of a snowshoe hare. His riches were rumored
to be immeasurable; his castle undiscoverable. Although he had
appeared to humans of all ages, it was children who tended to vanish with him. No one knew where those children were taken—
some described a castle built of stones and secret wishes. Others
referred to "the winter island" or, more simply, "the woods." The
more that I read, the more I began to visualize this place, this fairy
realm, with yellow moss as soft as silk rugs and trees as old as the
soil they grew in and cold, pewter-colored waves spraying a gos-
samer mist over the rocks.

But I needed to tunnel back further than the explosion of
memes and posts in the year before the crime. I needed to determine his origin if I wanted him to appear to me. Remember: *origin*,
from *originem*, from *oriri*: to become visible. In many of the stories
people posted, I discovered hints of ancient roots—rumors of his
appearance in the hieroglyphics of Egyptian pyramids, or spec-
ulation about his role in the Children's Crusade. I studied photographs of sixteenth-century woodcuts and giant Scandinavian
landscape paintings, seeking out the clues that others claimed to
have found there. And yet, although I searched and scrolled until
my eyes teared up and my temples throbbed, I could never track
down the basis for the rumors, the documents that anonymous
users on monster blogs claimed to have held in their own sweaty
hands. Who had named him? Where did he come from? How could
I fight what I didn't understand?

In the evenings, Jack and I hunched over tepid microwave dinners that we didn't eat. The room smelled of plastic, and the silence between us grew dense and thorny. He never spoke first.

"I tried to contact them," I said. My voice sounded feverish even to me. "I emailed all their screen names. But my messages bounced back."

Jack dragged a fork through lukewarm chicken pasta. "Leave it, Syl," he growled. He refused to look at me. "I don't want to talk about the fucking Kingman."

In those gray, strained weeks before he left, he was already sleeping on the sofa bed in the spare bedroom. He'd moved there three days after Faye's arrest. I spent half the night battling nightmares in a cold bed, and the other half scrabbling for answers online. My hair was falling out, carpeting the pillow and clumping in the shower drain. I wasn't eating. I was close to something: in my peripheral vision, I glimpsed quaking branches, cold white waves, stars colored brightly as jewels. Sometimes, from my bedroom window: the crest of a black cloak coiling around a corner of the garage. I didn't want to tell Jack because I didn't want him to prescribe something that made me lose sight of these things. Obviously they meant something, led somewhere. I just needed time to decipher them.

I'd started leaving rambling voice mails for Officer Pine, reading aloud from anonymous reports and describing haunting woodcuts in minute detail. I wanted to tell her things about the Kingman that she didn't know. I needed her to see how Faye had been preyed upon and swayed.

"Everything started with the Kingman," I informed Jack, jabbing my knife into the plastic film on my tray. "If he wasn't on the Internet—if Faye hadn't found him—"

Jack shot to his feet and his chair clattered to the floor. "*Stop it, Sylvia*," he snarled. "Just *stop*. Don't you see? This all started with *us*. If we hadn't—"

He caught himself. He leaned over, lifted the chair from the floor, and carried his container to the sink. With his palms flat on the countertop, without turning back toward me, he reminded me that he'd once suggested we could be happy without children. "You don't know what you're going to get," he said, his words aching with the weight of an emotion that I couldn't name. "There's so much you can't control."

I wanted to tell him that this was true of everything: of lightning strikes and stock markets and marriages. Only a few months earlier, I would have laughed if someone had inspected the lines on my palm and told me that soon Jack and I would go a week or more without speaking to each other; that he would start disappearing for unexplained hours; that a black silence would descend like a shroud over the house, transforming us into ghosts of ourselves, a kind of walking dead.

But my chest was buckled too tight for words. I lunged from my seat and stamped out of the kitchen, pretending not to see the way he crumpled over the sink and pretending not to hear his fathomless, shuddering grief.

It took Jack's departure to draw me back from that virtual abyss. In the years since, I'd worked hard to keep the Kingman from my mind. I'd sold the computer; burned all my notes. And so when I rolled open the door to Faye's closet and saw the corners of newsprint taped up behind the clothes, I wasn't expecting to shove aside the hangers and find his name lodged in the headlines behind her blouses and her coats.

The articles, clipped from local papers within the past year, reported a rash of Kingman crimes. Wisconsin, Tennessee, Arizona, Wyoming, Oregon, Maine, Florida. The children used different kinds of tools—poisons, fires, baseball bats—and they attacked different kinds of guardians—teachers, neighbors, the parents of friends—but they all claimed the same motivation. They did it for the Kingman. They said he had been watching them. They said that he needed them. There was something very important waiting for them, they insisted, in the woods.

I can't remember how I made it out of that closet with my limbs turned to water. But somehow I flung myself from the room and landed on a kitchen chair and looked up to see a pale face studying me through the window.

Steady, I told myself, clutching the table and lurching to my feet. *It's only in your mind.* My gaze pierced through the wobble of my own reflection and shot savagely across the parking lot. I poured myself a glass of water and sat down again.

For more than a decade the Kingman had lain dormant. Why were these crimes occurring now? And to learn of them in Faye's own apartment, a day after her daughter appeared at my door—it could not be coincidence.

There was only one person in the world who knew the Kingman like my daughter did. So, once I'd caught my breath, I tugged my phone from my pocket and dialed a number that I still knew by heart: the home of Faye's oldest, closest, most devoted friend.

My daughter had never been a social child. If a schoolmate invited the whole class to a birthday party, Faye would be included—but never to anything more intimate. On the way to those birthday parties, Faye would grow pensive, subdued. When we arrived, she'd slither out of the car and trudge up the walkway with the gift bag gripped in a white-knuckled fist. The glance she'd cast back from the front door reminded me of a fox whose foot had been seized by a steel trap. Everybody knows that friendship among girls requires persistence and courage, so I continued to propel her toward the chocolate cupcakes and the poolside games with a performed enthusiasm she refused to mirror. Neither of us minded when the invitations began to dry up.

I admired the fact that Faye didn't seem to need anyone, to long for anyone, the way I had when I was young. Independence was a quality, I believed, to be cultivated. Besides, I liked having her nearby: sprawled with a book along the porch swing, her bare feet propped up at one end; cross-legged in the grass with a sketchbook, drawing roses in fairy-tale gardens; dragging string across the carpet for the cat, baking batches of cookies in a twilit kitchen, or bent over the dining table with an atlas and a novel, drawing maps of imaginary places.

And then, in third grade, she found Anna: a wiry, nervous girl, with sharp elbows and grass-stained knees and eyes like asters. She always whispered "please" and "thank you." She and Faye spent most of their time outdoors, conspiring among the rosebushes or disappearing through the gate in the fence to the rich woods of the state park and down the winding path to the creek. When they returned to the house, they made peanut butter sandwiches and locked themselves in Faye's room to listen to music, the walls pulsing with eerie harmonies.

Yes, they also went online. But the computer was wedged into a corner of the dining room where Jack and I could walk by anytime and glance at the screen. Nothing was hidden. And anyway, the girls didn't even spend all that much time on it. Instead they rode bikes to the library and watched movies after dinner and knotted friendship bracelets out of colored thread. They trained the cat to sit and retrieve. They skipped down to the creek to catch tadpoles, and they returned with armfuls of chicory and wild daisies, which they deposited in mason jars and distributed in such vast quantities throughout the house that the hallways smelled like meadows.

After everything happened, I received letters from strangers who wrote to tell me that I didn't love her, that I didn't watch her, that I didn't know her. But they didn't understand a thing. I loved her ferociously, with the kind of ruthless, unflinching devotion you see on wildlife documentaries. Sometimes I'd find myself wishing for danger so that I could prove myself like the mothers I saw on local news stations. I dreamed that Faye would become trapped beneath a car so that I'd have a chance to lift it from her; I imagined tackling a rabid bear who slashed through the tent that she and Anna had set up in the backyard. But Faye was too cautious for trouble. She extinguished candles that I'd lit. She smothered campfires in ashes and wore a life jacket to the creek. It was she who checked and double-checked the locks on doors and windows before she went to bed. If anything, she seemed more aware of danger than I did, more attuned to the shadows that lurked beyond the floodlights of our lives together. "Mom," she would cluck at me from the passenger seat if I backed out of the driveway with my seat belt unfastened. "I wish you'd be more careful."

As Faye grew older, she looked more and more like me: the angled features and the translucent skin. She was bone of my bones, flesh of my flesh. And so I was tricked into believing that I knew her, that she wanted what I wanted. The home, the family, the fortress I'd built—I'd thought that I was keeping her safe. But all that time, what if I'd been trapping her inside?

Monsters, Ink: "King of the Woods"
Episode Aired May 12, 2008

—Good morning, everyone, and welcome to *Monsters, Ink*—the radio program in which we chat about the latest urban legends, scary stories, and horror movies. Today we'll be talking about the monster that made headlines last month, thanks to the two little girls who tried to kill for him. I'm Dan, here with my cohost, Esme—

—Hey, everyone!

—And today, we're talking about the Kingman. Now, Esme, had you heard the Kingman's name before you learned about the crime last month?

—Oh, for sure. He's only the most popular urban legend circulating through culture right now! I'm guessing that most of us already know the basic facts: He's associated with trees, with darkness, with riches, with magic and power. He lives in a castle somewhere in the North Woods of Minnesota, where he's concealed his fantastic treasure— precious gems and coins dredged up from shipwrecks on Lake Superior. That's his home base, but he travels, maybe teleports, all the time. Wherever we are, he's often close by, watching us with a face that looks something like a crude eyeless and mouthless mask—but we rarely know he's there. We're told that sometimes when we think we're looking at a tree, we're actually looking at the Kingman; and sometimes, when we think we may have seen the Kingman, and we feel that surge of terror and wonder, we blink and find ourselves facing nothing but a tree.

—I just got chills.

—Yeah. The Kingman will do that to you; he's a creepy dude. But he's also got some allure, obviously.

—I've heard lots of people wondering why he's so appealing right now. How would you answer them?

—Well, first of all, most of our days, our routines, are dim and predictable. But legends and fairy tales—they're spaces of possibility. Mermaids walk on land; swans turn into long-lost brothers. I bet this is why we so often associate the tales with children: because young people are more attuned to the potential for magic, because they haven't yet lost this sense of wonder, thrill, seduction that deserts us as adults.

—Maybe that's why the Kingman has this kind of Pied Piper mystique that speaks to certain kids, that draws them to him. The girls in North Carolina are a great example.

—I like the Pied Piper comparison. But you know who else he reminds me of? Peter Pan.

—What makes you say that?

—For me it's the idea of a place far away where adults can't find you; a place that promises to be magical, but which also contains a definitely dark and grown-up violence.

—I see.

—And in my opinion, that's essential to the Kingman's massive popularity right now. Literature scholars say that the monsters of any era are expressions of specific fears, desires, preoccupations. It's probably not a coincidence that in the age of "helicopter parenting," kids are dreaming of a dark and distant place to hide. And it's not a coincidence that a creature of inexhaustible but evidently unnecessary wealth has begun to stalk through our late-stage-capitalist anxieties. Finally, it's probably no coincidence that a monster of the primeval forest finds himself revived on the Internet, which is itself a kind of black woods with bottomless caverns and secret treasures and trees of knowledge and sinuous paths. Isn't the Internet, too, a place where a young girl could easily take a wrong turn and find herself lost?

Elizabeth the Good

When someone called her old name, Elizabeth's pulse picked up speed. It was just after noon, and she was headed to philosophy. Her old name was an English classic, common as clover, and she reminded herself that the person who said it couldn't be talking to her. So she didn't turn her head, and she prayed that no one could see the vein throbbing in her neck. *One foot in front of the other*, she said to herself, her steps robotic, her eyes on the pavement. *Keep walking, keep walking, keep walking.*

But then she heard it again, closer now, and whoever had said it was following her. The footsteps picked up, slipping a little on the first leaves to blanket the sidewalk, and even though she started to move more quickly, too, she didn't want to break into a sprint. Every day, her goal was to not call attention to herself. She refused to lose her cool.

"Anna!" called the voice for a third time, and now a hand clasped her shoulder.

"I'm sorry," she said automatically, lifting her arms as if to shield herself. These were the words she'd practiced. "You've mistaken me for someone else."

But the minute she saw the woman's face, she knew that the game was up. She dropped her arms. Faye's mom had aged about a hundred years since Elizabeth had seen her. Her hair had turned white, but her eyes were still flecked with gold. In the courtroom she'd looked like a cardboard cutout of a mother. Nothing like the mom who used to wake them after sleepovers with bacon and orange juice, whose hugs had been hard and warm, whose hands braided their hair and flipped their French toast. She made a move like she might hug Elizabeth right then, out of some ancient habit, but she halted herself midgesture and stared instead. Her gaze raked the cropped, dyed hair, the glasses Elizabeth wore even though her eyesight was perfectly fine. Her disguise had finally failed her.

"Oh," Elizabeth said. She swayed on her feet, and Mrs. Vogel's arm flung out as if to catch her. "It's you."

She got the idea from a history book that she read in the detention facility. Her aunt and uncle didn't want her reading fiction during those years, but they also didn't want her reading only trashy magazines and newspapers. So they sent the history books. At first Elizabeth was skeptical. But once she saw that history was simply stories by another name, she changed her mind. She couldn't read them fast enough. She was starved for stories back then, desperate for them, deprived as she was of Faye—who'd been sent someplace else—and so it didn't matter to her that everything in these books was true. Her world had lost much of its mystery, but it was probably a *good* thing, she decided, that these stories couldn't turn twigs into fingers. They couldn't reach out and grab somebody.

When she read about the Viking kings—Gorm the Old and Cnut the Great, that kind of thing—she thought: *If I'm going to change my name anyway, why not add an adjective like that, too?* On registration forms and class rosters, she was Elizabeth Good because the documents didn't include an option for an article. But in her heart of hearts—and in her textbooks, her journals, her handwritten name tags at mixers and such—she was Elizabeth *the Good*. Her roommate even called her that when she was pissed at her.

And she tried to live up to the name. She volunteered at after-school programs. She sorted canned goods in soup kitchens. She carried extra change in case someone on the street asked her for money. Every day the school hosted a service in the chapel, and even though it was not mandatory, she always went. As soon as she sat down in a pew, she clasped her hands and she bowed her head and she said a silent, fervent thanks to anyone who might be listening. She'd been given a second chance. She'd been cloaked with anonymity, invisibility.

Because if people found out who she was? What she'd done? The very thought left her reeling.

That's why Faye's appearance last spring threw her into a tailspin. She'd been studying for finals. The windows were open; the trees were blooming. Even though there was still a bite in the air, people were sprawled in shorts and tank tops all over the campus lawn.

She'd wanted to escape her history. She'd tried so hard. But when she heard the knock at her door and found Faye standing in the hallway, her eyes shining like the Kingman's famous jewels, Elizabeth did what she'd always done. She opened the door wider and invited Faye in.

She told Faye's mom that she couldn't talk because she had to get to class. But Mrs. Vogel fell into step beside her and asked if they could please just have one coffee together. Wasn't there a place they could sit down?

Elizabeth's aunt and uncle taught her to be nice. Write thank-you notes, chew quietly, look people in the eye, and accept invitations even if you don't want to go. *Elizabeth the Good*. So Elizabeth led the woman to the packed student union and zigzagged through the din to a booth in the back, partially blocking the windows. Mrs. Vogel secured two cups of coffee and slid in across from her.

"How did you find me?" Elizabeth asked.

"I called your aunt and uncle."

"And they just *gave* the information to you?"

"It wasn't easy to convince them. But I told them it was an emergency." She tilted her head toward the students, the windows, the buildings outside. "Has Faye been here recently, Anna? Looking for you?"

Elizabeth stiffened. "My name's not Anna anymore. It's Elizabeth."

Faye's mom didn't react. Perhaps she'd changed her name, too.

"And anyway," Elizabeth reminded her, "the judge said we weren't allowed to see each other."

But Mrs. Vogel didn't buy it. She leaned forward. "When was Faye here?"

Elizabeth wanted to seem indifferent, but her shrug felt forced even to her. "Last spring."

She reluctantly described how Faye drove straight onto campus and left her hatchback double-parked in front of the dormitories, how Faye climbed the four flights to Elizabeth's room and rapped on the door again and again until she opened it. It wasn't until they were both inside, facing each other across the battered floors, that Elizabeth thought to ask: "How did you find me?"

Faye had waved a hand dismissively. "I saw you downtown one time," she said. "You didn't see me. I followed you here."

Elizabeth was desperate to know more—when exactly had Faye seen her? Where?—but she'd been terrified that her roommate would come home and start asking other questions. So she'd told Faye that they should go down to talk in the courtyard.

She could see the night again as she recounted it: Faye like a coiled spring, her figure trembling, glowing in the shabby stairwell. Elizabeth looked out the window of the student union now and remembered how Faye had alighted on the edge of a bench, her gaze flicking again and again to the dim outline of a car parked beneath one of the old-fashioned lampposts that dotted the darkened quad. The trees had been mostly bare, skeletal, their limbs growing, stretching as the girls passed by. Had Faye seen them beckoning to her? Had Elizabeth?

"Hey," Faye's mom said, waving her hand in front of Elizabeth's gaze, looking spooked. "What do you see?"

When she blinked, the vision vanished. "Nothing."

"What did she want from you?"

Elizabeth shifted on the bench. "Money," she finally said. "She'd been working at a garden center, but the pay wasn't great. She told me that she was going away for a while and that she needed help getting there."

"How much did you give her?"

"I didn't have anything to give. I had to move out of the dorms the following week, into a summer sublet off campus. I needed every dime."

"Did she tell you where she was going?"

"No."

"Did she tell you that she had a daughter?"

Elizabeth looked out the window again and longed to be anywhere but there. The din of the student union clattered between them.

"Elizabeth?"

"Yeah, she did."

"Was Amelia with her?"

There was the scene again: the sky black and starless, a radio from a window above them spitting out rock songs. Elizabeth sighed. "She was waiting in the car."

Of course Faye told Elizabeth that she'd had a child. She described a little of her daughter's birth: the nurses with their starched expressions, the hospital lights glaring. She said that she'd watched something on television about Amelia Earhart a few days before, and so the missing aviatrix was soaring through her mind.

"She went missing," Faye told the nurses. "Poof! In midair! And nobody ever found her."

The nurses' faces remained placid. Faye could not get over their lack of interest in this decidedly interesting fact.

"Poof!" she said again. "Poof! Poof! Poof!" When she began to laugh loudly and unevenly, the nurses moved to restrain her. She fought them off, spinning her arms like propellers. The nurses lunged forward, tried to pin her limbs down. The intercom sizzled, Faye had said, the call button sang. The monitors bleated in time with her contractions.

Faye made everything sound maddening and gorgeous. Like something out of this world.

And so when she asked if Elizabeth wanted to meet the child, Elizabeth realized that she did. She wanted to see what her best friend had made. She trailed her out of the courtyard and over to the car, where they found the little girl waiting for them in the back seat. The child's hair was neatly combed, her eyes like mirrors, her small chin raised in something like defiance. She looked just like her mother.

"Listen," Faye had said, jolting Elizabeth from her reverie. "I need a favor."

After the crime, during her teenage years in the detention facility, people often asked Elizabeth why she went along with it. She learned to cry and say that Faye had pressured her. They liked that because it made sense to them. They didn't want to hear about monsters or Great Lakes or pine forests or secret treasures or shoreline fortresses. They didn't want her to describe how sunlight can wriggle through leaves in a way that makes it look as if the trees are hiding something. She seemed like a fairly normal kid—no signs of darkness or madness. That's why they wanted assurance that everything was someone else's fault. But history doesn't work like that, Elizabeth knew. It's layered, it's tangled, it keeps coming back.

Because her own parents had died when she was young, she was raised by her aunt and uncle. They lived in Chicago before her uncle lost his job and they had to move down south. The house was cramped. Her cousins wrestled, and her aunt and uncle argued. She started spending the whole day outside just to hear herself think. That's how Faye noticed her on the bus: she had twigs in her hair. Faye swooped down out of nowhere and started pulling them from Elizabeth's ponytail without asking permission. The girls who had been whispering together two rows behind her suddenly fell silent. The bus bumped in and out of potholes, but Elizabeth didn't feel them. On that day the heat didn't smother her and the exhaust fumes didn't make her sick. All that mattered were Faye's fingers combing through her hair and the surprising sense of peace that bubbled over her.

Once the two of them became friends, the other girls stopped kicking pebbles at Elizabeth during recess. They stopped blocking her cubby in the classroom, stopped stealing her water bottle, stopped hiding her backpack from her. It wasn't that they *liked* Faye. It was that she unnerved them. She had this way of peering past them that made them look compulsively back over their shoulders. If they laughed at her, she didn't seem to hear it. If someone said her name, she often responded ten seconds too late. Elizabeth didn't know where Faye went when she was gazing out the classroom window, but wherever it was, Elizabeth wanted to go there with her.

With Faye, everything changed. Other people, boring people, woke up and ate cereal, went to school and to work, came home and watched television and then went to bed and did it all again. Other lives, Faye explained, were routine. Predictable. But that's only because most people didn't know where to search, as she did, for mystery.

Sometimes Elizabeth wished she could tell someone about the elaborate parties Faye organized in her bedroom for the characters in the stories that they read, for the creatures in the drawings that they made. She wished she could describe the way Faye held an invisible brownie between her thumb and index finger, the way she laughed at the jokes that she imagined being told. Elizabeth used to sit as close to her as possible, raising her cup when Faye raised hers. Sometimes they'd sing with guests whose voices they couldn't hear, or dance with people whose feet they couldn't see. Nobody at those parties cared that Elizabeth's clothes were the wrong size or that her sneakers had holes or that her parents were gone. Not even her.

But it was impossible to explain the magic of those hours, or how safe she felt with Faye in a world of their creation. Nothing bad could happen to them here; they simply wouldn't let it.

"Elizabeth," Mrs. Vogel said. "Put yourself in my position for a minute. Please. My daughter is missing. Are you saying you don't have any idea where she's gone?"

Elizabeth pressed the coffee cup to her lips and took a giant gulp. She wondered if Faye's mother saw her life without Faye the same way Elizabeth saw her own: drab and bland, all the magic drained out of it. A cup of coffee, in Faye's cool hand, could be an elixir, a potion, a poison. But in that dreary building on that postage-stamp campus, a cup of coffee was nothing but a cup of coffee. Lukewarm and bitter.

"She needed money," Elizabeth said again. "I didn't have any."

"Who else could she have asked?"

Elizabeth waited. It took several seconds for Faye's mother to figure it out. Adults, Faye had said once with that bewitching, clear-eyed confidence of hers, are distracted and self-centered. They've forgotten how to pay attention to their surroundings. They miss things, important and powerful and dangerous things, that kids can still see.

"Why else would stories like these," Faye had asked, tapping a fingernail on the cover of her giant, gorgeous book of fairy tales, "be specifically labeled for children?"

Eventually Mrs. Vogel saw what Elizabeth was saying. Did that mean that she'd betrayed Faye's trust? In that moment, Elizabeth couldn't say. She could only melt back into the sticky booth, her limbs like jelly, her head singing with strangers' voices, as the woman across from her stood up from the table and walked out the door.

Interview with Bailiff Roger Brouwer

Recorded on November 17, 2018

Hard to believe that I'd never heard of the Kingman before that crime.
The proceedings turned me into a real expert. I've seen so many
pictures of that monster that I could spot him in a woodcut a mile away.
I know all about his history before the Internet, and all about how he
slunk his way online. First he appeared on web pages about conspiracy
theories. Then web pages with horror stories. Nothing super credible
yet—just fringe groups making a little noise. But after that there were
encyclopedia stubs and dictionary entries. He turned up in homemade
videos and blurry photographs. The stories multiplied, and before long,
he was all over the damn place. At least that's what they said. Years have
passed, and I still don't own a computer. Never will. All that Kingman
crap sealed the deal for me.

The girls were sent to separate detention centers, to be released
when they turned eighteen. But I don't think I'm alone in feeling like
justice hasn't quite been served. In that courtroom, huge and shining,
those two looked *tiny*. The one named Anna cried a lot. The one named
Faye stared at the air above the judge with an expression you might call
dreamy. It was only on the third day of the hearing that I realized she
was watching pigeons wobble back and forth on a high window ledge.
Character witnesses said she was an animal lover, and I guess she'd
heard the Kingman sometimes traveled with a wild dog. Was that part of
the appeal?

If I were you, I wouldn't make a movie about him. That's what you
said that you were doing, right? He has a way of—getting in your mind.
Messing with your head. There were days I had a tough time following
the arguments because I could've sworn I saw a wooden head popping
up and down behind the furthest bench. When I went home at night,
I barely slept. There was a constant tapping on my doors. Sometimes,

without any reason, my posters fell off the walls in the middle of the night. Once, the lamp turned on by itself. If I did manage to get some shut-eye, I had nightmares of being alone in forests where I had to duck and run to escape the branches that were grabbing at me.

Yeah, I see you smiling. I know you don't believe me. I'm not saying the guy is real. I'm just saying—I don't know what the hell I'm saying. Just look out, okay? Just keep your guard up. Some things don't need to be real to destroy you.

Sylvia

After tucking Amelia into bed, Jack trudged down to the porch and resumed his place on the swing. The late-summer heat blanketed the house, and the cicadas hummed around us. The warm strum of a banjo drifted from the radio he'd left on in the kitchen.

Earlier, I'd watched from the living room as Jack made dinner with Amelia's assistance. He'd hauled a chair over to the stove and handed her the box of pasta to dump into the stove pot. He'd shown her how to stir the sauce. She'd received the clean plates from him cautiously, reverently, clutching each one to her chest as she crossed the floor from the cabinets to the table. Her face, when she turned toward me, was washed in the last of the afternoon light. Her skin was rosy, her expression briefly exultant.

I wanted to freeze the three of us right there, in that moment, like figures in a snow globe. I'd forgotten this part of parenthood: The yearning to stop the sun from sinking any farther to the ground. The longing to hold on to someone who, minute by minute, has already ceased to exist.

"What are you thinking about?" Jack asked from the other side of the swing. He couldn't read my face in the dark.

My thoughts were roiling like hurricane winds, churning up images that I'd worked hard to submerge: Faye perched on the kitchen counter, swinging her legs as she helped me stir together the flour and sugar for a piecrust; her thin figure disappearing into the empty wooded lot at the end of the road, returning hours later with ragged hair and dirty knees; her hands in the courtroom, man-acled and motionless.

"I'm thinking about what Anna—what Elizabeth said," I told him. I'd already described the scene to him, in bits and pieces before din-ner, when Amelia had been occupied with other tasks. I'd explained the way the light in that dingy student union hit Elizabeth's face at such an angle that she could have been nine years old again, clear-eyed and honest. She'd glanced over her shoulder before reminding me that Faye needed money. Her tone: guttural, conspiratorial.

Jack arrived at the same conclusion I did. "Do you know where to find him?" he asked. His elbow brushed mine.

"No," I said. "But I know who does."

He swiveled toward me. "You're not thinking of driving out there, Sylvia," he said.

"I'm thinking of it."

"It's three hours each way. That's the entire day. What are she and I supposed to do?"

A pair of dry wings whispered past the porch. "You said you'd help me, Jack."

"I thought—" He stopped himself.

"What?"

He shrugged and shifted, the swing groaning beneath him. "I thought that meant we'd—I didn't think that you'd—" His sigh was explosive. "Well, I didn't expect you to call me down here just so you could leave me every day, just so you could take off all over the goddamn state. You weren't honest with me. That's what I'm saying."

"Then I'm sorry I called you." My bitterness rose. "I know it's an inconvenience. But the sooner I find her, the sooner you can get back to your mountains."

For a full minute, he didn't speak. Then, quietly: "You're right, Sylvia. Go to Windy Cove. Get Faye. The sooner I'm gone, the better."

He rose and stalked off the porch. I stayed where I was. My heart cracked again, and I pressed my palm against my chest to keep the pieces together.

Three months before Faye was scheduled for release from the detention center, her juvenile court counselor had called to ask us what we planned to do next. Jack and I were both on the line, listening from our separate lives.

"Have you thought about what it would be like to bring an eighteen-year-old into your house?" the counselor asked when I told her that I'd assumed Faye would simply come home. "An eighteen-year-old who's been locked up for nearly eight years?"

I snapped like a wolf trap. "You're talking about our daughter as if she were a stranger."

The counselor shuffled her papers and clicked her pen. I waited for Jack to agree with me, but he said nothing.

"Jack," I said. "Are you still on the line?"

He cleared his throat. "She made a bad decision," he said. "These are the consequences."

That's when the counselor cut in. "Trust me," she insisted. "This will be best for *everyone*." She assured us that a youth development center would provide the structure and care that Faye needed to finish her high-school degree and ease her transition back into the world.

"Is Anna—her friend—does she get to go home after she's released?" I demanded.

"That's between the young woman, her psychiatrist, and her family."

"I assume that's a no."

The counselor sighed. "You know as well as I do that of the two girls, Faye was found to be the leader and her friend to be the follower." When I didn't reply to this, the woman cleared her throat and brightened her tone. "And, of course, Faye will continue her therapy. She's been doing marvelously so far. Dr. Karen says that there's been no mention of the—the what's-his-name—"

"The Kingman," I snarled. I could hear Jack suck in his breath. Though we were hundreds of miles apart, I knew he'd winced as if I'd struck him.

"Yes, that's right, the Kingman." The woman's tone was approving. "Your daughter hasn't said his name in years."

Things that Faye adored at age four, age five: light-up sneakers, tulle skirts, face paint, animals. The white cat followed her everywhere. She was always the first to volunteer to bring home a class pet for holidays or long weekends, which is how we found ourselves laden with guinea pigs or gerbils or droopy-looking betta fish. She could squat beside an anthill for hours, watching them work. She had a gift for spotting birds' nests and animal tracks, which she pursued for hours, tirelessly, through the woods.

When she was seven, her teacher told her class about the monarch migration that crosses the Southern Appalachians in the spring and fall each year. Faye returned home that afternoon bursting with facts about the butterflies' diet and habits and anatomy. Her enthusiasm was so infectious that by the time we'd finished dinner, we were making plans to drive into the mountains the following week in the hope of catching the tail end of the migration. We packed snacks and road maps; Faye brought an armful of books, a floppy hat, a disposable camera. The three of us piled into the car, and several hours later we poured out of it again, Jack and me swinging our arms and stretching our backs as we followed Faye along the trail.

Sometimes, even now, I startle awake to find that I've been dreaming of that grove again: the piney tang of red spruce and balsam fir; the October breeze spinning briskly down from cobalt-colored peaks. The flames lapping against the trees were butterfly wings, and the branches bristled with antennae. Jack and I, pausing on the edge of the trail, watched Faye glide forward until she reached a golden clearing. There she stopped, and stood, and turned her face skyward to the monarchs gathering in a bright orange cloud above her. A few of them fluttered down to her hair, her shoulders, her long-fingered hands, and her laughter pealed between the trunks. I remember that my eyes were stinging and that Jack's hand was crushed in mine and that I was marveling at this vision of my daughter and thinking: *Where could this wondrous, glowing stranger have possibly come from? How is her face so like mine?*

Windy Cove wasn't too far up the coast from the town where I'd been born. As I stepped out of the car in front of the rambling, rundown beach house, I drew in a fortifying breath of briny air. The breeze whipped my hair into my eyes, so I couldn't see that someone was watching me from the porch until I'd approached the steps. He was leaning against the chipped blue siding, his arms crossed over his chest and a baseball cap pulled low over his forehead. As I drew near, he stiffened. Then he leaned forward, scrutinized me more closely, and rested his hand upon his chest.

"Sylvia Vogel," I said. "Faye's mother."

"Sam," he drawled. "House director. If you're looking for your girl, you've come to the wrong place. She moved out a couple of years ago."

"I know."

"Then what're you doing all the way out here?"

The gulls screamed from the telephone wires. Two blocks to the east, the ocean folded against the shore. "I'm looking for someone else. A guy who used to work here."

The three-story house sagged behind him, its white trim flaking and a whale-shaped weather vane spinning on the patchwork shingles of the roof. Wind chimes rang discordantly.

"That information's private," he said.

I braced myself with another gulp of sea air. "I believe that the guy I want to find left here in kind of a hurry."

"What's that supposed to mean?"

Instead of answering, I waited.

"Listen," he finally said. "We called you right after we found out about those two. I know that you talked to her on the phone. I know she told you how it was."

I remembered that call: Faye's voice sliding through the telephone line. "Settle down, Sylvia," she'd said. The sound of my name in her mouth had rattled me more than the news itself. "There was nothing nefarious about it. It was just one of those things."

Oak leaves rustled above me. "All I know is that my eighteen-year-old daughter was under your care," I said, "and after less than a year of living in this house, she found herself pregnant."

"We talked about this four *years* ago," the director insisted. "I called you. We split the doctors' bills. The guy was young and stupid. You and your husband said you weren't going to report it."

"That's right." I shot him a humorless smile. Jack and I had been leery of reporting anything to do with Faye. "That's what we said."

I knew most of the story, but the director grudgingly filled in the rest. Amelia's father had been employed at Windy Cove right out of college as a groundskeeper and handyman, but he had been fired as soon as Faye started to show.

On the night that he was ordered to pack his belongings, he refused to leave. The director had to call the police to pry his fingers from Faye's metal bed frame. As the police dragged him away, he screamed out to her. Faye, the director said, sat cross-legged on her thin mattress, a holey shawl wrapped tightly around her shoulders. Her gaze, violet in the hum of the fluorescent light, remained fixed on her lover's face. Everything else—the shouts of the police-

men, the threats of the director, the gasps of her fellow residents—
went unheard, unheeded. She sat as still as the icon of Saint Jude
that was tacked to the right side of her window, her hair trailing like
a black veil down her back.

According to the hospital record, Amelia's father was not present when she was born. Faye called a taxi when her water broke.
Shortly after giving birth, she returned to Windy Cove. This was
early December, during a cold snap unusual for the coast. As she
crossed the front yard, she followed the billowing cloud of her own
breath. She stepped over the threshold with her baby swaddled and
tucked under one arm, her suitcase under the other.

The director claimed that he didn't want to take her back, that
dependents weren't allowed, but when she promised that she
would be good, her teenage face was so earnest and so clear that he
could only run his fingers through his thinning hair and acquiesce.
He was a Christian man, he assured me, and when Faye turned up
at his door in the dead of winter, the stars flung across the frozen
sky behind her, her expression illuminated by the feeble light of
the entryway and her newborn whimpering softly at her side, he
could not send her away.

It did not hurt matters to have discovered that afternoon, as the
director did, that Jack had sent the rent check early that month,
with a little extra to account for the child. And so he agreed to let
her return to her room.

For the remainder of Faye's time at the house, her behavior was
impeccable. She took up yard work: planting vegetables and raking
leaves. She filled her room with books and kept her daughter close
at hand. After a month or two, Faye received permission to take a
few early morning shifts at a diner down the block. The director
kept an eye on the baby. When Faye had saved up enough, she
purchased a battered two-door hatchback. And a few weeks after
Amelia's first birthday, she moved out.

"And the boyfriend?" I prompted. "The child's father?"

The director didn't blink. He admitted that after the boyfriend was forcibly removed from Windy Cove, he didn't give up on Faye. For the first few weeks that he was gone, he called and called and called. The director had to yank the phone jack from the wall at night in order to keep the house quiet.

By the time the baby was born, the calls had dried up. But the director kept tabs on Amelia's father, updating his address book whenever the man moved.

"For everyone's protection," he said. He shrugged. His hair was wispy, his eyes watery, his face rutted with exhaustion. "The guy did well. Joined some kind of new Internet company a few months after leaving here, made a ton of money. Last spring, I saw an announcement in the paper that he was getting married. I figured that was the end of it."

"Do you have his most recent address?"

The director heaved a sigh, ambled inside, and returned a few minutes later with the information scribbled on the back of an envelope. He handed it over. "You promise this is it?"

"I swear." A speckled lizard darted up the banister, missing my fingers by a millimeter.

"It's not an easy job," the director said. His posture and his tongue had loosened up, and he slouched over the porch railing. "You know. Trying to ease these kids back into the world after what they've seen. What they've done."

The closet, the map, the pushpins. The glint of a knife through sun-soaked leaves. A child's face at the window, pale eyes peering out into the dark.

I crushed the envelope in my fist. "I believe it."

He shook his head. "Most people who come through here— they had a tough go of it. They fell into drugs or out of school early. They had violent neighbors, violent siblings. Family members who were hard and mean as fuck."

He was speaking more to himself now than to me. "In my twenties, I lived next door to a couple of dealers. The two little girls who lived in that house played outside and waved at me when I came home. Wolfish guys knocked on their door at all hours; their parents' fights would keep me up at night. I gave the girls a bottle of bubble mix once, and I remember thinking, as I watched their bubbles rise, that they didn't have a prayer in the world. The odds were stacked against them. Any day now I'll probably open up this door to find myself face-to-face with one or both of them, all grown up, everything smashed around them."

For a second, I could no longer hear the sea. I sensed what was coming next, and already my ears were ringing.

"But Faye"—his gaze narrowed on mine—"she had every advantage in the world. Nice parents, nice house, nice school. From the second she was born, she was loved. You could tell just by looking at her." He shifted his feet, and the wooden slats groaned. "So why's a kid like that want to go and make her easy life hard?"

I knew how the verdict would come down. Everyone did. I knew the judge wouldn't take long to reach it.

The night before closing arguments, I lay awake a long time, watching shadows slinking from the window to the ceiling to the door, and I thought about what I wanted to say to my daughter. I imagined every possible scene between us; I saw how each one would go. Finally, I settled on the truest, simplest sentence I could think of.

"Faye," I said, right before the bailiff led her out of the courtroom for the final time. When she turned to look at me, her eyes were unusually glassy, and her cheeks were flushed with unexpected color. Her delicate wrists were trembling in their handcuffs, and all I wanted in the world was to lift an arm and sweep her toward me so I could feel my child's heartbeat pounding next to mine. "Faye," I said again. "My little sparrow. I love you."

What had she responded? Why couldn't I recall? As I stood on the walk facing Windy Cove, the sand blowing over my shoes, I replayed that memory three times over in my mind, straining to hear my daughter's reply. But there was only the wind in the tall grass and the waves in the distance and the gulls keening over the shore.

Interview with Lara Vasiliev, MD, PhD
Recorded on January 29, 2019

—You know I can't speak to you about my diagnosis of those girls, specifically. That information is legally, medically confidential.

—Of course, Doctor. But the label you've assigned to your diagnosis—the Kingman Effect—became central to the hearing and leaked into popular culture and vernacular. So, perhaps without speaking specifically about the girls—now young women—could you explain in general terms what you meant by "the Kingman Effect"?

—The term refers to the phenomenon by which this mythical being pulls people—almost always young people, but not exclusively—so deeply into his lore that they lose their ability to distinguish between fiction and reality.

—And can this phenomenon take place anywhere? Online, offline?

—I suppose it *could* take place offline, but that's not as likely. Offline, there are more boundaries between self and others, self and stories. You can look up from a book and recognize that the world in front of you is different from the world on the page. You can control the story and even the storyteller by closing the cover or shelving the volume. But the Internet dissolves those boundaries. The Internet is designed so that you click and keep clicking, so that you tunnel deeper into a world that *feels* real but is only virtual. The Internet makes it harder to look up, to step back, to reflect on what you're absorbing.

—And why did you call your diagnosis the Kingman Effect?

—Because around the time of that infamous crime, it was the Kingman who was leading young people into that dense thicket of legends and lore. He would stretch out a hand and beckon with fingers so laden with precious stones that it was impossible to see the skin beneath. He would point you toward tales that were ever more horrifying and places that were ever more chilling. He would give you the sense, as you trailed him through chat rooms and forums and web series and photo galleries, that you were headed toward a final treasure, an ultimate truth, that would bestow you with such dark knowledge and power that you would never need to return to the world you had left.

[Silence. The camera zooms slowly in on the doctor's face. Her gaze is focused on something distant, something beyond the walls of the conference room.]

—Dr. Vasiliev? Are you—is that—are we done?

Sylvia

The house towered over the shoreline, glassy and dignified. As I waited between two massive columns for the front door to swing open, I gazed through the side yard to a teal horizon.

The last time I'd seen my mother outside the hospital was when we'd driven to visit her immediately after her diagnosis. My father had passed away years earlier, but the house teemed with magnanimous aunts and cousins who had come bearing frozen meals. I crafted a hasty gin and tonic in an unoccupied corner of the kitchen and carried it two blocks to the beach, where my mother reclined beneath a striped umbrella with a romance novel and a bird-watching guide. Both books lay half-buried in the sand beside her chair while she shielded her eyes with one hand and watched Faye, a toddler at the time, playing along the shoreline. Faye had caught sight of a squadron of pelicans floating just offshore. She kept launching herself into the waves, and Jack kept fishing her out and tugging her back to safety.

"That child is not afraid of anything," my mother said.

"Isn't that a good thing?"

"Depends." Her sunglasses concealed her expression. "Fear is useful. It can keep a person safe." She accepted the drink from me. "You know what I mean, Sylvia. After all, you were afraid of *every-thing*."

"Was I?"

My mother's laugh hovered between us, rich and mellow. The tonic sparkled in her glass. "Yes," she said.

I sank deeper into the sand. The night before, Faye had raised her dark head from the pillow and gestured to the gauzy curtains that floated over the window frame.

"Someone's there," she'd said, her pupils like embers, her expression serene. I was the one who'd shivered, who'd approached the curtains with wobbly knees. When I'd pulled back the fabric to prove that there was nothing to fear, I'd been embarrassed by the relief that washed through me.

Faye slithered through Jack's arms, slick with seawater, and lunged for the pelicans again. I glanced up to find my mother watching me. She lifted her hand to my face and thumbed away a bead of sweat that was trailing from my temple to my ear. Her arm was thinner than it should have been, her figure gaunt and haunting. My gaze grew damp, and she shimmered before my eyes. I was afraid that if I blinked, she'd vanish.

When the front door opened, my mother's ghost slipped away, darting through the seagrass to the water. The woman standing before me was tall and impassive in translucent black silk. "Can I help you?" she asked.

I squinted against the blinding white siding. My head ached. "I'm looking for my daughter, Faye," I said. "I think she might have been here?"

The woman's gaze snapped from my sneakers to my hair and back again. Then she looked past me as if seeking someone who might be standing in my shadow. When she saw that I was alone, her shoulders slumped.

"You're too late," she said. Her lipstick was the color of peonies.

She started to close the door, but I wedged my toe into the frame. "So she *was* here?"

The woman's nose was so close to mine that I could see the

freckles concealed beneath her powder. The shadow of a gull skimmed across her face.

"If you'll excuse me—" she said.

"Please," I said, reaching for a reason to detain her. "Just for a minute. I'm . . . feeling a little dizzy. It never used to get this hot in September."

Her figure glittered before me. At first I thought it was an illusion, a mirage brought on by sunlight slanting off the sand. But then she dropped her forehead into her palm, and I saw that she was trembling. Thousands of tiny black beads sprinkling her dress quivered in the light.

I asked if she was all right. After a moment she recovered herself and stepped aside so that I could enter. I followed her down a tiled breezeway to the kitchen, where she poured two glasses of iced tea.

"David's not here," she said, sinking to a chair in a cloud of rose perfume. "But he would have wanted me to help you. He was the kind of person who would have helped anyone."

Her name was Jane. Somehow Faye had come across their wedding announcement, placed in the paper six weeks in advance of the ceremony. She'd been clasping the brittle sheet when she arrived at the church the last weekend in May. She eased out of her taxi, the spring sky stretched thin above her, her shadow guiding her across the lawn. The wind tugged her hair free from its knot, stealing her wide-brimmed hat and sending it spinning away. The groomsmen, standing on the grass beside David with their jaws slack and their cigars forgotten, told Jane later that she strode toward David, whose face had gone as white as a bridal gown, and insisted on speaking with him alone. Jane was applying makeup with her bridesmaids in the church basement, and so she knew only what her husband and his friends told her later: that this ex-girlfriend appeared out of nowhere, demanding money.

"For his daughter," Jane said. "Or so she claimed."

Jane told me that when Faye showed up, Amelia's father was so eager to get rid of her that he pulled out his wallet and handed her the stack of prepaid debit cards that he'd purchased for the honeymoon. Then he strode across the lawn, yanked open the door of the idling taxi, and gestured wildly until she climbed inside. The groomsmen said that he watched the car until it rounded the curve behind the church, and then continued watching the road until they approached him, ringed him, and guided him away. They placed a tumbler of whiskey in his hand and slapped the color back into his cheeks. By the time the ceremony began, everyone agreed that he was behaving as much like himself as any man on his wedding day.

"He was jittery, sure," Jane said. She set down her glass with a clatter. "But happy. We both were. Two days later, we left for Peru."

"Peru?"

"For our honeymoon. He wanted to climb Machu Picchu."

"And the prepaid cards?"

"He got more."

Jack and I had honeymooned in Scotland. We wound our way through the countryside on rickety train cars while flocks of sheep drifted across the moors like clouds. We slept inside the stone walls of old farmhouses and hiked through the ruins of ancient castles. On Loch Ness, I ran a hand along the edge of our boat and came away with a splinter. Jack turned my palm toward the sky and pulled the splinter out from the base of my thumb with his teeth. Beyond the oars were only soft waves and mossy hills bleeding into a charcoal sky. I'd believed then that everything good was ahead of us, but I see now that my sorrow was already hurtling down the tracks. With a whistle and a billow of white steam, it was already on its way to meet me.

Storm clouds gathered at the corners of Jane's eyes. "David was a good person," she said. "She bewitched him. Then he left that place. Six months later he met me, and we started to build a life together." She waved her hand toward the cathedral ceilings, the massive refrigerator, the view of the ocean rolling along the shore. "And then she shows up on the day of our wedding? Demanding money? Raving about a rash of unsolved crimes, rattling off book titles, babbling about some king she knows—"

I jerked forward and knocked over my glass. The ice cubes skated across the table and clinked to the floor. "She mentioned the Kingman?"

Jane swayed to her feet. She retrieved a towel from the sink and began to sop up the spill. "The groomsmen just told me she was talking about a king."

"What did David tell you about it?"

"I didn't ask him."

"You didn't *ask* him?"

Her gaze bored into me even as her hands continued patting the towel. "He had enough to deal with. The whole honeymoon, he wasn't himself. After we got home, he was distracted. He wasn't sleeping. I'd wake up and he'd be at the window with the curtains pulled back, staring so hard at something outside that he didn't hear me when I called to him. Sometimes I tried to look over his shoulder, but nothing was ever there." She slumped toward the table. "I assumed that he was thinking of her."

"Of Faye?"

"Or the daughter. Or both. I don't know."

I posed my question more gently this time. "And you didn't ask him?"

"I never got the chance." She bowed her head. "One night, when he couldn't sleep, he got up to go for a drive. While he was out, a thunderstorm rolled in. His car was found smashed against a tree." She took a shuddering breath. "That was it. He was gone before the ambulance arrived."

In the months before he left, Jack, too, used to disappear from the house without warning or explanation. I'd hear the jingle of car keys, the rumble of the engine in the garage, the crackle of tires over the pebbled driveway. He'd be gone for an hour, maybe two, and if I asked him where he'd been, he'd say "Nowhere" in a voice that was so hollow, so strained, that I began to picture *nowhere* as a specific place: a damp pocket of forest, an undulating shadow, a blanket of pine needles where my husband would go to get away from me. Was he alone there? In my mind's eye, his body was taut and vigilant. I saw him straining to hear the crack of a twig, the feet sweeping through leaves, that would herald the arrival of a tenebrous companion.

Jane said that in the weeks after David died, as the summer slouched toward autumn, she became obsessed with finding Amelia. She spent hundreds of hours trying to track her down. She needed to touch the little girl's face, her hands. She needed to look into her eyes and see David looking back.

"I stopped going to work," she said. "I couldn't sleep. Friends called to check up on me, but I stopped answering the phone and the door. I had a single focus: finding that child."

"Couldn't you have gone to Windy Cove? The director had their forwarding address."

Jane smiled faintly. The crescents beneath her eyes were growing more pronounced. "You don't understand. I wasn't looking for Faye. I was looking for her daughter."

"Faye was *with* her daughter."

"No." She shook her head. "When David asked her where the girl was, she said she'd left her with a friend because she couldn't take the girl where she was going. That's why I searched day cares and preschools. I rode my bike in circles around parks. I called high schools and colleges, superintendents, and alumni organizations, but no one had ever heard of Faye or her friend. I began to feel as though I'd made them up."

"Jane, this is crucial," I said. "Amelia appeared at my door three days ago. But you said that when Faye was here in May, she didn't have the girl with her. So where was Amelia between May and September?"

Her lipstick had transferred to her cup. The light shifted, and her skin dimmed. She hunched over the table, diminished. When she finally spoke, her voice was liquid in the darkness.

"That's what I'm telling you," she said. "I have absolutely no idea."

Interview with Jules DuBois, Former Art Teacher at Star Academy
Recorded on February 8, 2019

Of course the tools are sharp. They're made for cutting linoleum.
Cutting wood. When I introduce the printmaking unit, I spend a whole
class on safety demonstrations. I show them how to cut in the opposite
direction of their hands, their torsos, their classmates. I distribute
bench hooks to keep their blocks from slipping. I hang up sign-out
sheets for the tools so that I know exactly who has which knife, which
gouge.

I'm aware that other art teachers would say that fourth graders are
too young for this kind of work. I disagree. I trust my students. I taught
that unit for thirty-two years, and I only had the one issue. It was a big
issue; I'll grant you that. But if the girls hadn't stolen the tools from the
art room—don't you think they would have found similar implements
elsewhere? Wouldn't they have had access, for instance, to steak knives
from their own kitchen drawers?

I don't absolve myself completely. There were signs I could have
read. But they seemed like good kids. Attentive, focused. They always
sat next to each other, usually at a table by themselves. Faye excelled
at drawing and painting. Anna's clay figurines, once we reached the
sculpture unit, were whimsical and otherworldly. So when they started
telling me about this person, this thing they'd encountered on the
Internet, I suggested they channel it into their prints. They really went
for that idea. They sketched prototypes of a northern shoreline; a castle
in the woods. They gouged crude trees and jagged waves. Even now,
years later, when I picture the Kingman moving through the world, it's
as if he's risen right from their blocks: slashes of arms and legs, inky
cloak, face empty of features but for the lines and whorls of the wood
grain itself.

The first sign that something wasn't right, I guess, was that they stopped talking to me as much. Before, they'd enjoyed telling me about their projects. But once they got into those Kingman carvings, they clammed right up. Started eyeing me with something like suspicion. I'm a pretty straight shooter, so finally I asked them what was up. They covered their work with their arms and said: "The less you know, the better."

That's probably why I started snooping around their cubbies after class. I'd call that the second sign: the fact that I felt the need to ink up their blocks and see how the prints turned out. It was an invasion of their privacy, I know. But I didn't feel like myself when I was doing it. I was a little delirious, maybe. It was late and the building was empty and I'd turned out all the lights but for one over my worktable. My shadow seemed elongated—weirdly animated and separate from me. I figured I must have been coming down with something. When you work with kids, that happens.

While I was rolling the ink over the carvings, I only saw the trees. But when I turned the blocks over, pressed them to the paper, and studied the marks that they left, all the hair rose on my arms. It was the faces in the trunks that got me: misshapen ovals, wide-eyed and screaming. There must have been five or six at least in every print. I didn't expect them. Who would? I was still breathing hard when I noticed the wavy lines of a cloak beneath the trees. The knife-blade crown. The knobby, branch-like fingers beckoning me, commanding me to lean in.

After that, I must have fainted. I have no idea how I got home. When I came to, it was a weekend morning and my dog's tongue was lapping at my hands to rouse me from my bed.

The following Monday, back in the art room, I looked for the prints I'd made but couldn't find them. I looked at the blocks but didn't see the faces. Didn't see the Kingman, either. I was distracted all week—blurry, disoriented. The littlest sounds would make me jump. I was focused on trying to hold myself together.

That's why I didn't notice that the tools went missing. It wasn't until the weekend that I heard the news and realized they were gone.

Elizabeth the Good

Although Elizabeth hadn't called Faye's house in years, her fingers remembered the digits. Three rings, half of a fourth. When a familiar voice finally answered, a little out of breath, Elizabeth's tongue was so dry that it was hard to speak.

"Hello?" Faye's mom said. A pause, and then more impatiently: "*Hello?*"

"It's Elizabeth," she tried to say. The words came out in kind of a shout.

She'd been awake the entire night before. Then she'd spent the day trying to write a paper, but her wrists kept slumping over her keyboard, and her blood kept pumping so loudly through her ears that she couldn't concentrate. By the end of the day, there was nothing she could do but confess.

"Listen," she said. "I didn't tell you everything."

But Mrs. Vogel already knew. "You had Amelia with you for *four months*? And you never thought to contact anyone? To turn her in? To *call me?*"

"How did you—" Elizabeth started. But it didn't matter how the truth had come out. "I thought—I didn't—" she stammered into the receiver. Her roommate was peering over the top of her bunk, so Elizabeth dropped her voice to a whisper. "Faye said she'd come right back."

"Faye *said?* And you *listened* to her?"

Elizabeth tightened her fingers around the receiver. She didn't have an answer. After everything that happened, why was she still shielding Faye? Why, when Faye showed up at her door with that outrageous request, didn't Elizabeth simply say no?

"Haven't you learned *anything*?" Faye's mom was saying.

"I—"

"I've had a very long day, Anna—"

"Actually, it's Elizabeth—"

"In fact, I've had a very long decade. And now Faye is missing and my granddaughter is here and the Kingman is back—"

The desk lamp flickered. "What do you mean, 'back'?"

"I don't mean *back*, I just mean, he's in the headlines again, and—"

Elizabeth couldn't keep her voice from cracking. "What headlines?"

"The new *crimes*, Anna! The ones in her closet!"

"In her—"

"And I'm *worried* about her. I thought that I was only a few days behind her, wherever she went, but I'm actually *months* away. She could be anywhere. With anyone. Anna—" Finally, she caught herself. "*Elizabeth*. What has she been doing all this time?"

Elizabeth strained to remember: Had the North Woods come before the Kingman, or had the Kingman come before the North Woods? Had they found out about their monster after they'd already zeroed in on the Upper Midwest, or was the rumor of his fortress what brought them there? *Probably*, she told herself, *it doesn't matter how it started*. What she did remember were the hours they spent poring over the atlas, studying the vast green stretches that represented woods and the blue baubles that stood for lakes. She remembered that when Faye asked her if she could see the eyes that blinked at them from deep inside the map, Elizabeth told her that she could. She *wanted* to fear what Faye feared. She wanted to believe her when she promised that they could face any danger as long as they were together.

"But where will the danger be coming from?" Elizabeth had once asked.

Faye had squinted at the roses on her wallpaper as if willing them to stop moving for a second so that she could corral her thoughts. "From somewhere long ago," she said.

Elizabeth didn't understand. But before she could ask for clarification, Faye added: "And also, somewhere cold."

That was when they started talking about snowdrifts and icicles. It was when her dreams frosted over, when she began imagining herself into wintry places as Faye told story after story about treasure hunters and ship captains and ice explorers who fell off their maps and vanished.

"Their families thought they died," Faye said. "But the truth is that they didn't *need* to go home because they found a different kind of home. One that they didn't even realize they'd been looking for."

Elizabeth wanted to help Faye's mom. She wanted to tell her what she knew. The sentences were bubbling up in her chest, fizzing on the tip of her tongue. But then her roommate was climbing down from her bunk and moving toward the mini-fridge, pretending to rummage around for a pack of baby carrots or an iced tea when really all she wanted was to hear this conversation better. So Elizabeth waited too long to reply, and then there was a snap in her ear and the connection was cut and all she could hear was a crackly white static that sounded a little like music and a little like words and a little like a message that someone had told her once before.

From the Memoirs of the Honorable Ernest B. McKinley

Published 2011; Reading Recorded on February 22, 2019

I'd been on the bench for about a decade when the Kingman circus
came to town. The girls, the families, the reporters, the tourists, the
writers, the gawkers—the whole thing was mayhem, absolute mayhem,
the sort of chaos Maurice Sendak describes in *Where the Wild Things
Are*, which comes to mind because it happened to be the book my
son was insisting that I read to him every night. *Let the wild rumpus
start!* I felt like calling out every time I entered, my robes swishing at
my ankles, my notes in one hand and my gavel in the other. When I
sat, the whole courtroom sat with me. The lawyers paraded all kinds
of characters down the aisle and up to the stand: teachers and police
officers and psychiatrists and neighbors. And yet we never heard from
the parents.

The parents were there, of course. Or some of them were. The
smaller, more anxious child came with a gaggle of sullen relatives who
looked like characters straight out of Roald Dahl. The other one had only
her mother. The woman sat three rows behind her daughter, who was
slender and grim. The mother was drained of life and color. She knew
that after this, she would become a pariah in the community, held up
as a model for what a mother shouldn't be. How could a parent let this
happen? That's what people were whispering behind her. I could see
their lips moving, even from the bench. The woman, the mother, sat
with her back as straight as a tree trunk, and never once turned.

I wondered for a long time after that, as my own son was growing
up, what had happened to the father. If my son had committed such a
crime—what would Hallie and I have done? Forgiven him? Disowned
him? To me that must have been the most monstrous part: deciding
how to proceed. Trying to see where you went wrong.

At the end of Sendak's story, the wild things cry out for Max to stay.

"Oh please don't go—we'll eat you up—we love you so!" That's what they say. At that point in the story I always reached for my son's foot and pretended to put it in my mouth. He laughed and laughed and laughed. How funny it was to him: that peculiar, savage link between love and violence.

Sylvia

It was late when I returned from the coast, but Jack was waiting for me. The living room windows leaked light across the driveway, and his silhouette floated back and forth across the frame. I'd been yearning for him the whole drive home, my body bent over the steering wheel as if leaning in his direction would pull me there faster. I had so much to tell him.

But when I opened the door, he stopped pacing and spun toward me. His black eyes burned.

"What happened?" I demanded.

"Where the hell have you *been*?" he growled. "You're five hours later than you said you would be. When you didn't show by dinnertime, I tried to call—"

"My phone died."

"And so I waited, and waited—"

I stepped toward him, but he started pacing again. "It's a long drive," I said. "You know that. And after Windy Cove, there was Jane, and before I left I needed to persuade her to—"

"Who the fuck is Jane? And where the fuck is Faye?"

"What *happened*, Jack?" An unexpected stab of fear. "Is Amelia all right?"

"She's fine. She's asleep."

The wind coursed through the leaves outside, and an unlatched shutter banged somewhere against the siding. A storm was sliding in. Jack's face, shadowed and haggard, concealed whatever he was thinking. When he finally spoke, his voice was hoarse.

"This isn't what I came for," he said.

I didn't know what he meant, but his anger had shaken my own frustration loose. "Do you think I wanted this? That I planned to spend the week racing all over the state, scrambling to get inside Faye's head? I'm sorry that I dragged you down here. I should've known better than to call you, than to force you to take some responsibility. Once again, this is all my fault."

We glared at each other from opposite sides of the living room. In a different lifetime, a different version of myself had gazed into his face and seen a vision of Faye. Now, no matter how intently I scanned his features, I found only exhaustion and age. *Don't do it*, I wanted to tell my former self, who was still tilting toward Jack in the optical shop with her heart in her hands. *If you marry this man, it will ruin you.*

Finally, Jack lifted his duffel bag and swung it over his shoulder. Hot tears prickled in the corners of my eyes, but he was out of the door and inside his truck before I let them spill over.

As his headlights winked out of sight, I couldn't stop myself from remembering the way I'd burst into his office an hour after my breakup and pinned him against the wall of the examination room. I remembered how, when we walked out of the building together, his hand gripping mine, the sidewalk glittered in the late afternoon sunlight like a promise. In that moment, I saw my future unfolding before me, warm and golden.

See? I said to my former self, trudging up the stairs to check on the child. *The future is nothing but a mirage, a projection. A trick of the light.*

Once, around the time of the hearing, Jack and I had been called to a psychiatric hospital to meet a group of doctors who were fascinated by Faye's situation. They asked us what kinds of books we'd read to her as a child, what sorts of movies we'd watched as a family. They inquired about imaginary friends and future aspirations.

They angled over their clipboards and took assiduous notes in a pinched script.

I was remembering the white glow of the computer screen, the blogs and videos and chat rooms I'd inhabited in the months since the crime. I'd learned that the Kingman had a tangled, storied history. This was not a creature that my daughter had invented. He'd come from somewhere. That had to mean something.

"But the Kingman—" I began.

"Sylvia," Jack warned.

The doctors considered us from behind several pairs of glasses, their eyes reptilian.

I tried again. "I mean, she wasn't the one who made him up. He exists outside of her experience. Lots of other people—"

Jack was on his feet before I finished the thought. He abandoned me among the pixelated prairie scenes, across from a row of doctors who stared at me with the frank curiosity of botanists whose favorite flower had sprouted wings and taken flight.

A few days later, over breakfast, I'd asked Jack about Joan of Arc. All night I'd dreamed of Joan, remembering scenes from an old film I'd seen years ago. The actress's hair was razed to her skull; her luminous face overflowed the screen.

Jack dumped a tablespoon of cream into his mug and watched it snake its way through the coffee. "What about her?"

"She heard voices."

He glared at me. "You're comparing our daughter"—the words *our daughter* spat out bitterly, vengefully—"to a saint?"

The cat padded through the kitchen and twined herself around the table legs. Then she rippled to the doorway and stared intently down the hallway. She frowned back at me and meowed.

"That's not what I'm saying," I said.

But Jack wouldn't let it go. "You're saying that Faye could have heard something real."

"I'm just trying to understand—"

"What happened to Joan of Arc, Sylvia?"

I looked back at the cat, who was still peering down the hall-way, her head turning as if tracking something's movement. "She burned at the stake," I finally replied.

"She burned at the stake," Jack repeated. The blood drained from his face. "And her voices burned with her."

When the phone rang, I thought it would be him. Instead, a young woman was saying, "Listen—" but by then I was too rattled to hear her.

"You had Amelia with you for *four months*?" I shouted. "And you never thought to contact anyone? To turn her in? To *call me*?"

She said something after that, but a white noise was fizzling through the line, and I couldn't make out her words.

"Elizabeth?" I said. "*Elizabeth?*"

Then the line went dead, and she was gone.

Upstairs, a lumpy shape inhaled and exhaled below the blankets on the sofa bed. When I stepped closer, I made out the head of a stuffed elephant resting on the pillow, its trunk tangled up in her hair. The elephant was new to me, as was the star-studded fabric of the pajama sleeve beneath her downy cheek and the stack of folded shirts on the carpet. In the bathroom, an alligator-shaped toothbrush leaned against mine in its ceramic cup, and the sink bore traces of sparkly toothpaste.

I brushed my own teeth, retrieved my laptop from my desk, flipped on the bedside lamp, and propped myself up against the pillows. I shuffled through the papers I'd acquired from Jane, searching for the correct web address to type into my browser. She had been slow in handing over the log-in details for the prepaid debit cards her husband had ceded to Faye.

"Why do you want that?" she'd asked.

"Because then I'll be able to see where Faye used the cards," I'd explained. "Even if I don't know where she's going, I'll know where she's been."

Maybe Jane wanted to be the one to track down Faye. Maybe she was worried that the cards would reveal something about David. Whatever the reason, she dragged her feet. Stars dangled faintly over the sea by the time I finally returned to the car with the papers clutched in my hands.

Now a circle of white light from my bedside lamp beamed over the keyboard as I typed in the card number and password. While the page loaded, flickering to life with letters and figures, my heart thudded inside my throat, and my temples throbbed. Let's say I did discover where she was. What exactly did I plan to do once I'd ensnared her in my arms?

Here's something that I never dared to tell anyone, especially not Jack: the more I read about the Kingman during those months after the crime, the more real he became to me. I saw him in the shadows that crept into the bedroom at night. I saw him flicker between the oak trees at the edge of the backyard. When, in my loneliness, I dragged out ancient family photo albums, I saw him there, too: standing behind Faye at the swing set, or sliding out of the frame as she puffed her cheeks and extinguished the candles on her birthday cake. It was then that I realized the Kingman had always been with us. Why hadn't I noticed him before it was too late?

That night I dreamed that I was unlocking the door of my old bookstore on an early winter morning. The black sky was barely pink and the spines shuddered on their shelves as if, when the door blew open, the breeze had woken and chilled them. I'd had to surrender the management of the shop after the crime because so many people were jostling through the door to gawk at me, to yell at me, that the business suffered. I maintained my ownership and received quarterly checks with my cut of the sales, but I no longer set foot in the store except in dreams.

In this one, Faye was floating through the shelves. She used to spend every afternoon and weekend with me there, working her way methodically through the children's section, and then the young adult, devouring stories with such fierce urgency that customers often stopped, astonished, to watch her read. In my dream, Faye spun toward me with an inscrutable expression, her arm bent around a stack of books that she balanced on her hip bone. The letters on their spines shone in the gloom, and clouds of dust drifted from the ceiling, as ghostly as snow at night. Faye extended her arms as if to hand over the books, but my own arms were clamped to my sides and I couldn't catch them before they fell. It was when they thudded to the ground that I startled awake, lurching up from my damp pillow with clammy skin and a riotous heart that refused to settle back in its cage. For a long time I sat rigidly in the dark, listening to the silver fingers of rain tapping on the roof and remembering how vividly I used to dream about my mother in the months after she died.

The sky cracked with lightning, and the wind howled around the roof. Downstairs, the birds twittered wildly. Worried that Amelia would be frightened by the storm, I rose from my bed and stepped into my slippers and drifted toward the end of the hallway.

When I poked my head into the spare bedroom, I found that the night-light had gone out. I couldn't make out the sofa bed, the chair, the lamp—they were nothing but bulky, unfamiliar shadows. It was only when another round of lightning sliced open the darkness that I could see the outline of her figure on the windowsill.

I shuffled over to Amelia and placed my palm against her back. Her shoulder blades tensed and trembled like wings.

"Are you all right?" I whispered.

She pointed, pressing her fingertip to the glass. She tapped once, twice, three times. I knelt beside her and mirrored her position, squinting out at the yard in the rain, trying to distinguish the boulders and the shrubbery from the shadows. Dense clouds spiraled overhead, smoky and green. Water sheeted into the pond, and I could have sworn I saw the neon flash of a long-dead fish. Was that what she was looking at?

But no. When I followed her gaze, I could see that she was focused instead on something at the edge of the yard, among the oaks that lined the driveway. The trees floated above the ground, their limbs rippling and spectral. I blinked, and someone shifted between the trunks. My fingers went cold.

"Amelia," I said darkly. "What do you see?"

Her pale face glistened like a crystal ball. My muscles tensed, as if to flee.

"Can't you tell?" Her voice was her mother's voice, too. "He's coming back."

That's when I knew that I was dreaming.

In the morning I found her sprawled, sleeping, on the carpet beside the sofa bed. Her hair, pooling across the pillow that had pursued her to the floor, gleamed beneath her face.

I made coffee and carried the mug to the porch. I was waiting for something, but I had no idea what. The wind shivered through the leaves and birdsong jangled from the trees. The sun had risen, but the shadows were still lanky and blue. I stood there for what felt like hours, the coffee cooling in my cup, the mist rolling through my mind, looking at a magnolia that Jack had planted with Faye. If I narrowed my eyes and peered just so into the light, I could still see her kneeling in the grass, cupping handfuls of dirt over bare roots, talking to herself as she worked.

When my coffee had gone cold, I returned to the house to wake Amelia. I combed her hair with trembling fingers and dumped too much cereal into her bowl. The flakes snowed onto the tabletop. She watched as I swept them up, as I poured her juice and slid into the chair across from hers. She was still watching as I laid out the printed pages of that night's research, her expression keen, but she removed her gaze when I instructed her to eat.

Faye's first purchase had been a bus ticket in Raleigh. For two days after that, I could track her progress north by locating the towns where she'd spent small sums in gas stations or fast-food restaurants. Rocky Mount, Fredericksburg, Baltimore, Youngstown, Cleveland. I tried to imagine her view of the Great Lakes in Toledo or Gary or Milwaukee: a turquoise backdrop for billowing smokestacks and railroad tracks and the red-orange rust of abandoned factories. When the bus hit Wisconsin, it veered west to the capital and then began its slow ascent to the north, skirting small silver lakes and gliding through state forests. By the time I'd reached that portion of the map, I didn't need to read the rest of the charges to know where Faye had landed. She'd been heading toward the same place she'd tried to reach on foot when she was nine years old, her backpack stocked with granola bars and the tip of her knife still beaded with blood: Minnesota.

"Land of lakes and ice and snow," I said to Amelia, who was chewing her cereal with a thoughtful expression. Her jaw halted, midbite, when I spoke. I remembered the torn headlines in Faye's closet, imagined a crown of knives. "Most importantly, legendary home of—"

I stopped myself in time.

At first, we had allowed the girls to play in the woods on their own. They never ran into trouble; they always returned safely. But a few months before the crime, we'd heard of a devastating case in Virginia where a boy Faye's age had simply—vanished. He had been plucked from his own neighborhood, off his own bike. News outlets broadcast the story everywhere, and the parents gave such heart-wrenching interviews that for weeks it was all anyone could talk about. Sometimes at night Jack had to shake me awake, to rescue me from nightmares of abductions and disappearances. It was he who suggested we hire our neighbor Brittany to accompany Faye and Anna through the park, to the creek. She was sixteen, a piano player and a stargazer, and we rested easier knowing that the girls were not alone.

Once or twice she hoisted her telescope out of her trunk and set it up in our backyard so that she could teach Faye and Anna the names of the constellations. At the detention center weeks later, when I asked Faye what she had seen, she'd lifted her chin and considered me through the Plexiglas. "A star king," she'd replied, and a gust of cold wind had whipped around my heart.

That morning, when the girls said they were going to the woods, we called Brittany to see if she could pop over. Everyone knows what happened next: the picnic breakfast of powdered doughnuts on a quilt in the backyard, the walk around the fence into the park. You probably know that the girls asked her to leave them alone, but she didn't. How they leapt at her. How they held her down together in the leaves, the creek gurgling beside them, while Faye raised the knife she'd smuggled out of the art room. You've heard the nurses talk about the five puncture wounds, and so you know how narrowly Faye missed rupturing a major artery, slicing a vital organ. That hiker has given a thousand interviews in which he describes what it was like to see Brittany dragging herself out of the woods, a half mile down from our house. You might even know that Faye and Anna were two miles away by then, splashing their hands and faces with cold water in a grocery-store bathroom, holding their bloodied T-shirts beneath the faucet until the stream ran clear. You know that they were picked up in a ditch that ran along the highway, but you probably don't know exactly what they were intending to do next. That was something we had to piece together later.

What you need to understand about my daughter is that she waited to take her first steps until she was fourteen months old.

She was biding her time. She'd been plotting for weeks and weeks so that when she finally pulled herself up on the coffee table, she could cross the whole living room and stride through the dining room to the kitchen, tug on the leg of Jack's pants, and startle him into dropping his sandwich.

Do you see what I'm saying? Faye has never lifted a foot or a finger without a good reason. And so, when she set out through the crisp yellow grass with Anna, ignoring the cars flying past them on the highway, her skin already close to burning, her destination was clear in her mind. She was on her way to find the Kingman. It was only twelve hundred miles to Minneapolis. She had packed snacks and maps, and she had a loyal friend at her side. Children in chapter books were always setting out on adventures. There was no way that those kids were any faster, smarter, or more resourceful than she.

I brought Amelia out to the porch swing to get some fresh air; to think. She paged through a women's magazine that she'd opened across her lap, pausing to inspect the faces of makeup models. When a truck turned down our road, her chin snapped up and the magazine slipped from her fingers as she tracked the rumbling crescendo of its approach.

The carousel of milk-scented infants; the open beak of a heron chick; a castle on a great gray shore; a shaft of golden light between the trees. We never escape our childhood dreams. As soon as I had found Faye's child on my doorstep, as soon as I had seen those crimes tacked to the plywood walls of her closet, I should have known where my daughter was going.

Interview with Anders Olsen, Proprietor of Royale Lodge
Recorded on March 28, 2019

—This lodge has been in the family for a hundred years at least. Usually, business isn't great. The island's remote. Bitter cold in the winter, thick with flies and skeeters in the summer. You gotta take a ferry or seaplane from Michigan or Minnesota. My grandma said that this place isn't for the faint of heart, and she wasn't wrong. The resort seekers, the beach readers, the massage lovers, those kind of people— it's better that they go down to Florida for a shrimp boil or what have you. Isle Royale is for something else.

—But in 2008, things changed. Isn't that right?

—Sure is. Suddenly we got more requests for reservations than we could handle. We had to bring on extra staff to clean, to cook. We switched on the NO VACANCY sign in May and didn't switch it off for a couple of years. Things have settled down again now.

—Can you tell us what caused the surge of interest in your property? In Isle Royale?

—Sure can. It was just after that stabbing. The crime down in North Carolina, with those two little girls. That's when everybody started talking about the Kingman. Rumor had it that his castle was on an island in Superior, just off the coast, wooded and rocky and dark. People assumed it was Isle Royale.

—And you believe that they were wrong?

—Well, I don't believe a legend is the kind of thing a person can be right or wrong about. That's kinda the whole point. But I'll say this: if I were out looking for legends, I wouldn't waste my time here on Isle Royale. I'd try my luck on Isle Philippeaux. You know—the phantom island? Two hundred years ago, it showed up on maps. But it's not on any maps today. Lots of people have gone searching for it with no luck. Doesn't mean it's not there; Superior is not an easy place to navigate. Depending on her mood, she'd just as soon sink you as look at you.

—Have you ever gone searching for this phantom island yourself?

—Me? I'm a little too busy for that kind of thing. This lodge doesn't run itself. But—well, I don't know.

—What were you going to say?

—Well, I don't want to speculate, or cause trouble for parents. Kids are impressionable. They'll talk to anybody. Believe in anything. Hell, my own boys have the wildest imaginations. Half the time they come down to breakfast, they're talking about the weird things they saw out their window the night before. A shadow shuffling back and forth across the beach. Bigmouthed faces in the trees. A couple of times they've said they heard the lapping of a rowboat in the water, and they've insisted that we walk out and find it.

—A phantom rowboat from the phantom island?

—So they say.

—Have you found it?

—There's nothing there to find.

—So you don't believe in the Kingman?

—Well—I believe that the mind can play tricks. There have been nights, when I've been walking the rocks in winter, that I've seen the lights of boats where I know no boats could be. There are times when the wind through the trees sounds to me just like a child crying. There are hikers who go out and never come back again. But it's rugged up here, and lonely sometimes, and that Great Lake's a killer. It doesn't take a Kingman to make a person disappear.

Jack

Jack didn't turn around to look at Sylvia before he left. He started up his truck and soared over black highways until he reached the hills, then the mountain pass. Finally he spotted his cabin hunkered down among the pines. The sky was soft and dark. A strip of daylight waited beneath the horizon. He yanked his keys from the ignition and strode onto the porch. It was cooler up here, as he knew it would be, without Amelia's searing gaze and Sylvia's smoldering fury. He kicked off his boots and stomped toward the bedroom. His life was a hell of a lot easier when there weren't other people in it.

Of course he knew that she'd shouldered more than her share of the responsibility. In such situations, it's the mother who's blamed. In former times, when people still believed that monsters came from humans, they wrote scientific treatises about all the things a pregnant woman could do that would deform the child in her womb. If she had sex while menstruating, her child would be monstrous. If she had sex in strange positions, her child would be monstrous. If her blood were impure or her thoughts were sinful or if she looked at or ingested or even smelled something she shouldn't, well—her child would be monstrous then, too.

In the aftermath of Faye's crime, everybody hoped to find out that Sylvia drank too much bourbon while pregnant or that she and Jack kept Faye locked up in the attic. That's why reporters interviewed their neighbors and colleagues, tracked down their browsing history, and lurked in the shrubs outside their windows. The reporters wanted to catch the two of them fighting or drinking. Selling drugs or stolen cars. If people could figure out exactly how they'd failed as parents, everyone would know what not to do. They wouldn't wind up with a kid who stabbed her babysitter with a printmaking knife and pledged her allegiance to a creature who'd crept out of the Internet. They needed to protect the world from monsters like Faye.

In the weeks leading up to the hearing, Sylvia kept asking where they'd gone wrong. So Jack thought about it. He admitted that once he'd chastised a kindergarten teacher for suggesting that Faye try to color in between the lines. He'd raised his voice near the cubbies with Faye's rubber boots dangling from his hand and the scent of crayons filling his nostrils. He'd insisted that his daughter's freedom and creativity were more important than arbitrary constraints. But maybe that had been some kind of test. Maybe he was supposed to tell Faye about the value of rules, the importance of fitting into social structures, and the dangers of forging her own path.

Sylvia listened to his description of the scene in silence. Her face glowed in the gray light of the computer screen. When he finished, she leaned forward in her desk chair as though she intended to say something; but Jack wasn't about to take the blame.

"It's not our fault that Faye made a bad choice," he said.

Sylvia twisted in her seat. "But she's *our* child."

"That doesn't mean she's an extension of us." He knew that he sounded cold. "We raised her the best that we could, Syl. She's not an adult, but she's not a toddler, either. She knows that this was"—he wanted to say *horrific*, but instead he said—"wrong."

Sylvia remained silent. She was drawing into herself again. Over her shoulder gleamed pictures of fairy-tale forests and faceless kings. He needed to pull her back to him.

"Turn that thing off," he said, more sharply than he intended. He tried to soften his tone. "Won't you, please?"

The filmmakers had knocked on his door once, too, demanding an interview. He'd lost his temper. He'd raised his voice, ripped the cord out of their microphone, wrenched the camera from their hands, and smashed it to the ground. Afterward he peered down at the shards of glass and metal and wondered which parts of the story they'd already captured and which parts he'd just unleashed again.

"Hey, man!" the skinniest one shouted. "That thing was fucking *expensive*! You better be planning to pay us for that!"

He took one step forward and all three of them stepped back. He could feel himself growing taller, more menacing. He wondered if he looked to them like the wild man he was in the process of becoming: terrific beard, scruffy flannel, boots caked with mud. His voice was hoarse from disuse, but he cleared his throat anyway.

"Who gave you the right to make a movie out of someone else's pain?"

They muttered something about art. When he took a second step toward them, the heel of his boot slammed against the weathered boards of the porch. That was it. They took off, hurtling toward their car like they were the ones who were victims.

In the end, he wound up watching the documentary. He couldn't stay away. They'd managed to get interviews with almost everybody: police officers, psychiatrists, teachers, jurors. They staged dramatic readings of news reports and memoirs. There was even a scene where Anna's aunt spoke directly to the camera. She wasn't wearing makeup. Her skin was puffy and spotted. She looked like she'd been on the verge of tears for five years straight. Sylvia had told him that at the hearing, the woman had sobbed so hard that people couldn't hear the lawyers' questions. The judge had to ask her to leave.

"She was living this whole other life inside her head," Anna's aunt said to the screen. Jack imagined the tripod in her living room. The filmmakers sinking lazily into her pleather couch. "But lots of times kids don't differentiate between fantasy and reality. That's how they play." She paused, blinking at the camera. The moment felt rehearsed. "How do you know what's normal and what's not?"

He was making dinner when he realized she was gone. Bagged salad and frozen pepperoni pizza that he'd picked up after discovering that Sylvia had little to eat in the house. Amelia had been sitting at the kitchen table, flipping the pages of a wildflower field guide that he'd found for her in the bookshelf that ran beneath the living room window. But when he turned around to set a plate in front of her, she wasn't there.

He tore through that house like a hunting dog. He ripped closets open and yanked blankets from the beds. He tried the bathtub, the pantry, the cobwebbed corners of the attic. Then he barreled out to the porch and slammed through the screen door to the front yard. Sylvia could have rolled up the driveway any minute. He pictured her face when she learned that he'd lost their only child's only child.

I asked you to do one thing, he imagined her saying. *One goddamned thing. How many times do you intend to let me down?*

Of course Sylvia would never say something like that. In that whole horrifying year after the crime, she'd never so much as suggested it. No. Instead, she'd gone silent. Sometimes he'd shown up at the bedroom door after she returned home from the courtroom. He'd waited at the threshold to see if she wanted to talk. But the minute she felt his presence, she turned to face the wall. Eventually, he stopped going to her. It killed him to brush her arm when they passed in the narrow hallway. He knew that he had to get out of there.

It was easy enough to spot Amelia once he was in the yard. She was standing at the fence, her back to the house, peering between the pine slats as if there were something more interesting than trees out there. She didn't protest when he swept her inside and deposited her in front of her lukewarm pizza. She took a bite out of a slice and chewed without complaint.

But Jack couldn't shake the weight of Sylvia's imagined anger. He had come because he wanted to be close to her, but also because he needed to prove something to her. Unfortunately, he didn't yet know what that was.

As he lay on his own bed that night, too sapped to sleep, a memory came for him. Faye had been a little older than Amelia, and they'd driven to Boston to see his family for Thanksgiving. The Saturday after the holiday, he and Sylvia had bundled Faye into a winter coat and an earflap hat borrowed from a northern cousin. Then the three of them had set out for the art museum. It wasn't a long walk from where they were staying: one mile, two at most. The sky was soft with pending snow. White lights twinkled in brownstone windows. They could see the puff of their breath as they strolled. Faye was darting ahead, skirting patches of ice on the sidewalk. Every twenty steps or so she dropped to her knees to draw a chalk arrow on the pavement. Each one pointed in the direction from which they'd come.

"Faye," Jack remembered saying. "Why aren't the arrows guiding us toward the museum?"

She peered at him as if he were even more foolish than she'd initially expected. "Daddy," she said. Her tone was scolding. "This is for later, so that we can find our way back home."

Interview with Lillian Pine, Former Durham Police Officer
Recorded on June 29, 2018

I don't know why I drove over to the detention center on the day that Faye Vogel got released. I felt invested, I guess. I'd spent years thinking about her. That talk I'd had with her at the station stayed with me. A couple of times I stopped by the courtroom during the hearing to see what people were saying about her. About her monster.

I didn't think she'd recognize me after all those years had passed. But as soon as she emerged into the lobby, she cracked a half smile at the sight of me. She left her caseworker standing by the metal detector and she glided my way.

"Congratulations," she said, indicating the basketball beneath my shirt.

"Thanks," I said. I felt the baby twist. "You must be looking forward to seeing your folks."

Her expression shuttered. "Yeah," she said. "But I'm not going home with them. They're not even married anymore."

Outside, an orange sky stretched across the distant highway. A car door slammed. A scraggy shadow lengthened in the parking lot. "I'm sorry to hear that," I said, and I was. I could be sorry even if I wasn't surprised.

"Nothing has turned out the way I thought," she said.

Then her mother walked in the door. She looked much older, but she was dressed for an occasion with a colored silk scarf and low yellow heels. The father followed a few steps behind her and stopped in the doorway.

There were a lot of reasons for me to quit the force. The darkness, the violence, the fear. The baby on the way. But I don't think I made the decision to leave until that day. That hour. It was something about witnessing that reunion. All three of them stiff and formal, their faces pained and their shadows trembling. Somewhere deep inside, the baby bucked and writhed.

Sylvia

I'd thought about boarding a plane a thousand times or more. Marching up to the ticket window with nothing but a rolling carry-on, demanding the cheapest flight to Europe, to South or Central America. *Just point to a place on the map*, I'd announce, *and send me there*. I'd stride down the aisle and grab a window seat and sleep the whole way, my head tilted back, my lips parted, the beverage cart clattering all night long. When I sat up and removed my eye mask, the former Sylvia would have vanished. I'd step outside the airport to find myself transformed.

Jack had done it, hadn't he? He'd evolved from a mild-mannered eye doctor to a rugged mountaineer. I promised myself that when I finally left, I'd do even better. I wouldn't simply distance myself. I'd disappear completely. I'd start over.

But I couldn't disappear—not yet, not then—with Amelia breathing softly beside me and Jack's truck hurtling around the bend in the driveway. He tumbled out of the driver's seat before the gravel dust had settled and jogged toward the porch, his shaggy hair flopping. Amelia slid from the swing and mashed her forehead to the screen door, her face split open in a grin. I remained where I was, the porch swing wheezing beneath me while Jack slowed and pulled open the door, catching the girl with one large hand to keep her from toppling down the steps. When he turned to face me, she folded herself against his leg.

"Did you forget something?" My tone was barbed.

He peered at me. The midmorning light striped across the porch floor. "No," he said. "I came back because I promised I'd help you."

"But you said—"

"I know what I said, Syl," he said. "And I'm sorry. I was overwhelmed. I got scared."

"You got scared?" A crisp breeze gusted through the screens. I remembered crouching with Amelia at the window. I imagined the Kingman, spindly and regal, slipping from shadow to shadow. "Scared of what?"

He blanched and shifted his weight. Amelia slithered to the floorboards and then reattached herself to his leg like a limpet. He trailed his fingers through her hair.

"I don't know, Syl, let's start with—scared to find out what Faye is up to. Scared to see where the next crime pops up. Scared of the police, the reporters, of the way Amelia sometimes stares at something I can't see. Is that enough?"

My gaze dropped to Amelia, her face shining, her chin tilted toward Jack. In the courtroom, Faye's expression had been polished and cold. If she'd felt fear, she'd buried it.

"I shouldn't have said all of that," Jack muttered. "And I shouldn't have left yesterday. I'm sorry. But not everybody can be as brave as you."

I was startled into looking at him. *Brave.* The word glimmered between us, gorgeous and honed.

When I arrayed the cash-card statements before Jack, he agreed with my analysis. "Minnesota, all right," he said. Amelia, watching cartoons in the next room, glanced up at his grim tone. "That's where she's always wanted to go."

A vision of the girls trekking north along the highway: the map, the snacks, the photographs in their backpacks.

"That was thirteen years ago," I said. "Why would she leave now?"

Jack fidgeted with his water glass, sliding it back and forth between his palms. "I didn't want to bring this up," he said. "But over the past few months, there've been some incidents."

The closet walls papered with yellow headlines. "Kingman crimes," I said.

"That's right."

"You don't think that Faye—"

"I don't know *what* to think about Faye."

I waited.

He drew in a breath and then added, "Sorry. It's just—this was hard enough the first time around."

I extended my hand to touch his. The gesture was instinctive, the urge to reassure him so deeply embedded in the fiber of my being that I wasn't even aware that I was reaching out to him until I'd done it. My fingers brushed his knuckles, weathered and cracked. Before I could pull my hand back, he'd flipped his over and clasped my palm firmly against his. The slap of our skin startled me, the warm pressure dizzying. I don't know what he saw in my expression when he raised his gaze to mine, but he loosened his grip and released me.

I cleared my throat and tried to focus on the question at hand. "What do you make of this charge, here?" I asked, tapping the sheet in front of me. "Six hundred dollars to the University of Minnesota?"

Jack scanned the list of charges. "It says registrar," he said. "She's taking a class."

"Why travel all that way just to take a class?"

Jack looked thoughtful. He drummed his fingers on the table and shot a glance toward Amelia, sprawled across the couch with her head on a cushion.

"There's somebody who teaches up there," he said. "In Minneapolis. A scholar who's done a ton of research on"—he stumbled, but swallowed hard and picked himself up again—"the Kingman. He's working on a book."

A light flared in my mind. I might have known this once. "How did you find that out?"

He hesitated. "Well—listen, Syl. I needed to know what they had said about us."

Of course: the documentary. The youthful filmmakers emerged from the fog of memory, slouching on the front steps, pushing their cameras into my face, lobbing their questions like grenades. I remembered how hard I'd struggled to shut the door. "Did you talk to them?"

He grimaced. "I told them to fuck off. But then, when it came out last year, I saw it. I had to watch it in several sittings—I could only take small doses." He laughed dryly, and the sound sent a tremor through me. "It's been thirteen years, and I still can't wrap my mind around why she—well. But I thought that if I watched the doc, maybe—I don't know." He shrugged. I tried not to stare at the movement of his shoulder bone beneath his black T-shirt. "Maybe I'd finally have some answers."

"And do you?"

He chuckled again, and my whole body loosened. It took all my strength not to topple toward his torso and melt right into him.

"Nope," he said. "But it does make me wonder. Maybe Faye is looking for answers, too."

When I was alone, I used to keep myself company by populating the house with alternative versions of myself. The Sylvias who had boarded imaginary planes in order to escape their isolation and despair, who'd soared over the glitter of city lights or the wide, crashing seas between the craggy mass of continents. The Sylvias who had married men who were not Jack. Or the ones who had chosen not to have children. What had happened to the shades of myself who made the decisions that I did not? How were those other paths laid out beneath the one I chose?

Another Sylvia might have listened to Jack when he claimed

that he was content without children. "Would it be so terrible if it were just the two of us?" Jack had asked me once.

Perhaps I should have drawn him close, twined my arms around his waist, and loved him even harder. Perhaps that could have been the end of it.

Jack showed me how to stream the documentary. He clicked past the first thirty minutes and paused when a pair of thick blue glasses filled up the frame. Behind the glasses, a man blinked into whatever light the crew had rigged above them. The man was clean-shaven, wearing a crisp button-down shirt and a skinny black tie. The camera crew followed him out of his office, trailing him through a windowless corridor, pale green and dim. At the end of the hall, he yanked open a door and strode into a lecture hall brimming with students. Since most seats were occupied, some of them had settled cross-legged on the floor or opted for leaning against a painted brick wall. They rotated their heads like owls as the professor passed, their gazes pursuing him down to the lectern. Most didn't give the camera a second look. LECTURE ONE rolled across the bottom of the screen in white block letters. Then the professor began.

> First, you must suspend your disbelief. Unwrap it like a scarf from your shoulders. Hang it on a hook in the hallway. Leave it at the door, swaying above the floor, and enter a world where everything is still possible.
>
> This is and is not a biology class. This is and is not a history class, a poetry class, a chemistry class, an art class. This is and is not a psychology class, although at times you will certainly find yourself plumbing the depths of your own consciousness, analyzing your own nightmares. You're here to study monstrology. Much like Frankenstein's monster, this class has been built out of pieces from other bodies, other minds, and other disciplines. Herme-

neutics, alchemy. If you don't know those words, you'd better look them up.

Our classroom may appear, on its surface, to be normal enough. The rows of ragged ergonomic chairs. The humming fluorescent lights, casting their sickly green glow. The podium, the projector, et cetera, et cetera. And yet, this course demands that you abandon your modern outlook, your contemporary comforts, and journey back with me to the world of the ancients. I want you to imagine yourself into a place and a time when dragons breathed fire just beyond mud-brick city walls, when centaurs cantered through holy cedar groves, when sailors feared the leviathans they knew were lurking in the deep. You probably believe that you are smarter than the ancient travelers who dug up pterodactyl bones and believed that they had found evidence of griffins or phoenixes. You probably think that you know more than they did, simply because you live *now* instead of *then*. Well, my friends. *Think again.*

Jack's finger jabbed at the space bar, and the lecture stopped. "Don't do that, Syl," he warned. "Don't lose it on me."

"I'm fine," I lied. "Play the clip."

What if, in a different story line, Jack and I *did* have a child, but I'd paid more attention to her? What if I'd been there to remove the knife from her hands, to ruffle her tangled hair, to drop a kiss onto her cheek, and to hug her so hard that she forgot what she was doing? What if I'd accompanied the girls to the woods that morning? Darted through dark trunks beneath an honest spring sky? Wouldn't I have been able to save them?

Instead of those other Sylvias, those stronger, wiser, warmer Sylvias, there was only me. The one who drew back from Faye when she entered the police station, the one who never reached out to touch her in the courtroom. The one who let Jack leave without a fight. The one who nearly shut the door in the face of her own granddaughter because the sight of that child chilled her to her core.

Now, what do you know of the word *monster*? Where does it come from? Any ideas? No? No one wants to hazard a guess? Have I already frightened you into silence? Fine, fine. Well—excuse me, I didn't see your hand there. What did you say? All right. Did everyone hear that? "A creature half human, half beast." I won't deny that this is the way in which the term is often used. Centaurs, Minotaurs, mermaids, and the like. So, you're not wrong. At the same time—can we all agree that the word is frequently applied to humans and nonhumans, too? A serial killer on trial is called a monster, as is the fantastical sea dragon of Loch Ness. The Old French *mostre* signified on the one hand "prodigy" or "marvel" and, on the other hand, "misshapen being." The Latin *monstrum*, or "portent," emerged from the verb *monere*, "to warn." At its core, then, a monster is an omen, a sign—something both significant and foreboding. I've written those words on the whiteboard. Memorize them.

So. What, exactly, do monsters signify? Where do they come from and what do they foreshadow? If these are the questions that have driven you here, to this particular classroom on this cool morning, then, friends, you are in the right place.

As you can see by the readings listed on the syllabus, we're going to start with ancient history. Then we'll go hurtling through the Middle Ages, the Renaissance, modernity, et cetera, et cetera. Seven weeks in, you'll take the midterm. Then, for the remainder of the course, we'll build upon that historical foundation in order to hunt down the monsters of the present. The memes, the movies, the Internet lore. We'll end with the monster who happens to be my personal favorite, the monster who haunts the dreams of parents flung far across this country, the monster who emerged out of the rich earth of the Fertile Crescent and stalked through the shadows of the centuries, sliding through civilization after civilization, story after story, until he found us. You might have heard tell of his castle nestled in the black-spruce forests that run along the North Shore of Lake Superior, and I'm sure you are familiar with the string of crimes associated with his name. You know who I mean. Yes, I can see the gleam in your eyes, the expectant tension in your shoulders as you lean forward in your seats. I'm talking about the—

Jack lurched toward the computer and struck the space bar again. The clip froze over an image of the professor locking the door to his office and crossing a tree-lined quad. Students sprawled on the grass before blocky brick buildings, their backpacks tucked behind their heads, their books spilling out onto the grass.

"That's Minneapolis?" I confirmed, pointing to the screen. "He works at that university?"

Jack had been watching me watch the documentary. Now he nodded toward Amelia, who was inspecting photographs of birds in the next room. The teakettle whistled.

"We'll hold down the fort," he said. "Call me when you land."

After her crime, when the police questioned her, she said that she'd had to do it in order to protect her family. He was going to come after her parents if she didn't do as he instructed, she told her interrogators. Who was *he*? they asked. She shook her head and didn't answer.

After I'd packed my suitcase, while Jack was still on the phone arranging the ticket with the airline, I tugged the laptop onto my knees and pressed play on the documentary. The recording from the interrogation room was crackling and snowy, but it was clear enough to see Faye bow her head. I could hear her start to cry.

That's when I leaned forward, squinted at the screen. My Faye never cried, I reminded myself. So who is that girl who walks like her, talks like her? What has she done with my child?

PART II

The Professor

In 31 BC, Caesar Octavianus defeated the famous Antony and Cleopatra, both of whom took their own lives rather than allow themselves to be captured. Octavianus seized their children and transported them from Egypt to Italy. Although two of the children—the young boys Ptolemy Philadelphus and Alexander Helios, aged six and ten—warned Octavianus of an invisible guardian, someone who would surely come for them as soon as they called his name, the emperor dismissed their stories as child's play. He, too, had been a child once. Yet the journey out of Egypt was plagued by troubles: camels were struck dead without warning, food and water supplies vanished overnight, and iridescent desert beetles ate entire tents, robes, and blankets. Then, during the Mediterranean passage, seven different men threw themselves overboard. Witnesses said that right before they jumped, they went mad. Each of them claimed to see a figure, glittering as black as obsidian, beckoning to him in the distance. The men spoke to mirages, wrestled with nightmares. Rumor had it that Octavianus slept fitfully on the voyage, too. Perhaps this is why he neglected to keep an eye on Ptolemy Philadelphus and Alexander Helios. Whatever the reason, he lost them. No one remembers where or how. All we know is that one day they were there, and then the next day, they weren't. This is the earliest case of missing children in written history.

Sylvia

I stood in the back of an empty lecture hall, gazing over a sea of padded chairs to the murky outline of the podium and the moonbeam glow of the whiteboard. Then my phone rang.

"You made it okay?" Jack asked.

He'd shuttled me to the airport several hours before the sun rose, easing the truck along a black-ribbon highway while Amelia slept in the back seat. At the curb, he'd stepped out of the driver's side and dropped my bag at my feet and pitched forward as if intending to embrace me before I skittered out of reach.

"Yeah," I said. "Thanks."

"Any luck at the university?"

Although he couldn't see me shake my head, he felt it. He grunted and then went silent. He'd scrolled through the department website. He'd found the course title and location. We'd both hoped it would be that easy, that twelve hours after my departure I'd be arriving home again with Faye by my side. In my imagination, Faye followed me onto the plane with a paperback book and a sheepish expression. Once she'd buckled herself into the seat beside me, she tucked a strand of hair behind her ear and apologized for the trouble she'd caused.

It sounds foolish, fantastical—but parenthood is founded on fantasies. We spend years of our lives imagining what our children will become: journalists or ballet dancers, park rangers or nurses, engineers or public defenders. I never dreamed that Faye would become a pariah, a case study, a criminal.

Of course I've read about kids who smuggle guns into school and slaughter their classmates. The con artists and dictators and arsonists and hit men of the world were once children, too. Is it foolish or arrogant or shortsighted of us to believe that our own kids will be different from that, better than that, better than *us*? Or perhaps the question is this: If having children really did improve the human condition, then wouldn't most of our problems have already been solved?

"Professor Wolff isn't here," said the woman at the front desk of the department office. Her face was lined and jowly, her floral shirt rumpled, her lips coral red. The black-and-gold nameplate on her desk read KATHY.

"His class is supposed to be meeting right now, just down the hall," I said. "Do you know where I can find him?"

"Nope. Won't answer his phone." She jabbed at her computer keys. "Nobody's seen him for two weeks or more."

"But the class—"

"Canceled for the fall semester."

The office blurred at the edges. "Do you mind if I sit for a moment?" I murmured belatedly, already slumping into the chair across from her desk.

Kathy lifted her fingers from the keyboard with the poise of a concert pianist. Her gaze sailed along the length of my body, from the top of my oily head to the luggage sagging against my ankles.

"If it helps, you're not the only one looking for him." She leaned forward, cheerfully conspiratorial. "He was supposed to have published his book this year, and the department's losing patience."

I gazed blankly toward a raincoat on the coat hook. It extended its plastic arms, reaching for me.

Kathy coughed to regain my attention. Eyeing me over the rims of her glasses, she declared: "My point is, the professor isn't here. Is there anything else I can do for you?"

On the drive to the airport, when Jack had asked me if I was plan-ning to call my sister while I was in Minneapolis, I'd glared at him in the dark. A love song trickled from the radio, and Amelia sighed in her sleep. I'd waited until the truck had glided forward another mile or two before I answered.

"I never understood why she did that," I snapped. The surge of anger felt childish, ancient, reassuringly familiar. "Of all the places she could have chosen to live, why Minnesota?"

"She got a job offer, Syl," Jack said. "You're acting like she moved halfway across the country just to upset you."

Six months after the hearing ended, Rosie had sent me a note—an email—with her new address. No explanation; no apol-ogy. She'd gone from living three miles down the road to another life entirely. First Jack, then Rosie. The people I loved couldn't get away from me fast enough.

"For a school psychologist, she isn't very good at talking to peo-ple," I muttered. "We haven't spoken in more than a decade."

Jack shrugged. "You and I haven't spoken to a lot of people in more than a decade. Hell, we've barely even spoken to each other." He slashed a grin in my direction. "And look at us now. Just a cou-ple of old pals on the road again."

Twice a year, Jack and I used to pack up the car and wind our way up the coast for his sprawling family reunions. We stretched the drive to Boston over two or three days, watching city skylines rise and fall like ocean waves. Faye's favorite stopping point was the aquarium in Mystic, where, as a two-year-old, she'd stuck her hands into an open tank with a cownose ray. Every time she approached that tank, taller and nimbler with each passing year, I remembered how her toddler face had kindled when the ray's silky wings had skated across her fingertips. Over dinner at a sea-side clam shack, the sea billowing in the distance, I'd gazed at her across the table and doubted the aquarist's assurance that despite their name and appearance, these rays did not possess the power to electrify.

"Rosie doesn't want anything to do with me," I told Jack now. The highway lights streamed together. Jack twisted the radio dial, and the music mellowed.

"What makes you think that?"

"Well, there's the fact that she hasn't called me in thirteen years."

"Have *you* called *her*?"

I knew I sounded petulant. "Yes."

"When?"

I hadn't planned to tell him. But what more did I have to lose? "A few days after Faye was sent to the detention center," I said. "The night that you left."

He went silent. All he knew of that night was that I'd stood at the screen door, framed by the golden square of the living room, until he'd driven out of sight. He didn't know that I'd waited there, rooted to the welcome mat, my gaze fixed on the place where his taillights had vanished, for several hours more. And he didn't know that when I finally collapsed on the cold tiles, convulsed with sobs I couldn't conquer, I'd cradled the phone to my breastbone in the stupid hope that he would change his mind. When the receiver remained silent, I'd broken down and dialed my sister. She didn't pick up, and she didn't call back—as if she were the one, I remember thinking bitterly, who'd been betrayed.

"I know I wasn't at the hearing when she testified," Jack murmured. "And I remember how angry you were with her when you came home that night. But, Syl—"

"I don't want to talk about this."

"—I also know how much she loves you. And I'm certain that whatever she said, however she sounded—"

"*Jack*—"

"—that she never intended to hurt you."

My face was blazing. *"You weren't there."*

Sixty-three streetlamps ticked past my window before Jack spoke again. I counted them.

"I know I wasn't." His voice was so low that I couldn't hear it. I could only feel the words as they thrummed through my seat. "But I still think that you need to call your sister."

At first, his suggestion had seemed outrageous. But by the time I'd left the English department, I'd run out of ideas. Leonard Wolff was missing. Faye was somewhere in that crisp, autumnal city. But Kathy wouldn't release her address from the school directory, especially not after I'd admitted that I didn't even have her phone number.

"Your daughter won't let you call her?" she'd asked, her gaze shooting toward the photographs of ruddy Norwegian-looking children on her desk.

"It's complicated," I said.

"It's policy," she replied.

And so I found myself sinking into the back seat of another taxicab, flying over the muddy green band of what must have been the Mississippi, bike riders and Rollerbladers rippling like pennants past my open window. I scrolled through my contacts until I located Rosie's information. After I'd given the driver her address, I rested my head against the foggy window and thought about all the mornings I'd trailed my sister to the beach to spot her while she swam laps along the shore. I used to carry toaster pastries in paper towels and sit cross-legged, the sand warming my thighs, straining to see her tiny, red-capped figure reach the end of a lap and stab an arm toward the sky in greeting. The sun inched higher over the horizon as she sliced between salty waves. With no one else on the beach at that hour, it was my job to call out if I caught sight of a dorsal fin poking through the surface or the shadow of a stingray swishing in the shallows.

When she spoke at our wedding, Rosie described what it had been like to come up for air and see my watchful silhouette on the shore. "Sylvie always had my back," she told the sixty guests assembled in the small Greek restaurant, their faces blurring in the candlelight. I was leaning against Jack, my head tucked into his shoulder, the folds of my dress cool and heavy on my thighs. His breath in my hair was sweet with champagne and frosting. Outside, thunder cracked, and cars sprayed through standing water, their headlights like rhinestones.

Rosie had to raise her voice in order to be heard over the rain pummeling the roof. "In high school, when I started sneaking out and getting into trouble, it was Sylvia who waited up for me. She covered for me when our mother asked for my whereabouts. She listened for my knock on the glass, lifted the sash, and drew me back in. I was nine years older than her, but she was the one who looked out for me." Rosie slowly raised her glass. "Sylvia's love is a fierce love, an unyielding love, a loyal love. It is a gift that cannot be taken lightly."

In the years after the crime—when I lived without Jack, without Faye, without Rosie—I turned my sister's words over and over again in my mind, obsessively, despairingly. Was my love too stubborn? Too demanding? If it was truly such a gift—then why had I ended up alone?

The front yard of Rosie's house was lined with sunflowers gone to seed, the lawn prickly, thick with milkweed and chicory. Outside a blue front door, I pressed the bell and waited. When it opened, an unfamiliar woman was standing in the entrance, squinting into a pale sun suspended directly behind me.

"Can I help you?" she asked.

"I'm sorry," I said. "I must have the wrong house."

The woman inspected me. She wore a sweatshirt over green scrubs, her hair tied back with a thin white scarf. I was about to retreat down the broken brick walkway when I noticed the name of my sister's college stamped across the sweatshirt.

"Ro?" the woman called back into the dim hallway. "I think there's someone here for you."

"I've got the wrong house," I repeated, stupidly. This had been a terrible idea. Of course Rosie wouldn't want to see me. "I should go—"

But it was too late. Rosie appeared behind the woman at the door, shaking her curls out of her face and wiping her hands on a balled-up dish towel. If she was surprised to find me on her doorstep, she didn't show it. The woman snaked an arm around her waist, in an act of possessiveness or reassurance, but Rosie didn't react.

"Sylvie," she said. "Hi. We were just finishing up dinner. Would you like to come in?"

The woman's name was Leila, and she worked as an emergency room doctor. She and Rosie had been married for two years.

"Going on three," Leila called from the sink, elbows deep in soapy bubbles. "Our anniversary's in October."

Rosie studied me. "You're surprised?"

"That you're married? Of course I am."

She had the grace, at least, to glance away. "It was small. Ceremony at the city courthouse, reception at the corner bar. That kind of thing."

"Congratulations," I managed. And then, in a murmur that she might not have heard: "I thought you would have told me."

My sister turned toward her wife, who was crossing the room to join us at the table. "Sylvie's wedding was gorgeous," she reported airily, as if we'd just celebrated yesterday. Then, to me: "How's Jack?"

The last time she'd seen him was the night before she testified at Faye's hearing. Jack had loomed over the charcoal grill in the backyard, watching a black cloak fall over the woods, gripping his spatula like a talisman but forgetting to flip the burgers, so that when they finally reached our plate, they were charred and tough. I'd chilled the red wine beforehand, since that was how Rosie liked it. She'd asked me a few questions about the store, the house. We had avoided the subject of Faye.

"We've been through hell," I said.

She considered me with that familiar, inscrutable gaze. Why was I telling her this? She already thought I was a failure as a parent. It could come as no surprise that I had failed at marriage, too.

"I'm sure you're wondering why I'm in Minneapolis," I said. "And I'm sure you'd rather I wasn't here." I flicked a quick look at her face, which remained opaque. "It's just..."

I didn't know where to begin. The missing professor? The new Kingman crimes? The bus inching northward up the map, the glass house on the shore, the bank cards, the apartment, the child at my door?

"You came here looking for Faye," Rosie said.

I thought I'd misheard her. "Excuse me?"

"Faye," Rosie repeated, with a flash of impatience. "You know she's here, right?"

Leila was looking from one of us to the other. "I'll make us some tea," she said. She rose to her feet and nudged her chair back against the table.

"How do *you* know Faye is here?" The voice that was speaking didn't sound like mine. "Have you seen her?"

Rosie shook her head so hard that her cheeks went pink. Leila carried a kettle to the sink and turned on the tap. "No, I haven't seen her. But she—" Was the lamplight flickering, or was her chin trembling? "She told me in an email."

It took a second for Rosie's words to sink in. The stovetop clicked as Leila lit the gas burner. "You two *write* to each other?"

In the courtroom, Rosie had worn a tailored blazer, a pencil skirt, and a pair of glasses that had magnified her fierce intelligence. I'd eased into my usual seat with more hope than I'd felt in weeks. This was my sister; my daughter's godmother. She had known and loved Faye since the hour Faye was born. She had agreed to serve as a character witness. She was going to tell the judge what Faye was really like, and after that he was bound to see the crime as the anomaly it was.

"Not often," Rosie said quickly. "A couple of years ago, when she had just gotten out, she wrote me a note to say happy birthday. Since her birthday was the day after mine, I wrote to say thanks and best wishes to her, too. The next year, it was the same."

All this time, I'd assumed that if Faye wasn't talking to me, she must not be talking to any of us. "I would have written back," I said, hollowly. "If she'd written to me."

Rosie heard the sound of something break inside me. "It was just once a year, Sylvie. Just happy birthday, really, and a couple of sentences of news. This year, she said that she was up here."

I struggled to keep my voice from shaking. "So you've known since June? And you didn't think to say anything?"

"We don't—" Rosie's gaze slung toward Leila as if Leila would toss a life preserver across the kitchen. "We don't talk to each other. How could I have told you? I have no idea how much you speak with her, or how much of what she says is mine to share. Plus, I—well, I didn't think you'd want to hear from me."

Outside, footsteps shuffled through leaves. Leila placed a mug before me, the minty steam rising like fingers. Is that what Faye thought, too? I wondered. Did she assume that I didn't want to hear from her? That this state of silence, of isolation, was something I had *chosen*?

I jolted out of my chair, knocking my head against a low-hanging chandelier. The beams vaulted against the walls as both women hurried to help me. "I'm fine," I snapped, batting away their hands. The last thing I wanted was Rosie's assistance. "I'm tired, that's all. I'm fine."

It was Leila who guided me upstairs. By then I was blinded by tears. It was her arm that bolstered me up. It was she who lowered me down onto the bed like a child, she who removed my shoes and pulled back the covers, she who drew the blinds and lifted the quilt to my chin.

"There, there," she said, her voice unfamiliar and maternal and laced with a longing that I could not yet place. "Get some rest." She slid cold fingers across my forehead. When she lifted them away again, Rosie's silhouette was filling up the doorway.

I closed my eyes. I felt Leila rise from the edge of the bed, and I heard her slippered footsteps pad out the door and down the hall-way, and I heard the bedsprings protest again as Rosie eased herself down beside me.

"You know what I think?" she whispered.

I pressed my eyelids more tightly shut.

"I think you've spent thirteen years blaming yourself for some-thing that isn't your fault." Her words crashed toward me as if a dam had been broken. "I think you've isolated yourself on pur-pose, as some kind of penance, because I think it's easier for you to do that than it is to admit that you can't control everything or to accept the fact that sometimes a person can do everything right, and her life will *still* fall apart."

I turned my face toward the wall so that she couldn't read any-thing in it. I wished that I could slow the rush of blood to my cheeks.

"Anything else, Dr. Gray?" I said.

I could hear the swish of her hair as she shook her head. "Just this, Sylvie. Even if you *did* fuck something up—and I'm not saying that you did—it doesn't make you a monster. It just makes you—I don't know—" The rustle of an exasperated shrug. "It makes you human."

My fingers warmed beneath the sudden, unexpected pressure of her hand on mine. Then she stood, and the mattress bounced back into place, and she was gone.

After she left me, I lay awake in that unfamiliar bedroom and remembered a night I'd lain awake in a camping tent between Jack and Faye, listening to the snap of twigs in the dark as the stars slowly rotated across our mesh skylight. I'd felt a terrifying surge of love for them, a visceral urge to defend them from the dangers beyond our nylon walls. What I couldn't see back then, of course, were the dangers that we carry with us: all the secrets and the dreams that have planted gnarled, stubborn roots inside our hearts.

Most people know the story of the Pied Piper. He arrived in the German town of Hamelin to find it infested with rats. The townspeople offered him a mighty sum for taking care of the rodent problem. So he played his pipe and led the rats away to the river, where they all drowned. When the townspeople refused to pay him, he played his pipe and led the children away to a mountain, which swallowed them up forever. What most people don't know is that this supposed fairy tale is grounded in historical fact. One hundred and thirty children in Hamelin really did disappear in 1284. In 1384 the town erected a stained-glass window in the main church that told the story of their tragedy. The line in the town register that describes the placement and unveiling of the window states simply: "It is one hundred years since our children left." The window has since been lost—or destroyed—but contemporary accounts of it describe the image of an individual standing just outside the town gate, dressed not in "pied," or multicolored, robes but in a shimmering black cloak and a goldstone crown. His face was made of a single piece of clear square glass, so that when you looked at him you could see through the wall to the woods that used to stand not far from the church. There was no pipe portrayed in the window. So what happened to the children? A plague? A landslide? A mass drowning? The Children's Crusade? Today, speculations abound. But what scholars really want to find is that window, which may be the earliest known representation of the Kingman on the European continent.

Sylvia

I slept until noon. When I staggered down to the kitchen, bleary-eyed and disoriented, Rosie was sawing slices from a loaf of seeded bread.

"How are you feeling?" she asked. Before I could answer, she pointed her chin in the direction of the cell phone I'd left near the cutting board the night before. "Your husband called. I answered. Hope that's all right."

"He's not my husband." I tumbled onto a stool at the butcher-block island. My head was thick with fog. Rosie nudged a mug of coffee in my direction, and I lifted it to my lips.

"You went through with the divorce?"

"I don't know why you sound surprised."

"He sure sounded like your husband on the phone," she said, layering cheese and tomatoes between the slices. "He was worried that you hadn't called last night. He wanted to know if you'd remembered to eat something. He insisted that we let you sleep in."

I took another, longer swallow of the coffee. The fog began to retreat. "Was he surprised that I was here?"

"Nope." She popped the lids onto her glass storage containers and slid them back into the fridge. Then she wrapped the sandwiches in wax paper. "Seemed like he was expecting it."

"How is it possible," I asked, unable to conceal my exasperation, "that you were *both* expecting me to show up here, when I had no intention of doing so?"

At that, Rosie laughed. If I closed my eyes, I might have been a child again, hearing the sound through the thin walls of my bedroom, wondering whom she was talking to and what had been said to delight her. I finished my coffee, and the kitchen sharpened.

"Sylvie," she said then, staring at the wrapped sandwiches. "Did you ever think that Faye—well, that she might not *want* to be found?"

"Yes," I said. Somewhere in the house, a grandfather clock chimed the hour. I waited until the sound had died away, and then I added: "But it's also possible that she's in trouble. That she needs me. So I can't stop trying."

Rosie sighed. "Then you better get dressed," she said. "We'll eat these in the car."

"Where are we going?"

She laughed again, this time more darkly. "I promised Jack I'd help you out." She raised an eyebrow until it vanished underneath her bangs. "Husband or not, he sure seemed keen to get you home again."

Lately I've been wondering if I would have been strong enough to confront Faye that morning if Rosie hadn't gone with me. I'd like to think that I would have hunted down her address on my own, that I would have found my way to that ramshackle bungalow on that run-down street of student housing, crossed the packed dirt of the front yard, and pounded on the door until she opened it. Sometimes I imagine myself waiting alone on the concrete step, studying the chipped green siding around the entrance, glancing up at the curtains drifting from the attic window and recognizing them as my daughter's. Even now, when I lift my hand from these pages, I can hear the skipping of her footsteps down the stairs and picture her face at the crack at the door as if it were a memory, and not a fiction.

I know that this isn't how it happened. I haven't lost my mind.

Still, I'll admit that as we approached the house, I saw less and less of our surroundings. I was imagining her face when she opened the door and discovered me there. I was picturing her hovering at the threshold, blocking my entrance, pinning me in place with her granite gaze. I was consumed by the question of what I should say to her.

You've got to come home to your family. You need to take care of your child. You have a responsibility—

I could hear her laughter pouring in beside me, filling up my sister's car.

Hypocrisy. From the Greek *hypokrites*, or "actor." Meaning: someone who judges from underneath a mask.

Two boys opened the door to us. They slouched in the entryway, brushing lanky hair out of their eyes, until we told them we were looking for Faye. Then they grew tense.

"What makes you think we know her?" the taller one demanded.

Rosie frowned. "Because she gave me this address," she replied. "She told me she was living here."

The boys conferred together in a language that I didn't recognize. Fearing that they would move to close the door on us, I uttered the first words that came to mind. "I'm her mother."

As if the word *mother* triggered a wordless sense of filial obligation, they inclined their heads and gestured us inside. The taller boy dragged the door open wider and tossed a limp hand toward the peeling floral wallpaper of the hallway behind him. "You have to go up the back stairs."

That's how we found ourselves tunneling through a warren of dank rooms, shuffling around threadbare futons and crushed soda cans and a mismatched set of lawn chairs crammed around a tiny television. On the flickering screen, a video game had been paused on a soldier pointing his gun into an empty warehouse. We followed the boys through the kitchen, across a sticky vinyl floor, before halting at the base of a staircase. The light was anemic and everything smelled like pizza. They waved us toward the steps, so Rosie and I climbed to the attic.

Beneath the eaves, everything changed. The room, spare and clean, rippled with fresh air. The planks of the floor were unfinished but swept, and a tattered rag rug rested at the top of the steps. Two skylights and two windows permitted dusty sunbeams to tumble over the contents of the room. A single plate and mug reclined in the drying rack beside a tiny sink. The sheets on a twin mattress had been neatly tucked into a rusted metal frame. A threadbare armchair faced the window that opened to the front yard, a flimsy card table beside it. Beside one of the chairs, a stack of books surged upward.

Rosie slid a finger across the cover of the book on the top of the pile and inspected the trail she left in the dust. I knelt down to examine the titles. *Legends of the North Woods. The Encyclopedia of Supernatural Sightings. Global Folklore. The Cambridge Companion to Monsters. Theories of Visions and Nightmares. The Lives and Deaths of the Brothers Grimm.*

"She was taking a class at the university," I told Rosie. "With a professor who studies the Kingman."

"Leonard Wolff?"

"How do you know that?"

My sister shrugged. "He was in the documentary."

Of course she'd watched it. Everyone had watched it. Through the narrow window, I could see a distant sliver of gray river between the buildings. What if I hadn't stuck my head in the sand? What if I'd kept tracking down the Kingman all those years ago? What if I'd insisted that Faye come home?

A lamp on the nightstand turned on without warning. When I spun to look at it, something swooped across my field of vision.

"Rosie, did you see—"

But Rosie was emerging from the gloom of the eaves, approaching the lamp with a sheaf of lined pages that had been torn from a spiral-bound notebook. "Look at these," she said.

I would have recognized my daughter's work anywhere. The Cyclops, the unicorn, the yeti, the phoenix, the dragon—each of the beasts had been painstakingly drawn in ballpoint pen, their outlines crisp, their details precise. The dragon's scales had been shaded so carefully that I was startled to run my finger over the crosshatched paper and find it smooth. The yeti's hair was matted, his gaze attentive, his fangs hanging over plump lips that were half-parted as if he were about to speak. What had Faye wanted him to say?

"She's always had such a gift," my sister murmured, her expression half-lit, her gaze admiring, "for bringing things to life."

In the kitchen downstairs, the taller boy introduced himself as Chue. "And that's my brother, Nhia," he said. They'd placed a chipped bowl of crackers on a folding table. Nhia carried an armful of sparkling waters from the refrigerator, and Chue poured two of them into glasses that he nudged across the table toward us.

"This is kind, but unnecessary," I said, hovering behind a chair. "I only wanted to ask—"

"You are her mother," Chue said. "Please, sit."

I pulled out the chair. "How long has it been since you've seen her?"

Chue crunched through a handful of crackers. "Two weeks," he said.

"And have you been to the police?"

At this, he snorted. "No."

Nhia's face was a perfect circle. He was heavier than his brother, slower moving, but his dark gaze was penetrating. When he finally spoke directly to us, indicating the drawings I was still clutching, his voice rose and fell like piano notes. "Can I see those?"

I fanned them out across the table, and all four of us studied them. Chue glanced up after half a minute, but Nhia lingered over the wavering figure within a stand of pine trees, some kind of turret or lighthouse jutting up through the woods behind him. Beside him sat the shadow of a fox. On his faceless head: a barbed crown.

Upstairs, I'd shoved that drawing to the bottom of the stack, hoping Rosie hadn't recognized it. Now her eyes were fixed upon it.

Chue tapped the paper closest to him. Beneath his fingertip, the Loch Ness monster was rising for a gulp of air. "These were assignments," he said. "For Professor Wolff."

"You were in the class with her?"

"Over the summer. That's how we met."

Nhia was still tipped toward the drawings. He dragged his finger lightly over the inked black needles of a ragged pine tree.

"The assignment," said Chue, "was to make the monster feel real. You could do what you wanted. Some people used Photoshop. Nhia and I created audio recordings. She made these." He shrugged, as if this information wasn't interesting. "Professor Wolff gave out an award for the best ones."

"What kind of award?" Rosie asked.

"An internship. A chance to help him with his work." Chue eyed me. "She won. So she's helping him finish his book."

Two weeks. The pieces were beginning to fall into place. "So you think they're together?"

Chue nodded. "She's lucky; people say that he's a genius."

At this, Nhia scowled. He finally raised his gaze from Faye's drawings. "He's a lunatic."

Chue grinned good-naturedly and reached out to ruffle his brother's hair. Nhia ducked away, his expression like thunder.

"Where is his book, if he's such a genius?" Nhia demanded. "Everybody talks about it. But even Faye said that she had not seen it."

"His work is too important!" Chue said. "It's not something that you leave around the house!"

Alarm bells clanged through me. "When was Faye inside his house?"

The boys considered each other. The air between them sparked with silent messages.

"Many times," Nhia said eventually. "They worked together at his home. She also helped with the kids."

"The *kids*?" After Amelia had been abandoned on a college campus? While Amelia had been waiting in an idling car?

"It's okay," Chue assured me. "She likes kids."

Rosie placed a hand on my arm. "Do you know where the family lives?"

"I picked her up there sometimes," Nhia said.

Chue cast a warning look at his brother. "We need to leave them alone and let them do their work. I think that they're fine."

Nhia shook his head and skimmed his palm once more over Faye's drawings. "I think that you're wrong," he said.

"What's that one?" Rosie asked, pointing to an image in the center of the table. "I don't recognize it."

For a moment, we all studied the piece of paper she'd indicated. A twisted knot of human arms and legs. A tangled ring of rope or hair and a scattering of what looked to be teeth. In the center: a double-headed, double-hearted core.

"Soul mates," Nhia explained. "Plato said that humans used to be made in the shape of circles. We had four legs, four arms, four ears, four lungs. Two faces, two mouths, two stomachs. So we were stronger back then. Twice as smart, twice as fast. But the gods didn't want humans to be so powerful, so Zeus cut us in half."

Soul mates. I felt the pinch on my finger as a former version of Jack slid my ring into place. Snapdragons on the altar bobbed their fierce pink heads. Ceiling fans whirred across high wooden beams. Later that night, when the guests had gone home, he'd propped himself up on his pillow, and we'd talked for hours and hours, until the sky glowed rose through the window and I fell asleep on his forearm. Who would have thought there would come a time when we had nothing left to say to each other?

"That's why," Nhia was concluding, "we always feel incomplete. We're doomed to search forever for our other half. And if the two halves are reunited—"

In the weeks and months after the verdict, I'd tried to pretend that my heart wasn't splitting at the seams; my bones weren't hollowing; my skin wasn't falling from me in thick, glittering flakes as I transformed, against my will, into someone, or something, else.

"—we become monstrous again."

Once upon a time I'd been a mother, a sister, a spouse—I'd possessed more soul mates than one person deserves. But the Kingman had taken them all.

In 1587, English settlers established the Roanoke Colony in what we know today as North Carolina. Needing more resources and supplies from the Old World, they sent their governor back to England. When he returned for them three years later—after having been delayed by storms, finances, and wars—no trace of the ninety men, seventeen women, and eleven children remained. The governor was distraught, particularly because his daughter Eleanor and three-year-old granddaughter Virginia were among the missing. Were they killed by wild animals? Did they join local tribes? Or was the source of their disappearance something more mysterious, nefarious? Searches for the lost colonists have yielded only two significant clues: first, the word PHILIPPEAUX *carved into a fence post near the main entrance of town, and, second, a collection of twenty-three large gray stones, each sporting the same crude etching of a faceless man with a crown of knives. While a vocal group of experts has labeled the stones as little more than a modern-day "hoax," not everyone is so certain that they are fake. How could the Kingman have been transported to the New World? What did he want with it, with them? With us?*

Sylvia

Nhia told Rosie how to get to Leonard Wolff's house. On the drive over, when I asked her what else she knew about the professor, she shrugged. "Not much," she said. She kept quiet for three or four stoplights, and then she added: "I've only seen him in person once."

"You've seen him?"

"A few years ago. He was giving a talk at the college bookstore."

I kept my eyes on the pavement rolling ahead of us. "Why did you go?"

"Because he was talking about the Kingman." The sound of cold waves crashing on rocks rushed through my ears, then drew back. "Obviously, that name means something different to me than it did to everybody else in that room. None of them had a niece who—" She broke off.

"What was he like?"

"The professor?" Rosie pressed her lips together, remembering. "Tall."

A flock of bicyclists winged through the lane to our right. Beyond them, a slope of dried grass tumbled down to a tiny beach and a bowl of green water. In the far distance, a canoe flicked across its murky surface.

"Tall?" I repeated. "That's it? That was your takeaway?"

She swung the steering wheel hard to the right and I gripped the door handle to keep from falling into her. "What do you want me to say? He talked about the monster. He read some pieces of his research. He answered questions, and then he left."

I pictured Rosie sitting stiffly on her folding chair. The gluey scent of fresh books; the hiss of an espresso machine from the counter café a few shelves down. I heard, as if I were sitting beside her, pages rustling as the professor's fingers fluttered through his notes.

"When I got there, I thought I might say something to him," Rosie said. "That was my plan."

"What would you have said?" I asked.

She shrugged. "I'd heard an interview with him once, where he talked about why the monster became so popular. I suppose I wanted to ask him if he had any theories as to why two young girls would have—how Faye could have—well, you know. I just wanted to know what he would say."

"He'd blame the parents, like everybody does."

"Not everything is about *you*, Sylvie." My sister rolled her eyes. "In fact, he didn't talk about the crime at all. Mostly he talked about psychophysics."

"What is that?"

"It's a kind of psychology," she said. "It was invented by a German doctor who wanted to know why we perceive certain things and not other things."

In one experiment, Rosie explained, researchers played a sound for someone. They asked the person if he could hear it. He would say yes. Then they turned the volume down, notch by notch, asking the same question each time until he said no. Even though the sound was still there, he could no longer perceive it because his hearing wasn't sharp enough. His perception, in this case, was that the sound was gone. But objectively, that wasn't so.

"It's like how a dog can hear a high-pitched whistle, and a human can't," Rosie said. "Or how humans can perceive colors that dogs can't."

In another experiment, researchers showed the subject two swatches of blue in hues that were obviously distinct from one another. Navy and sky blue, for instance. And then they showed him two swatches that were more similar to each other, and then two more, and then finally there came a point when the hues were so similar that he couldn't tell them apart. The difference was there, but he was no longer able to perceive it. Psychophysicists, Rosie continued, were interested in precisely that turning point: the threshold between what you perceive and what you don't.

We drove another mile in silence. Then I returned to our earlier thread. "So what did he say when you asked about Faye?"

"I didn't get a chance to talk to him." Her fingers loosened, just a little, around the steering wheel. "The minute he started reading from his work, everybody in the audience went dead silent. No one breathed. We were transported, all of us, to the North Shore. The whole room grew darker and colder. I could hear the sound of Superior hitting the sand. Even after he stopped talking, after we'd landed back on those metal chairs on that hard carpet floor, it took me a minute to remember where I was. It was—" She flipped on her turn signal and rolled up to a curb. "I don't know. Magical."

The wheels crushed through a sheet of fallen leaves, and I studied the house numbers through my window. "He told you a story, Rosie," I said. "That's what stories do. They make you see things and feel things that aren't really there."

Rosie was shaking her head. "There was more to it than that."

"Are you saying he's some kind of sorcerer?"

"Of course not." She tugged the keys from the ignition. "I don't think he's superhuman. But my God—that guy knows how to set a scene."

Leonard Wolff's house crouched behind a line of fruit trees that curled around the property and concealed the windows from the road. Rosie and I stepped out of the car and over the curb and then we crunched single file across a path of wood chips that snaked between the trunks. Three concrete steps lifted us up and deposited us at the front door.

We'd rung the bell and been waiting for a minute or two when we heard steps crackling over the wood chips behind us. When I turned, a spotted dog was bounding toward us through the shrubbery, his tags jingling and his giant tongue streaming out behind him.

"Charlie!" called a woman somewhere nearby. "Here, Charlie!"

When the dog reached us, Rosie leaned down and snagged his collar between two fingers. "Got him!" she shouted. The dog sat back on his haunches and considered her, his ears pointed skyward. "What a sweet boy you are," she said.

The woman emerged from the bushes, jogged up to the bottom of the steps, wrapped her fingers around the wrought-iron railing, and doubled over to catch her breath. "Thank you," she said between gasps. Her fleece vest was caked with fur. "He's a real escape artist." After a few seconds, she straightened up and rested her hands on her hips. "It's his first week living inside a house, though, so I guess I can't blame him for being a bit wild."

The dog's tail thumped twice. "He's a stray?" I asked.

"*Was* a stray," the woman confirmed. "From somewhere out in the Dakotas. I'm just fostering him until he gets adopted. I've got another one in there." She jerked her thumb in the direction of the blue bungalow next door before taking the collar from Rosie and drawing the dog gently toward her. He licked her ankle, and she clipped a leash to his collar and patted his head distractedly.

"We're looking for Leonard Wolff," I said. "Is this the right house?"

She cast a glance over her shoulder, toward the street, as if half expecting to see him striding up behind her. "He's away," she said, turning back to us. "But his wife, Emma, should be back any minute. She took the boys to music class." After a pause, she added:

"You're welcome to come sit on my front porch, if you'd like to wait." She thrust her free hand at me. "I'm Steph, the neighbor. And you are—?"

"Sylvia," I said, my face warming in the sunlight. "And this is my sister, Rosie. We're hoping the family can help us find my daughter, Faye."

The woman's chin shot up. The dog whined to be released. "Faye?" she repeated. "I haven't seen Faye in nearly—" She paused, scrunching her eyes shut as if working hard to count back the days.

"Two weeks?" I suggested. I could see her attic room again as if I were standing in it: the rich September sunshine falling squarely from the skylight, the leaning tower of books in the corner, the shoes lined up along the imperfect floorboards.

Steph's eyes flew open. "Two weeks," she agreed. Faye's drawing bobbed up in my mind—the inky-black cloak, the barbed crown, the expressionless face. When I refocused, I was just in time to see a slender shadow slink around a corner of the house.

She insisted that we wait on her porch, settling us into splintered rocking chairs and carrying out a tray of coffees. A striped cat pressed her triangle nose against a window. A birdbath bubbled in the center of the yard, surrounded by a sea of swaying golden-rod. Once or twice Steph pointed at a bird perched on the stone rim, identifying a kind of woodpecker or chickadee. Every time a plane flew low overhead, interrupting our conversation, she apologized and cited our proximity to the airport. The air traffic noise, she said, was one of the reasons why Emma Wolff hated it here.

"She's originally from Germany. Met Leonard while he was on a research fellowship abroad during grad school. When she agreed to move to the States, I think she was imagining New York or Los Angeles. South Minneapolis is a far cry from the coasts."

We watched the wind roll across the yard next door, swishing through what Steph identified as pear trees. "They came here when he got an offer from the university. He'd been studying that monster, and his research took off when those two girls in North Carolina—"

My tone was cutting. "Yes, we've heard of them."

Steph looked at me in surprise. "Well, talk about good timing. In the flurry of interviews and articles and whatnot that came out afterward, Leonard found himself famous. A publisher offered him a book contract. The university gave him a job."

She indicated the flat cerulean sky and the scarlet leaves crinkling across the lawn. The city vibrated with color. "I think Emma assumed that they wouldn't be here forever. Only until Leonard established himself, finished his book. But it's been years, and there's no book in sight."

She told us that she became close to Emma after the twins were born. Steph made soups and lasagnas, picked up groceries and diapers. Leonard was always working. Emma suffered migraines and hallucinations, and she confessed to Steph that some nights when Leonard wasn't home, she'd see a stranger looming in the doorway.

"She said that she began to understand the parents of old German fairy tales," Steph said. "The ones who were so broken by their children that they abandoned them to the woods. That's what Leonard was studying, I guess, when they met."

Rosie was shaking her head. "She was obviously suffering from postpartum depression," she said. "Did she get any help? Did she talk to anyone?"

Steph shook her head. "She didn't go to any doctors, if that's what you're asking," she said. "But she did get help of a different kind. She got Faye."

From where we were sitting, I could see directly into the windows of the Wolffs' dining room. The edge of a table, the fabric tops of chairbacks. The houseplants arranged along the windowsill. I imagined the room at night: yellow gold, shimmering from within. The lanky professor reaching for a serving bowl; the wife pouring water into glasses. The dark-haired stranger in their midst, spooning mashed carrots into a child's mouth, swooping the spoon through the air like a seagull.

"She's good with the boys," Steph said. "And good with my dogs, too, even though they can be anxious sometimes, borderline aggressive. She'll come over and ask if she can take them for walks. They'll roll on their backs and nuzzle her hands, and when she leashes them up and takes off down the sidewalk, they trot right beside her, leashes loose, hackles down, docile as can be." She paused while another plane roared overhead. Then she said: "I thought it was strange that she left without saying goodbye. To the dogs, at least, if not to me."

"When did she leave?" I asked.

"I saw her getting into the car with Leonard the week before last."

"Was that unusual?"

"Not really. He often picked her up from her apartment or dropped her back there at the end of the day. I wouldn't have noticed them at all, probably, if the dogs hadn't been scrabbling at the window, barking like crazy."

"How did she seem?" I asked. Three bikers whooshed by. "When you saw her? Could you tell if she wanted to go with him or not?"

Steph lowered her mug. "They seemed normal enough to me. What's strange is the fact that I haven't seen them since." Then she raised an arm and pointed to a black sedan rolling up to the curb. "Look," she said. "Emma's back."

Few readers of American writer Ambrose Bierce are aware that his personal history is as startling and as haunting as his fiction. Having suffered severe neurological damage while fighting for the Union in the Civil War, Bierce spent several decades afterward battling debilitating migraines, frequent fainting spells, and—so claimed his wife and children—nightmarish hallucinations. Friends of his in San Francisco would often find him pacing the Pacific shoreline at twilight, tracking footprints in the sand that no one else could see. History books will tell you that when he headed south at age seventy-one, he was looking to join Pancho Villa's army. Shortly afterward, he vanished. Some suggest he was shot by Pancho Villa in Mexico; others say that he perished of pneumonia in Texas, or died anonymously in an insane asylum in Arizona. And yet none of these theories account for the reports of visitors to the Grand Canyon in June of 1915, who swore to have seen a weathered veteran in tattered blue fatigues roaming back and forth across the northern rim at dusk, babbling about a stone-faced king who was waiting for him near the river, looking for a way down into the bruise-colored abyss.

Sylvia

The summer that Emma met Leonard, he was living in a town called Marburg, in the apartment above hers. She used to wait all day to hear him coming home. His shoes rang on the stairwell in the hallway, and she could hear the emphatic yowl of his cat greeting him as he entered. In the mornings, she'd listen to the sounds of his life above her: his bare feet striking toward the shower, then water gushing through the ancient pipes. The slam of dresser drawers. The toothy whir of a coffee bean grinder in the kitchen. When he first invited her in, she looked around the place and felt as though she already knew every inch of it. They had not yet kissed; they'd barely touched. The brush of elbows, only, near the mail slots one day. And yet she felt as if she knew every inch of him, too.

"And he was there to study fairy tales?" Rosie prompted. We were inside Emma's house, balancing on the edge of a gray velvet couch, facing a cuckoo clock over the mantel. "Does that mean the Grimm brothers, or something else?"

"Die Brüder Grimm, yes," Emma said with a clipped nod. "Of course. But he was not reading their stories. He was reading their diaries to study their lives. Their family was very poor because their father had died when they were young. And so when they were old enough, the brothers moved to Marburg to study law. But once they arrived, something happened to change their minds. And so they chose to study stories instead."

"What changed their minds?" I asked.

She turned a glittering gaze on me. "That is what Leonard was trying to find out." She rose to her feet. "Follow me."

She led us through the dining room and the kitchen to the basement stairwell. We followed her down to Leonard's office, where three walls were lined with rows of books on makeshift shelves of cedar planks and cinder blocks. A massive walnut desk was pushed against the fourth wall, just beneath a small stained-glass window. It was wide enough to fit two chairs: the high-backed roller for the professor, I guessed, and the narrow wooden one for Faye.

Emma paced back and forth in front of the shelves until she found what she was looking for: *The Annotated Journals of Jacob Grimm.* Jacob and Wilhelm, she told us, tugging out the book, opening it to a bookmarked page, and handing it to Rosie, had three brothers who died. Two Friedrichs and one Georg. Although it was not uncommon to lose young children in the eighteenth century, there was something different about these deaths. In the journals he kept as a student in Marburg, Jacob describes them over and over again. The first Friedrich died before Jacob was born, but he was seven and then ten years old when the second Friedrich and the first Georg were taken.

"I say 'were taken' because that is the phrase that Jacob used," she explained. "After that, he says, his mother barricaded the doors and windows. In her grief, she refused to let her other children leave the house. Jacob believed that she feared for their lives. Yet what she feared did not seem to come from inside the house— illness, hunger—but from *outside* it."

Rosie was studying the page in her hands. "'The oak trees trembled,'" she read aloud, "'and my mother cried out, begging for us to be spared.'" She glanced up. "Spared from what?"

Emma looked at me, one eyebrow raised, the sides of her pretty face distorted by the tight pull of her braid. I remembered the glow of my computer screen, the wild search through Internet archives, the long black sleeve resting on the edge of my desk, just beyond the bounds of my vision.

"Is he talking about the Kingman?"

Emma's mouth stretched into the semblance of a smile. Her teeth gleamed, orderly and pearled. "That's what Leonard argued," she said. "That's what made him famous. And that's how we ended up here."

After they married and moved to Minnesota, Leonard started his job at the university and Emma found work as a translator. They didn't try for children, she said; neither he nor she wanted them. When she became pregnant anyway, she said, she was afraid to tell him.

"How did he react?" Rosie asked.

"He didn't say anything." Emma was peering into the distance. "For a while, he paced. But finally he said that everything would be all right." She returned her gaze to us. "I tried to cheer him up. I said at least we'd have someone to take care of us when we were old. But he said—" The baby monitor crackled. "He said that children don't owe anything to their parents. They didn't ask to be born."

Rosie closed the book, her professional interest piqued. "He's distant from his family?"

Emma shrugged. "In all the years that we are married, I have not met them," she replied. "I have never been west to see the red canyon where he was born. I know that his father died and his mother is unwell. I know that he is the oldest of seven, each one tall and pale. When I asked once what his siblings did, he said that they spent their days raising horses and praying for his soul."

"He's religious?" Rosie asked.

"Not at all," Emma replied. "But his family is, very much. They are insular, he says, and very strict, and—strange. That is why he does not see them. But—" I could see her weighing how much to tell us. "But I do not think that the loss was easy for him."

She told us how once, during the early weeks of their relationship, he accepted her invitation to attend her second cousin's
baptism. He teetered for several long minutes on the white stone
steps of the church before she could persuade him to come inside.
He didn't sing; he didn't recite. For the duration of the service, he
stood frozen beside her with his hymnal flipped open to the wrong
page, glaring so fiercely through the stained-glass windows that
Emma was half-surprised they didn't shatter.

Afterward, Emma took him to a sun-filled bakery and sat him
down at a table and waited for him to tell her what he had been
thinking during the service. But he didn't speak. He chewed the
cinnamon rolls and swallowed the coffee and then, after a little
while, he remembered to smile at her. When he reached across the
table, his hand was cold as marble.

"So I asked him about his recent work, about how it was going
with the Kingman," she said. "And his whole expression came alive
again." Her tone turned thoughtful now. "It has always been that
way with Leonard and this monster. It is more than a job for him.
It is a passion. A lifeline." She took Jacob Grimm's journals back
from Rosie and replaced the book on the shelf. "For a long time I
wondered if maybe that is why it has been so difficult for him to
finish his manuscript. Who would he be without it?"

By the time that Faye entered their lives, Leonard and Emma had
been parents for all of ten months. "I am not blaming my boys," she
told us. "But if I had not shuttered myself in the dark, or become a
ghost in my own life . . . If I had not been so drained by their needs
and their appetites, I would have had more to give Leonard. Maybe
I," she said, "could have been the one to help him finish his work.
For years he had struggled to write. Then she appeared, and it
was like a light switch flipped. He couldn't *stop* writing. The pages
poured out of him."

"Do you know what they were working on?" I asked. We had

returned to the living room by then. I was imagining Faye sitting on that sofa, gazing out that window.

"The final chapter," Emma said. "For years he had been tracking the Kingman through history. He had written about ancient Egypt, about Jacob Grimm, about early America. The end of the book was the hardest part, he said, because he had reached the present century. He needed to write about what the Kingman was doing, where he was living, in recent memory. So he and Faye were reading stacks of state records, city plans, and travel journals. He said they were looking for recent sightings and for references to the Kingman's castle in the North Woods."

The North Woods. If I squinted at the bars of light and shadow on the window blinds, I could almost see a black sea of trees, a pebbled beach, jeweled ramparts, spires that punctured the sky. I was closer to my daughter than I'd been in years. Why was she still eluding me?

"A few times I asked him if I could help," she admitted, "and he gave me things to read. Usually they were in German—accounts of explorers or traders arriving on these shores. But I never found any reference to the Kingman in them."

"But Leonard did?"

"In other accounts, yes. One night he woke me up to tell me about an island in Lake Superior that was rumored to be so rich with copper that French explorers kept trying to reach it even though most of the men who went there were never seen again. Leonard read aloud to me two pages he had just finished writing about a young Jesuit who did return with stories of a figure in a fur-lined cloak with a copper crown. The figure paced the shore at dusk and dawn, whipping up the waves to keep boats from landing. When I finally fell back asleep, I dreamed of ice castles and winter forests. In the morning, my pillow smelled like pine needles." She peered past us. "Isn't that odd?"

The house had grown colder as she spoke. It was impossible to tell how much time had passed. Even Emma's gaze, when it settled on me, seemed cooler and bluer than it had been.

"She was patient with the boys, and they loved her," she said. "But to me, there were things that seemed strange about her. Faye was cold when we were hot and hot when we were cold. She had a gift for predicting the weather, and a nose for finding objects we had lost. One time, she brought me a handful of stinging nettle that she said was for tea. The plant is known to leave an ugly rash, but her hands were unmarked."

"So?" Rosie asked.

Emma tapped her fingers against her armrest and then steepled her hands together. "Maybe this is why I did not trust her," Emma said, "even though she was good with the twins and good with Leonard." She cast a glance at me. "I am sorry if it is rude to say this to you. But maybe I did not like having her here in my house, growing so close to my husband, when I felt so tired and frail and she seemed so"—she had to search for a moment for the word that she wanted—"invulnerable."

Yet Faye was as vulnerable as anyone. Maybe more so. With a painful flash, I recalled the first-grade pool party where two of her classmates had pushed her down on the lawn and struck her with foam pool noodles until someone's parents called them off. Jack picked her up from the party, carried her from the car to the bathroom, balanced her on the edge of the tub, and scrubbed the dirt from her arms and legs with a soapy washcloth. I hadn't thought of that scene in years, and yet there it was in Emma's living room, as clear as the day that it happened: Jack, kneeling on the tile floor; Faye, dry-eyed and eerily serene, with the indifference of a life-size doll, allowing us to lift and wash and inspect her limbs. Her elbows were a little scraped, but her mind was someplace safe, someplace where none of us could ever find her.

"So maybe that," Emma was saying, "is why I let them go."

"Let them go *where*?" I asked.

Her eyes narrowed. "To the North Shore."

A wail spiraled through the hallway, high pitched and pleading. Emma surged to her feet and vanished around a corner.

Rosie squeezed my fingers so tightly that I knew she could feel my pulse through my skin. Could she, too, see those shapes emerging from the sand?

Before my sister could say anything to me, Emma reappeared with the boy on her hip. His curls were soft and gold, his thighs like sausages, his eyes filmy with tears. I imagined him in Faye's arms. I yearned to hold him; to feel the trace of her touch on his skin. I longed to see her, to conjure her up in this strange, stifling room. As beautiful as Emma's child was, Faye was a thousand times more dazzling. My daughter was a wonder, a lightning bolt, a solar eclipse: she'd burn your eyes before she'd let you look away.

I'd surrendered to the doctors, the social workers, to Jack, when they told me that it was too late, that she was too changed, that I wouldn't be able to reach her. But something was different now. *I* was different now. I had nothing left to lose.

In 1932, the Lindbergh baby disappeared. Although authorities claim to have found a body and although they pinned the crime on German immigrant Bruno Hauptmann, the case has never felt closed. Hauptmann went to the electric chair protesting his conviction and insisting upon his innocence. The evidence, experts agreed, was only circumstantial. Sources close to the family suggested at the time that the infant's body was a fake. Could this be why Charles Lindbergh himself insisted on cremation? His friends told reporters (at cafés and public parks, always off the record) that the family continued searching for their baby for years, long after Hauptmann's execution. Lindbergh and his wife both dreamed separately of their child standing in a clearing, holding the hand of a figure whose face they could not discern. In the heavy gray light before dawn, Lindbergh would climb into his plane and fly low over his property. His engine would roar as he looped around and around New Jersey in ever-widening circles. He was pursuing shadows, said his friends. He saw the flicker of lights in forests and fields where he knew there were no houses. "Hey!" he would cry, his voice whipping back into the sky. "Where have you taken my son?"

Sylvia

L eonard Wolff's summer class ended in early August. He marked up papers, fielded grade complaints. The end of summer unfolded, golden and dry. The colors began to shift. The nights grew longer and he grew restless, spending less time with his family and more time locked in his basement study with Faye.

In the first week of September, right before bed, he told Emma that he was nearing the very end of his work. He had traced the Kingman through the historical record. He knew of his origin, his evolution. What remained now was to write about his fortress. According to legend, his castle was concealed within the woods that blanketed the shores of Lake Superior. He needed to complete some interviews in the small towns up there. And he intended to take Faye with him.

Emma didn't like that idea. "There is nothing to see or research in the north, Leonard. You know there is no fortress. There is no castle. It is only myth."

His teeth glinted in the moonlight. "Fictions never appear out of nowhere," he said.

"But—"

"I have to finish the book, *mein Drachen*," he murmured. "Don't you want that, too?" And then he kissed her, hard, and she had no breath left to argue.

A few days later, she heard him dragging his suitcase down

from the attic. She watched him fill it with clothes. She asked him, feebly, where he was staying, and he told her that the plan was to keep moving up the coast of Lake Superior. They would begin in Duluth, he said, and work their way north: Knife River, Two Harbors, Castle Danger, Silver Bay. They had interviews to conduct and locations to scout. He also said something about the northern lights.

"Tracking them? Monitoring them? It wasn't clear to me," Emma said. She shifted her son to her other thigh. "For a while I could follow his location through our phone-tracking app. But I lost the signal at Split Rock."

"Split Rock?"

"The lighthouse."

Rosie tugged her phone from her pocket and pulled up a picture for me. I studied the image: an orange-brick cylinder topped by a black-iron turret. A pale sun threading through woolly clouds. The cliff edge; the sheer rock face glimpsed through pine boughs in the foreground; the lake, whitecapped and shimmering below. I imagined Faye pacing across the highest balcony, her arms outstretched and her face on fire, her gaze scanning the horizon, seeking the fortress that had once loomed inside her dreams.

I was so absorbed by this vision that Emma's voice, when she spoke again, startled me. "I have imagined certain moments between them so often," she whispered, "that these scenes have become real to me."

It took a minute for her meaning to sink in. Did she believe that Leonard was sleeping with Faye?

Rosie's expression softened. "We all tend to imagine the worst," she said.

Emma's son was babbling softly to himself. When she raised her face from his, her gaze alighted on me. "And sometimes we are not wrong."

————

My head filled with helium and floated back to the courtroom. Polished wood benches and guardrails gleamed. Rosie had taken the stand, and in the silence before the questions began, she was running her palm across the top of her head to flatten the flyaway strands of her hair. Faye slouched over the table only a few yards in front of Rosie, her face turned toward her manacled hands. She didn't look up when her lawyer rose. The woman's heels clacked on the marble floors, and her ponytail swung like a bronze pendulum.

The lawyer asked Rosie the questions that they'd practiced. Where did she live and what did she do for a living? How long had she been a high-school counselor? How close would she say she was to Faye? How much time had the two of them spent together? What would they talk about? What would they do? Did Rosie ever feel unsafe around Faye? Had she ever met Brittany or Anna?

In her well-rehearsed replies, Rosie sketched an image of a gentle girl, devoted to her family and her books, who'd simply taken a wrong turn on the Internet. It was the sort of thing that could happen to anyone.

What we wanted was for the judge to blame the technology, the blogs and the message boards, the warping of reality, the merging of fact and fiction, the dissolution of boundaries and the proliferation of illusions that occur every single day online. Why blame Faye instead of the forces that shaped her? Why not blame the Internet? The Kingman himself, or his creator?

When Emma's other child woke, it was time for us to go. As we passed through the hallway to the front door, I noticed the cardboard boxes stacked against the wall. In the entryway: a blue-and-white suitcase.

I turned back to Emma. "Are you going somewhere?"

"Home," she said. "To Germany."

"With Leonard?"

"Without him."

Something in her tone gave me pause. "Does he know?"

She glanced at a wedding photograph that hung just inside the front door. In a crowd of friends and family, a younger Emma beamed into the lens. Leonard, in a gray suit beside her, was looking somewhere beyond the frame.

"I had been startled, when I met Leonard," she began, "at how quickly love arrived. So perhaps I should not have been surprised at how suddenly it departed." She pressed her fingers to her sternum. "I can still feel the hole it left in my chest."

All of those mornings when I'd curled into my wingback chair with my coffee and my newspaper and I'd listened to Jack moving and washing through the ceiling above me . . . I knew how many minutes he showered. How many minutes he shaved. I knew the expression on his face when he rounded the corner into the room and saw me waiting for him. I knew the precise temperature and pressure of our first kiss of the day. There had been a time when I'd believed a love like that could never leave us.

"I have learned to love my boys," Emma added, looking thoughtful. "It could be that I only ever had a finite supply of affection to offer. But whatever the reason—his monster, your daughter, my children—I find that I no longer love my husband."

The night before her testimony, long after Jack had gone to bed, Rosie and I had remained on the porch swing. The room was cloaked in indigo, and our drinks glistened in our glasses. We were quiet for a long stretch of time before I worked up the courage to ask her my question.

"What did we do wrong?"

I hadn't cried yet. Not in front of Jack, not in front of the reporters, and not even when I was alone, locked away in the tomb of my bedroom. It was only when Rosie reached for me that I cracked open with the sorrow that had been pressing against my skin from the inside, straining for months to work its way out. She rocked me like a child while my shoulders heaved with the acknowledgment of my failure.

"Have you ever wondered if it's possible to love someone too much?" she murmured into my hair.

My words emerged in gasps. "You think it's my fault."

"That's not what I mean." After a few minutes, once I'd raised my head again, she placed her index finger beneath my chin and tilted it up so that I couldn't look away from her. Our noses were inches apart. Her eyes were gold flecked and damp.

"It is always a risk to have a child," she said. "You can't predict how she'll turn out. You took that risk and made that leap because you're braver than I am, Syl." She released my chin and pulled me to her chest. "But now you've got to let her go."

"Now it is my turn to ask a question," Emma said. She had set the boys in a playpen and followed us to the curb. Rosie unlocked the car, and we heard the obedient click of the doors.

"How much responsibility must a person carry for someone she loves?" Emma said. Her gaze roved up and down the street, but we were the only ones outside. The air nipped at my skin and goose bumps rose along my arms. "I remember reading about a famous author who hanged himself in his basement. His wife was the one who found him dangling from the noose. I remember thinking: *Did that woman wonder if it was her fault? Did she wonder if she had not made him happy enough?*"

Next to me, Rosie tightened her grip on her keys. I heard them jingle once before she silenced them against her palm.

"Maybe that is not the right example." Emma's eyes shone. "Here is a better one: A young woman believes that a legend is real and commits a crime in the name of a fiction. Years later, still in search of that legend, she travels north and dismantles a marriage."

Rosie stepped closer to me. A set of tires screamed near the stop sign on the corner.

"You knew?" I said. "And you hired her anyway?"

"I found out after they left," Emma said. "When I went down to Leonard's study and discovered the clippings hidden in the back of his desk. Her last name was different, but I recognized her face. At first I couldn't believe that Leonard permitted her beneath our roof for all those weeks. Then I realized that this was exactly what he wanted."

"What do you mean?" Rosie asked when she saw that I had lost the power of speech. "What did he want?"

Emma's laugh was brittle. "He's spent his whole life looking for the Kingman. At some point, the creature became more real to him than me. And who better to lead him to the Kingman's lair than she?" She shook her head hard, and then she fired her gaze into mine. "I'll say it straight out. Who is the real monster here, Mrs. Vogel? Is it the Kingman? Is it Leonard? Or is it your daughter?"

I'm always imagining alternative endings. After the hearing was over, I imagined that scene playing out a thousand different ways. In one of them, the lawyers stop asking questions after Rosie describes her relationship with Faye. In another, I deliberately set off the fire alarm, and we all stampede onto the marshy lawn. In yet another, a journalist has a heart attack and collapses in his chair, and the judge interrupts the proceedings to call for an ambulance.

In real life, of course, I did nothing. When the prosecutor stood to question Rosie, I remained rooted to my seat and kept my gaze fixed on the back of Faye's head. If Rosie ever glanced at me, if she tried to communicate something important to me, I didn't see it. I only heard her protests as the prosecutor asked her to tell us more about her job.

"I'm here as a character witness," Rosie said. "Not an expert."

"But you *are* an expert, are you not? A young woman has been violently attacked, and we need to understand why. So indulge us. Have you ever worked with a child who committed a crime like Faye's?"

"I work with teenagers. Not children."

"But you work with teens who have committed crimes, correct?"

"Small crimes, yes. Petty theft, vandalism. That kind of thing. I was a little wild when I was younger. I understand that it's not an easy age."

"And in your experience, why did the children commit those crimes?"

"It's complicated."

"Indulge me."

"Well, there are many different risk factors. Delinquent behavior can be linked to cognitive deficits that stem from birth or before. Other elements that increase the likelihood of delinquency include attention and hyperactivity disorders, substance abuse, depressive disorders, peer pressure, lack of social outlets, grade retention, school tracking, young mothers, single-parent households, family size, neglectful parents—"

"I see. And which of these risk factors do you see at work in the defendant?"

"I don't feel comfortable—"

"This is your area of expertise, Ms. Gray. Your statements earlier seemed to indicate that Faye Vogel was a happy, normal, well-adjusted child. She performed well in school and benefited from active, upper-middle-class parents who ensured that she had proper supervision. None of the risk factors you rattled off just now seem applicable here. So—in your professional opinion— what happened?"

"I am not Faye's psychologist."

"But you are a psychologist, and you are her aunt. Now, you mentioned neglectful parents—"

"As one of many risk factors—"

"—and I'm wondering if you could say more about Faye's relationship with her parents."

"I've never seen two people who loved their child more. Sylvia and Jack attended a thousand prenatal classes, they read a million parenting books. They were affectionate and firm and present."

"You're saying that what happened wasn't their fault."

"Of course it wasn't."

"But, obviously, something in this family went horribly wrong. Children who are raised well do not commit crimes such as this."

"Objection," said Faye's attorney.

"Sustained. Get to your question, Counselor," said the judge.

"Is there something essentially different about Faye?" asked the prosecutor.

"No." Rosie's voice faltered. "She's a normal kid."

"That's what we keep hearing, yes. But unfortunately the facts of the case simply do not bear that out. We have two choices here: nature or nurture."

"That's actually a false dichotomy—"

"Is Faye essentially genetically *defective*, or is she the product of her upbringing and her environment?"

"She's not defective."

"So it was her upbringing, then?"

Rosie's silence ballooned into the courtroom. People held their breath. I remained rigid, my gaze knotted to my daughter's greasy hair.

"Objection," Faye's lawyer said again.

"Overruled."

"The defense claims that Faye is a good kid who lost her way," the prosecutor continued. "They argue that, so long as she engages in intensive psychiatric treatment to rid her of her delusions, she should be permitted to return home. In your professional opinion—not as her aunt, but as a mental health provider—is this plan sound?"

When I think about it now, that scene at the hearing is layered over the memory of Rosie's visit to the hospital the day after Faye was born. She had stared at the infant in my arms with such trepidation that she'd made me nervous. I looked down at my daughter, too, peering into her wrinkled face and understanding, with the twist of a knife, that she would always be a stranger to me. I would never know for certain what she was dreaming or feeling. Blood is not telepathy. Much like my sister, my child would grow ever more mysterious to me.

Perhaps that was why Rosie's words in the courtroom drilled into my bones like the fulfillment of a prophecy. In the end, maybe love turns us all into monsters.

"No," Rosie finally replied. "She should never be allowed to return to my sister."

No one knows what happened to the SS Bannockburn *on her final voyage across Lake Superior. We know that the winds were raging, the snow was spinning, the waves were high, and the men were so youthful and inexperienced that local newspapers had nicknamed them the "children's crew." We know that the Superior Shoal was yet uncharted, and that lighthouses up and down the coast had been, inexplicably, turned off. But we also know that the ship emitted no distress signals, and that a wreck was never found. It was the crew of a nearby ship, the SS* Algonquin, *who described what it had been like to catch glimpses of the* Bannockburn *through the silver storm, cruising a few miles off the coast of Isle Royale. "Nobody believes me," Captain James McMaugh told reporters, "and I know it sounds crazy, with the gale and all, but I swear I saw somebody standing on the prow." To this day, some descendants of the vanished crew cling to the faint hope that their men were taken from the ship before it spiraled to the depths. They imagine those sons and brothers and husbands and fathers tucked safely away in the pines that twist along the North Shore. They exchange reports of familiar shadows watching over their houses, of ghost ships glittering along the distant horizon, of yellow lanterns at night, and of bells echoing like coded messages between the water and the clouds.*

Sylvia

It was Rosie who questioned Emma about the phone tracker, the rented cabin, while I waited in the car with my face turned stubbornly forward. Through the closed window, I heard their clipped goodbyes. Then Rosie was opening the driver's-side door and sliding behind the wheel and the engine was grumbling and we were leaving the Wolffs' house behind.

"You got the address?" I asked.

"The place where the tracker stopped working—yeah. And the name of the cabin that Emma thinks they rented. I guess she and he had been up in that area before." I could feel my sister's gaze on me. "Do you want me to go with you?"

I shook my head. We sped through a yellow light. In the distance, another lake bundled in bike paths and dotted with kayaks. The sun was low and the water was bronze.

"At least stay the night," Rosie said. "You can leave first thing tomorrow. You can borrow this car, and Leila can drop me off on her way in to the hospital."

"I'd rather leave tonight."

"You're not going to find them any faster in the dark." She braked at a stop sign, and the car jerked to a stop. "Please, Syl. Just for tonight? It's been a long day. I don't want to send you up there by yourself when you're so tired. It's too dangerous."

"Dangerous how?" Dangerous because Faye was unpredictable? Dangerous because Rosie didn't think I could control the situation?

"Dangerous because you have no idea what you might be walking into." Rosie cast a quick glance at me and tried to make her tone sound light, joking. "I won't allow it. I'm going to pull the big-sister card."

I knew that I was supposed to laugh. We were crossing the river now, with the ruins of warehouses and flour mills in the distance. My head ached and the highway tilted. Other cars continued swimming past ours, the sound of their engines reaching me slowly, gently, as if they were driving underwater. Rosie's voice floated toward me, her words gurgling without meaning. Through the windshield, I watched a long-limbed shadow leap down from a power line on the distant bank and dip into a spiky copse of trees.

"Maybe you're right," I said. "Maybe I'm overtired."

I could feel Rosie's relief. "Yes," she said, nodding with vigor. "Yes, you *are*."

The wash of sky was changing colors. I shuffled through my memories for images of the Kingman that I'd gathered during those feverish nights of research. Hadn't there been photos of his silhouette against an aquamarine sky? Hadn't someone written something about his icy force field, his electromagnetic pull?

"Emma mentioned the northern lights," I said. "Can you see them here? In Minneapolis?"

"I never have. I think you need to be further north." Rosie flicked on her turn signal, took a left into an alley, and eased through the corridor of garages and recycling bins. At the back of her house, she turned onto a concrete slab and shifted the car into park.

"Come on," she said. "You look terrible. Let's get you inside."

In the kitchen, we found Leila tossing a salad. Rosie dropped a kiss on her cheek and hung her coat on the back of a chair and directed me toward the cupboard so that I could set the table. Over bowls of pasta, Rosie described where we'd been and what we'd learned. Leila listened, sipping a little wine, thinking. Afterward, I made my way up to the guest bedroom and lay down on the mattress, intending to read for a while. But I must have fallen asleep immediately, because when I lifted my head from my pillow, the room was dark except for a shred of moon cutting through the window.

Another memory that twisted into shape before me: Jack, twenty-four years earlier, draining the whiskey from his cut-glass tumbler at someone's fortieth birthday party. He pulled his chair so close to mine that the wooden legs clapped together. Beneath the clatter of oversize serving utensils and the chime of ice cubes in highball glasses, he whispered: "What if I told you that I wanted to take you upstairs right here, right now? Would you do it with me, Syl?"

His breath smelled of pine boughs and maple syrup. I considered him: eyes black as thunder, chin coarse with stubble, curls tumbling around his ears. After a minute, his face split open in a grin. "Well, come on then," he growled, slipping his hand beneath the table and sliding it higher up my thigh. "Let's go."

We'd been trying to conceive for years by then, which meant that we'd had sex in every possible position, in every possible location, at every possible time of day. How could we have known what would work? How could we have known that it would be *there*, enveloped in the perfumed cocoon of other people's coats, veiled in the velvet darkness of someone else's bedroom, with my skirt hiked up to my waist and Jack's whiskey-soaked tongue rippling inside my mouth, that we'd finally succeed?

Of course I didn't know it when I rejoined the party a few minutes after Jack, my legs wobbling, my cheeks stinging from the cold water I'd splashed on my face to hide my heightened color. And I didn't know it when I drove Jack home through streets silky with fog, past row after row of slumbering houses. I didn't know it when I made him drink a glass of water with a pair of aspirin, nor when I burrowed down beneath the quilt beside him and rested the tips of my cold toes on his hairy shins.

The next day I brought him coffee in bed, and I leaned against him while he sipped from his mug and squinted into the translucent morning. We could hear the sound of our neighbors playing fetch with their dog in their backyard: the methodical thumping of the tennis ball against the fence, the jangle of tags. My hair was falling out of its bun and my pajama top was hanging off my shoulder and I knew that my eyes were blackened by mascara that I hadn't washed away the night before.

When the neighbors went back inside, Jack turned and gazed at me with something akin to wonder, his face youthful in the early autumnal light. He shook his head and let out a long, low whistle. "Sometimes I simply can't believe my luck."

Then he spilled a splash of coffee on his hand and uttered a string of jeweled profanities until I laid my head down on his thigh. My love for him was like a surgeon's scalpel, slicing through the center of my heart.

I rose from the bed in my sister's house and descended the stairs because I heard the clink of a spoon or a fork in the kitchen. There I found Leila stirring honey into a mug, the room unlit but for the three slender beams streaming from the oven hood to the stovetop below. She was standing just beyond their reach, and so I couldn't see her face.

"Trouble sleeping?" she asked. I nodded, and she turned to grab another mug from the dish rack. She filled it with hot water from the electric kettle and dropped in a bag that smelled of peppermint. She gestured toward a barstool and slid the tea across the counter toward me and held me in a direct, unswerving gaze.

"Rosie told me about the hearing, you know. About her testimony," she said.

I gripped the handle of my mug.

"Is it possible," Leila asked, "that you misunderstood Rosie's intentions?"

"No." I didn't care how childish I sounded. "She thought that

I had failed. She told them that Faye shouldn't ever be allowed to come home to me. Why would she say that unless she believed"—the anger abandoned me as quickly as it had come, and I ended my sentence forlornly—"that I was to blame for what happened?"

Leila extended an arm and covered my cold hand with her warm one. "Sylvia," she said fiercely, gently. "Listen to me. Nobody thinks that. *You* were not the one to wield the knife."

Hadn't Rosie said the same thing to me on the night before she testified? We'd already eaten dinner; Jack had gone to bed. We were drinking our cold red wine on the porch swing while sycamore leaves whispered thick as thieves beyond the screens.

"Sylvie," she'd murmured, her voice sounding so much like my mother's that I couldn't stop myself from scanning the yard beyond the porch, hoping to see my mother's ghost shimmering there. "Come on. I *know* you. I know that you did the best that you could with her."

When I looked at my sister then, I remembered her younger face in our shared bedroom mirror, round and pale as a clamshell. Her hand had swooped and dipped over her reflection as she rolled on coral-pink lipstick, rose-colored powder, inky-black eyeliner. I used to watch her flow through her window and spill down the drainpipe to the sandy soil below. In the distance, parked on a part of the road that she knew my parents couldn't see from their end of the house, the bulky outline of a station wagon was waiting for her, its headlights staring through seagrass. She never told me where she was going or whom she was meeting. I only knew that when she returned, she smelled of sugar and smoke. Her eyes were half-lidded and her lipstick was smudged. In the morning, her pillow bore the feathery stamp of her remaining makeup.

On the porch swing, the wine warming in our glasses and the cicadas buzzing through the screens, Rosie clasped my hand like we were children again. "The point is I don't want you to punish yourself forever for a crime that isn't yours."

How could I explain to Rosie then, or Leila now, that the crime *was* mine? How could I make them see that my child was both sep-arate from and inseparable from me?

My tea had cooled, and Leila was watching me, waiting for my response. *You were not the one to wield the knife.*

"You can't understand unless you're a mother," I said.

When I rose to carry my dishes to the sink and my bag to the car, Leila remained rooted to her chair. And so it was from a great height that I saw the sorrow wing across her features like the shadow of a seabird over sand. She flicked a wet glance at me and then looked away.

"The timing was always wrong." She turned her face toward the wall. "No matter when I asked, Rosie said she wasn't ready."

She lifted a hand and swiped at her eyes. When she turned back to me, she said, "Is it true, what Rosie said about all those babies you took care of when you were growing up? Was your house really packed full of them?"

I tried to picture the scene from Leila's point of view: the beach house swaying among the yellow grass, the cradles rocking in every window, the sweet scents of powdered milk and downy skin sus-pended in dream-dark corridors. Her face reflected the riches she imagined: all those infants waiting for her arms. In her clear gaze, I recognized my own ancient craving for a child and my own ill-fated future.

Once, in the years before Faye, we were visiting the Vatican and had gone in search of Michelangelo's *Pietà* in a tiny chapel of Saint Peter's Basilica. It was Tuesday morning, early, and the city had been swallowed by a fog so murky that traffic had slowed and tour-ists had lost their way, which meant that for a few minutes Jack and I were the only ones standing before these marble figures: the mother with her graven robes bearing the body of her son. Jack pointed out the way that her hand supported his chest, his ribs and muscles carved with such grace and care that it seemed at any moment he might draw a breath. I gazed into Mary's downturned face, wondering what she was thinking, wondering if her grief was any more or less difficult to bear since she'd been told that it was coming.

The tourists began to pile in around us, rustling their windbreakers and whispering to one another in a hundred different languages. I turned to find Jack watching me, his expression troubled. I smoothed out my face too late, knowing that he'd already read the thoughts flickering across it in the gilded light. He'd asked me not to think about children, and here I was, five thousand miles from home, thinking about children. When he squeezed my hand, I squeezed back. Then I let him guide me away. We ate a late breakfast in a café around the corner, leaning up against the coffee bar, taking tiny sips of bitter espresso and sharing a plate of *cornetti*.

If I'd been able to peer into her future, if I had known what she would do—wouldn't I have loved her exactly the same?

When I sift through scenes from my childhood, when I remember the pressure of all those infants in my arms, Rosie is rarely there. In my memory, it is only my mother and me who watch from the screened porch, time and again, as the social worker clips each baby into the same ragged car seat and goes rattling down the road in the same beat-up car. Rosie was never present when the infants arrived, either. I close my eyes and try to see her warming one of the bottles in the kitchen or humming a lullaby over a squished face in the bassinet. But no matter how many times I study those images, I can't find my sister in them.

"Did she give any reasons?" I asked Leila.

"She'd talk about the planet." Leila's voice was brimming. "She'd show me charts and stats to prove that having children was one of the worst things we could do for the climate. She'd ask me if that's what I wanted—to bring a child into a world where polar bears had gone extinct, where there wasn't enough fresh water to go around."

I'd seen some of these numbers. "She's not completely wrong."

"So then I'd tell her that it wasn't our job to fix everything that's broken, and I'd say that while we were alive I wanted to make choices that would make us happy, and she'd try to tell me that having a child *wouldn't* make us any happier, that studies have shown that parents actually rate their overall happiness and satisfaction much lower than nonparents—"

"They do?"

"—and I'd tell her that we were different from those people, and she'd say that that's what everybody thinks."

Leila sagged into the stool. She reached for her tea, but when her fingers touched the mug, they rested there without lifting it.

I was remembering the night that Rosie didn't come home. My mother received the call from the police station, and I'd watched from the window as her car tore down the driveway, the cracked shells popping and snapping beneath her tires. I'd remained at the sill for what felt like days, though the stars could not have shifted all that much by the time my mother returned with the pale orb of Rosie's face floating above the dark seat beside her. When my mother marched Rosie into the house, they both were silent. Rosie's elbows and knees were skinned raw, and her arms stung with scratches, but she wouldn't tell me what happened—not as I helped swab her wounds in the sickly halo of the bathroom mirror, nor when I brought her tea and toast the next morning. She was grounded for months, but it might as well have been for eternity. She stopped sneaking out and she refused any calls. Her capped lipstick squatted untouched on her vanity for years. It was not until I was emptying the house after my mother's death that I found it and, after letting the weight of it linger for several long seconds against the palm of my hand, tossed it into the wicker basket behind the door.

"Rosie got into some trouble when she was young," I said.

Leila bobbed her head. "I know. That's why she went into adolescent counseling."

"Right." I slid my finger across the countertop, trying to ease my way into my sister's mind. Why had she pretended not to notice all those infants in our house? Why had she resented our childhood so, when I had not? What had made her so angry with our mother that she would refuse to come when the woman was dying? I could have told Leila about the calls from that hospice room, my mother's face fading into her white pillowcase, Jack trudging in and out with coffee after coffee and wilted gift shop bouquets, and Rosie's distant voice on the other end of the phone, telling me she was sorry, she was busy, she simply couldn't make it in time—but how would this have looked to her wife?

Leila's voice broke up my thoughts, and the memories scattered. "Listen, Sylvia," she said. "I know this isn't—well, it's not a fair question. It's probably an impossible one. But—" A pause that felt eternal. The shuffling of footsteps overhead. And then the soft, urgent words: "After everything that's happened—are you happy that you had your daughter?"

Above us, water gushed through pipes. A car in the alley swung its headlights across the kitchen wall, and for half a second, I saw a shadow that I recognized. Didn't Leila understand that the very question was absurd?

"I'd sacrifice everything for Faye," I said. The voice that spoke didn't sound like mine. "I'd die for her. I'd—" My mind swerved through the dark, searching for something wild enough, sensational enough for this childless stranger to comprehend the boundlessness of my love for my daughter, the savage animal instinct. "I'd kill for her."

The clock continued to tick in the other room. On the second floor, the footsteps shuffled back down the hall. Leila shifted in her seat, and her face came into focus: thoughtful and bare.

"*That*," she said, rising to carry the mugs to the sink, "doesn't answer the question."

———————

A memory returns to me, unprompted and vivid: Faye perched on the edge of the kitchen counter, swinging her legs against the cabinets. Her dark hair tied back and her cheeks flushed with the warmth radiating from the oven. I'm remembering how she crushed the graham crackers into Jack's birthday cake batter with determined fingers. I'm remembering the jingle of mixing bowls, the hum of the electric mixer, the shine of egg whites whipped to foam. *Are you happy that you had your daughter?* I can still hear her lilting voice as she sang along with Jack's rock-and-roll station, and I can taste, even now, the sour sting of cream cheese frosting on my tongue. There are some moments that never leave us; some memories that we will carry to the grave.

Three days after his brother Wilhelm died, Jacob Grimm told a friend that he heard the scratching of his brother's nib pen in his office. But when he poked his head through the door to say hello, he saw nothing, and the scratching stopped. To his brother Ludwig, he wrote that maybe the sunken, infected corpse that had been carried out of the house the week before was not Wilhelm at all, but rather the misshapen carcass of an oversize elf. Changelings can be substituted for infants, so why not for old men? What if Wilhelm were alive and well in the woods, gathering herbs and collecting stories? "My brother wouldn't desert me before we had discovered the object of our quest, before we had found and named the monstrous shadow of our childhood, the mirthless, flickering figure who haunted our nightmares and our daydreams for decades. Don't you see, Ludwig? We had gone in search of stories when we were actually in search of him. We sought to ensnare him within the invisible threads of our narrative, to pin him down with words, and, in so doing, to keep him out of the woods." Ludwig wrote back, consoling Jacob for his loss and reminding him that his visions were only the products of grief. By the time the letter reached Jacob's house in Berlin, Jacob had disappeared. The house was empty, damp, and drafty, trembling on its foundations in the gusts of winter wind.

PART III

The Monster

Sylvia

In the years after Faye's crime, with nothing but my thoughts for company, I sometimes found myself wondering what would have happened to us if we'd had a second child. What if we'd had other lunches to make, other backpacks to stuff? What if there had been someone else in the house whose existence demanded that we get out of bed and face the world? We would have been forced to perform normalcy until it began to feel normal. We would have had to talk to each other. Make grocery lists. Watch sitcoms. Maybe, if we had been able to fill the empty space in other ways, it would not have crept into our hearts, our bed. Maybe it would not have swallowed us whole.

In the morning, when I descended the staircase with my suitcase in hand, Rosie was waiting for me. She dropped a piece of bread into the toaster and set a bowl of yogurt down in front of me.

"Keep your strength up," she said.

"You're sure it's all right for me to take the car?"

"Of course it is. You're sure you're all right going by yourself?"

"Of course I am."

I dipped a spoon into the bowl. Behind me, the toast popped up. After Rosie had retrieved it and turned back to the counter, I set the spoon down again.

"How did it all happen that night, when we were younger?" I asked. "When Mom went to pick you up at the police station?"

Her shoulders jerked back. "Excuse me?"

"I haven't thought about it in years. But yesterday I was talking to Leila and …" I didn't know how much to divulge about that conversation. "Why haven't we ever talked about it?"

My sister pressed her fingers to her closed eyelids. She inhaled and exhaled six times. When she opened her eyes again, her face was pale, but her gaze was steady.

"What do you want to know?"

I had been eight or nine at the time, which meant that no one told me anything. I'd had to pick up snippets of information from whispered phone conversations, from schoolyard rumors. "I know that there was a party, and that a girl died," I said. "I know that you were there when it happened."

Rosie arched over the countertop, her pajama top rumpled and her hair yanked into a severe brown-and-gray bun that made her look much older than she was. Behind her, white cabinets glistened in the dim light of dawn, and dry leaves rustled against the windows. I waited for the tapping of branches on the glass, but the sound didn't come.

"The party," my sister finally said, "was at a construction site along the shoreline. Well, it wasn't a party, really. Just some people drinking and smoking and throwing cups down from the top floor of what would become a condo building. I'd invited a group of kids from my senior English class. One of the neighbors must have called the cops. When we heard sirens, everybody scattered. I lunged for the stairs and tripped on the raw concrete and looked up to see an officer standing there. One of the girls I'd brought— she must have been too drunk, or confused, to know where she was going. It was so dark. She went scrambling toward a half-finished window and fell off the side. She went so fast that there wasn't time for her to scream. But we all heard the sound when she hit the rocks."

I imagined Rosie alone in her bedroom night after night. The faded floral wallpaper, the white glow of her bedside light, the discarded makeup on the vanity, the hot, heavy tangle of blankets. Often, when I'd knocked at her door with an offering of cookies or a book I thought she'd like, I'd find her tucked into a battered armchair by the window with the sash drawn up and the sound of the sea so close, so intense, that it could have been lapping at the roof. She'd never been reading, or listening to music, or doing anything but staring blankly at the houses across the street, in the direction of the water. She had been waiting, I now understood, for a ghost to appear.

Rosie shuddered, but kept talking, as though she needed to get to the end now that she'd started. "Mom wouldn't let me go to the funeral. She said that even though the girl was only there because of me, I wasn't to blame for her death."

The sun continued rising through the windows, and the room lightened and warmed. "Of course I knew that Mom was wrong," Rosie went on. "Whose fault was it, if not mine? But after a while, it was too hard to keep blaming myself."

"So you started blaming her?"

"If she'd paid more attention to us..."

The cry of a distant infant whirled through my memory. My mother, sitting at the table across from us, rose to her feet and sailed from the room.

"It still could've happened, Rosie. Even if she'd been with you every minute."

Did I really believe that? Or was I still convinced, in the deepest reaches of my being, that if I'd been with my own daughter that morning, I could have prevented all of it?

"I never understood how you could stand all those babies," Rosie said, her tone bruised. "Why was I the only one who cared that we came in second?"

The sweep of my mother's cool fingers across my forehead when she leaned down to say good night; the tingling in my scalp as she tugged my hair into braids. The sandwiches she sliced into moons and stars. The stacks of books she hauled home for us from the library. "There was plenty of love to go around," I said.

My sister shook her head. "Leila insists that love isn't finite. But we show our love through time and energy, and what is more finite than that? Every hour that she spent with those babies was an hour that she couldn't spend with us."

I remembered the hundreds of dawns I'd slid out of bed, abandoning the warm bulk of my husband, to retrieve a whimpering child from her crib. How many times had Jack opened his eyes to find me gone?

"Everybody believes that I'm the bad guy," Rosie said. "I bet you do, too, Syl. I bet you're thinking: *What's wrong with Rosie that she doesn't want to have a baby?*" Her words were full of water now, and three or four tears splashed to the table. She swept them savagely up with her sleeve. "I just don't want to love my wife any less. What is so awful about that?"

A few hours earlier, Leila had slumped over that very countertop. She had wanted me to tell her that she wasn't missing out on something wonderful. *Are you happy that you had your daughter?* She had been counting on me to say no.

Rosie buried her head in her arms. When she spoke again, the words were muffled, swaddled in cotton. "There's no good way to tell someone that you love her too much to have a baby with her," she said. "Believe me. I've tried."

As I rose from my chair and rounded the curve of the kitchen island to reach my sister, as I wrapped my arms around her for the first time in years, as I felt the drum of her pulse, her heartbeat, against my chest, I wondered if people are always bound to love each other too much or too little. What if the love that we give can never exactly equal the love that someone else needs?

Rosie hadn't been present for our mother's final hours. She hadn't listened to our mother's shallow, labored breathing; hadn't watched her conversing with the ghosts who floated near the foot of her bed. And so she hadn't heard our mother speak in fevered dream-tones about a little boy who fell asleep in his cradle and didn't wake up.

If you tunnel deep enough, you'll eventually come to the roots of a person's desire. If my mother hadn't lost her first child, then perhaps she wouldn't have needed to fill the house with infants. If she hadn't filled the house with infants, then maybe Rosie would have agreed to have a baby with Leila or maybe I would have agreed not to have one with Jack. Maybe Faye wouldn't have been born, and maybe she wouldn't have committed her crime, and maybe I wouldn't have found myself soothing an unfamiliar sister and hungering for an estranged husband while fearing, even now, that they would leave me again.

Soon I was motoring north toward Lake Superior in Rosie's rumbling sedan. Minneapolis diminished in the rearview mirror, finally vanishing, and the glass and brick of the city surrendered to scrubby trees and hungry skies. The clouds were pearl colored and woolly, and when I stopped fifty miles up the road for gas, the snap of cold surprised me. Inside, the cashier rang up my coffee and nodded toward the soft gray world beyond the windows.

"Sure *looks* like there'll be snow," she said, dropping the coins into my palm. "Though I know it's too early."

The first hour of the drive was easy. I had the map glowing on my phone beside me, but I barely glanced at it. I felt, rather, that I was being pulled by an invisible thread toward something or someone waiting up the road for me, and although I couldn't tell whether the sensation was sinister or benevolent, by then it didn't matter.

"I don't understand," Jack had said to me once near the end of Faye's hearing. He had walked into the living room to find me studying a set of Kingman images I'd printed out and spread across the coffee table. "Is he supposed to be something kids are afraid of, or something they desire?"

I didn't look up from the pictures of cloaks and pines and crowns. "Both," I said, irritated by the interruption. "Neither."

He remained standing in the doorway for several minutes after that. My body warmed in the heat of his presence; the skin beneath my nose prickled with the scent of his aftershave. But when I finally raised my gaze to meet his, he was gone.

At the time, the question had seemed irrelevant. But as I caught my first glimpse of the Great Lake ahead of me, the memory struck me differently. I'd thought that Jack had already made his mind up about Faye—that he'd condemned her, rejected her, and—in consequence—me. But what if all that time he'd actually, in his own way, been trying to understand?

I knew that I was approaching Duluth when the road began twisting beneath overpasses again and curving along the shoreline. To the left, a rust-colored downtown jutted at the foot of bluffs speckled with yellow foliage. To the right, bridges and causeways arched over and into Lake Superior. The road trembled beneath my tires and the radio crackled with static and I kept urging the car forward anyway, into the series of tunnels that swallowed me up and spit me out on the other side of the city.

From there, it was only another hour to the cottages Emma had described. The highway veered away from the lake, and for a while I lost sight of the water behind the thicket of trees. It was only when I turned off the main road to follow the gravel drive down to a rental office that I found it again: gray-blue and raw, the shoreline waves whitecapped in the wind.

The rental office turned out to be a vintage log cabin shouldered into a stand of pines. The yard was crammed with mangled metal sculptures and the walls inside bristled with taxidermied fur. As I made my way to the front desk, I could feel the eyes of long-dead animals on my back. How strange to think that my daughter could be there, on those grounds, just a few yards or walls away from me. I shot a glance toward a darkened dining room off to the left, half expecting to see her lounging at a table there.

But when I asked the woman behind the counter if she could tell me if my daughter was here, she shook her head.

"I'm not permitted to say what guests are staying with us," she said. And then, after a moment's thought: "But I don't suppose it's revealing too much to say that someone is *not* here. All four cabins are empty for the next two nights, actually. They weren't supposed to be, but what with the storm coming in, a couple guests checked out early this morning and a few others canceled their plans. People like the snow in December, but in September it just feels like an affront."

The vision of Faye in the dining room twirled twice before dissolving into air and dust. The breath slid out of my lungs in a warm whoosh, deflating me.

"I'm sorry to bear bad news," the woman continued. Her gaze settled on me, half-sympathetic and half-calculating. Her fingers deftly buttoned up her cardigan. "But the *good* news is that you can have your pick of cabins if you need someplace to stay tonight. How about I put you down for one?"

"I need to find my daughter," I managed to reply.

She squinted past me, toward the windows, where clouds were mumbling darkly together over the water. "Well, then let me help you find your way, at least," she said. "The forecasts are wrong a lot, but I'll admit that I'm a little bit concerned about what's coming." From beneath the counter, she drew out a paper map and began unfolding it between us. She pressed her hand across its creases and then stabbed an index finger at the shoreline to indicate our location. "Where are you headed from here?"

As my gaze roved across the map, I felt my knees growing weaker. My daughter could be anywhere, in any of these towns whose names

I didn't know, whose doors I couldn't knock on, whose windows I couldn't peer into. She could be lost in that stretch of woods while a storm whirled in from the water; she could be hunkered down in one of those tiny, battered cabins on the highway's edge. She could be frightened, cold, ecstatic, ravenous. As the floor bucked beneath my feet and the mounted moose curled its dead lips into a snarl and a familiar silhouette glittered darkly, bewitchingly, just beyond the margins of my vision, I asked myself for the hundred-millionth time how I had failed so utterly to keep her safe.

The cabin was neat and spare: a bedroom, a sitting area, a kitchenette, and a bathroom scrubbed and polished until the wood gleamed. Pine boards lined the floors and walls, antlers spiked above the bed, and a woodstove crouched in the corner. The woman from the rental office, whose name slipped my mind as soon as she shared it, showed me where to find the extra wood, the linens, and the dishware. She set down the suitcase that she'd insisted on carrying. Then she pressed the key into my hand, fervently wished me a good night's rest, and clomped out the door. I hovered for the space of several heartbeats in the sitting area, listening to the crack of branches beneath the soles of her boots as she crunched through dry leaves and struggling to accept the fact that, once more, I'd run out of leads.

My impulse, as always, was to call Jack. After a ring and a half, he answered.

"I lost her," I confessed, feeling dizzy, unmoored. "I'm sorry. I know that I was supposed to find her—she was supposed to be here—but there's too much woods, and I don't know where to look for her—"

"Sylvia—" Jack interrupted. He said something else, but his words were fractured. In the background, I could hear the buzz of an announcement through a loudspeaker and the rise and fall of strangers' voices.

I crossed to the window. "Where are you?" I asked.

More sounds: a symphony of beeps and horns, a whoosh of air. Jack tried again. "That's what I'm telling you," he said. "We just landed in Minneapolis. Can you stay where you are until we get there? I think we know where to find her."

His voice spiraled through my ears. I gripped the windowsill and watched the granite waves crack against a distant bluff. On the very edge of the outcrop, half-shrouded in trees, perched an amber-colored lighthouse, its stone base glimmering like garnets in the fading light.

"Who do you mean by 'we'?" I asked.

A scuffling noise, and then the line went dead. I remained frozen at the window, one hand gripping the sill, the other pressing the silent phone to my ear as if, through the sheer force of my will, I could capture and hold Jack's voice in my skin, my bones, my body.

Elizabeth the Good

Elizabeth had tried to get Faye's mom out of her head; she tried to stop thinking about Amelia. But she couldn't focus on her work. She couldn't sleep. She hiked up and down the steps of the dorm for hours, trying to jar the Kingman loose from her mind. At dawn she was standing outside the chapel, watching the sun bloom over the library, waiting for the doors to open so that she could exorcise the monster that was threatening to grab hold of her again. But she felt worse, not better, once she was inside.

A man who'd been dusting the sconces started at the sight of her. "You look awful," he said. "Do you want me to call someone?"

She shook her head, but that only made him narrow his eyes to scrutinize her face. Terrified, she got the hell out of there. Once in the quad, she stopped to lean against the warm bricks. Her back heated up and her pulse slowed down and her head cleared. She knew where she needed to go.

As she approached the house, she half expected to find the whole family inside: Faye, her mother, her father. She imagined the three of them as she'd last seen them together. When she and Faye had descended the stairs the morning they met Brittany at the edge of the woods, the trees beyond the fence had been dipped in blue-gray fog.

Faye's parents had been folded into each other on that swing. How many times had Elizabeth seen one of them resting a hand on the other's shoulder, forehead, fingers, thigh? How many times had she watched his gaze track her movements through the living room, the hallway, the backyard, or witnessed the thousand cups of tea that they carried to each other over the course of a single evening? That kind of love—so aching, so naked, so different from anything she'd seen at home or on TV—wasn't something she could wrap her head around. It was only something she could feel like a cold knife to the lungs. That kind of love never failed to suck the air right out of her. Never failed to make her feel like an outsider, looking in.

"One second," Faye had said. She gestured with the hand that held a doughnut, and the powdered sugar dusted her sweatshirt sleeves. "You go on ahead. I need to say goodbye."

Elizabeth lagged a little, dragging her sneakers toward the screen door. For the first time, she was harboring doubts. When the door banged shut behind her, she looked back over her shoulder, squinting against the sun.

"I'll be right there!" Faye called, as if concerned that Elizabeth would leave without her. Did she really think that that had been a possibility?

Elizabeth heard the creak of the swing and the rustle of a hug. She heard Faye's mom tell her to be careful, and Faye's dad say that he could see Brittany walking up the drive. She hoped Faye's parents hadn't noticed that her backpack was overstuffed or that her face was extra pale. She feared that they would suddenly decide to check the front pocket of her bag.

She heard Faye say goodbye. Then Faye turned and met her eyes through the screen with an expression of such grief that Elizabeth felt it like a blow to the heart.

When they were alone outside, Elizabeth tossed her arm around Faye's shoulders and tugged her close. She wanted Faye to know that she loved her, too. That when they reached the Kingman's castle, they wouldn't need anybody else. That if they could get to the North Shore, if they could prove themselves worthy, then they'd inhabit such a different world, a mysterious and glittering world—the kind Faye had always described for them, imagined for them—that it wouldn't matter what their lives had been or whom they'd left behind.

It was Faye's dad who answered Elizabeth's knock at the door. He needed a few seconds to place her, to add the years to the child that she'd been.

When he invited her in, she almost asked if they could stay outside, if they could just chat for a minute in the long yellow grass. But there were ghosts out there, too: Faye twisting daisies into crowns; her fingers dipping down into a murky pond for tadpoles; her arms scooping up the white cat mewling at her ankles; her mass of uncombed hair like a black galaxy, studded with forget-me-nots instead of stars. So Elizabeth followed him inside.

He poured her a cup of grapefruit juice because it was all he could find in the fridge. She watched him root through three different cupboards in search of glasses. Faye's mom must have moved them, because they weren't where Elizabeth remembered them, either.

"I heard that Sylvia came to see you," he said. "I'm sorry if—" He hesitated, choosing his words carefully. "I imagine that it must have been upsetting."

"I should have told her that Faye had left Amelia with me. I called, but"—she shrugged—"something happened with the phone."

"You had her in the dorms for all those months?"

"No. I had to move out of the dorms for the summer. I sublet the top floor of an old house downtown."

Because she'd been working concessions part-time at one of the parks, she'd been able to bring Amelia with her to work. She'd set the girl up at a picnic table in the shade with a picture book and an old MP3 player, where she could keep an eye on her while ringing up orders. During breaks, she'd carry over baskets of curly fries, and they'd feed the ducks together.

The summer had been sweltering, and the heat in their attic apartment was oppressive. Sometimes they'd eaten ice cream for breakfast to cool down. They went to the park five days a week, and on the two days Elizabeth had off, she took Amelia to the mall or the movies just to get out of the heat. She was a beautiful child. People were always stopping to admire her.

"And Faye hadn't told you when she'd be back?"

Elizabeth shook her head. That first night, while she had been arranging Amelia on the futon with a stained blanket and the television remote, Faye had made several trips back and forth with shoulder bags of clothing, toys, and books. When she had finished, Elizabeth eyed the towering pile of the girl's belongings and asked how long, exactly, Faye intended to be away.

"Not long," Faye had said, with a vague wave of her hand.

"Where are you going?" Elizabeth was waiting for a list of phone numbers, hotels. What if something went wrong? What if the child got sick, or needed help?

As if in answer, Faye had lifted her daughter up from the futon and swung her toward Elizabeth, who instinctively extended her arms to receive her. Amelia settled between the crook of Elizabeth's elbow and the curve of her hip as if she'd been molded to fit there. When Faye had reached out a hand and brushed her long fingers against the girl's warm cheek, Elizabeth had recognized the terrifying weight of her love.

Faye's expression, when she turned back toward Elizabeth, was unusually grave. "I've got to finish what I started," she said.

Two seconds later, her footsteps were drumming down the stairwell. When the building door slammed, Elizabeth had rocked on her feet. She had tightened her arms around the girl because she needed something to anchor her, something to hold, and together they moved to the window and watched from a great distance as

Faye loped away into the dark. The mist was draped between the trees and a silver moon was rising. Elizabeth was trying not to blink because she knew that once she did, the fog would swallow Faye whole.

In the morning, Elizabeth realized that Faye had left her car keys on the table. When she went downstairs to move the car, parking tickets papered the dashboard like snow.

"To finish what she started," Mr. Vogel was muttering. He said the words again, as if repeating them could strip them of their mystery. "And she didn't tell you what that meant?"

"No."

"And your roommate? Before you moved into the sublet? She wasn't suspicious about a stranger's child sleeping in your common room?"

"I made up a story about a cousin who was having surgery and a daughter who had nowhere to stay. Clara bought it."

"But then, last week—"

Elizabeth was waiting for this. She'd practiced what she would say. "I couldn't move back into the dorms with a three-year-old, and I couldn't afford to stay where I was." She hesitated, then added: "I worked hard to get my life on track. A kid was never in the cards."

"And you didn't want to go to the police?"

"No."

Elizabeth had no intention of setting foot in a station ever again if she could help it. So she heaped the back seat of Faye's car with snacks and she tucked Amelia into her car seat and she pursed her lips and pecked her sweaty forehead. Then she drove the car to the grocery store across the street from the station. She popped in a CD of Disney songs. She got out and poked her head back in and told Amelia not to worry. She didn't say she'd be right back. She never lied to her. She was not so much a monster as *that*.

And then she walked away, her sandals slapping gently on the pavement. When she turned, she could see Amelia's round face through the window, watching her go.

Obviously it's not a good thing to leave a child behind. Elizabeth knows that. Even if you don't go far. Even if you merely scurry over to the far side of the parking lot and cower in the tall grass on the edge of the road, which she did, gulping at the air like a fish flopping in the bottom of a boat. It was important that Faye's dad know that Elizabeth stayed near her. Even though the night was warm and sticky, she grew so cold over the hour that passed that she shivered for three days after. But she stayed until she saw a man lift Amelia from the car and carry her inside. She waited until the squad car rolled into the lot, its wet blue lights whirling. That's when she rose to her feet and retrieved the bike that she'd stashed two blocks down and pedaled away as fast as she could.

"You didn't think to bring her here?" he asked.

"I didn't—" How could she explain it in a way that would make sense to him? Would he understand her if she told him that the longer Faye's daughter stayed in her house, the more frequently she'd found herself dreaming of the Kingman?

She felt the monster's knobby fingers on her shoulders. "I didn't want to get tangled up with everything again."

He pinched the skin between his eyebrows. "But by then you were *already* tangled up in it," he reminded her. And then, after a freighted pause: "Anna, you'll never not be involved."

A sleepy cry came from upstairs and spared her the challenge of answering. After he left the room, she studied the peeling cabinets, the sun-bleached wallpaper, the fraying curtains. She could smell the ghost of ancient potpourri: rancid and sweet. She knew the place like she knew her own hands, her own feet. She knew where to step so the floorboards wouldn't creak. She knew that if she wanted cold water from the bathroom sink, she had to twist the knob toward hot. She knew all the shortcuts from the backyard to the creek. If she closed her eyes, she could hear the sound of murky water trickling over rocks, and she could taste the bubblegum on her tongue, and she could feel Faye's warm, dry palm slip into hers in order to pull her more quickly through the trees.

Faye's dad was right. *Elizabeth the Good*—what a joke. No matter how many times she changed her name or how many elementary-school students she tutored or soup kitchens she served, she would never outrun what she'd done.

"What's it like, to lose your parents?" Faye had asked Elizabeth once. She was painting tangerine wings on Elizabeth's face, which quivered at each cold touch of the brush.

The bathroom lights sharpened. In the mirror, Elizabeth's face was not her own. "Everybody loses their parents," she said, attempting indifference. "Sooner or later."

Faye lowered the brush and her own face went pale. "I guess that's right," she said. Elizabeth had never heard her voice like that: gravelly, grief-stricken.

For once, Elizabeth was the wiser one. The rush of power was unfamiliar, dizzying, intoxicating. She nodded with what she imagined to be solemnity. "It's only a matter of time."

When Mr. Vogel returned with the girl in his arms, Elizabeth couldn't keep her face from burning. The parking lot. The rattling engine, the distant sirens. The milky forehead through a foggy window. The images jostled for space inside her chest, their edges sharp and painful.

But Amelia beamed at the sight of Elizabeth. She wriggled in his arms until he set her down, and then she bounded across the floor. She hauled herself onto Elizabeth's thighs and curled herself like a question mark against her denim jacket. She wasn't angry at all. Elizabeth felt her heart slowing and her terror diminishing as the small form rose and fell with her breath. She stared down at the girl and wondered: *Is this what forgiveness feels like?*

"I know I'm involved," she said. "That's what I came here to tell you. I think I know where Faye was headed when she left here."

All the stories they'd told each other about the dense woods they'd never seen, the frozen shore they'd never touched. Faye had been looking forward to the cold, Elizabeth recalled. She'd wanted to see her breath turn into snow.

"To Minnesota," he said.

She hadn't expected this. "How did you know?"

"We think Faye went up to see someone at a university in Minneapolis. So Sylvia flew up there, but so far she hasn't managed to track Faye down."

Elizabeth chewed her bottom lip. "Mrs. Vogel said that there had been some new crimes, right? She said that the"—she dropped her voice and covered Amelia's ears with her hands—"*Kingman* is back?"

A muscle twitched in his cheek. "That makes it sound as though—"

"Okay, I don't mean *back*, exactly, but—the idea of him? If Faye was aware of that, if she was worried about what would happen if her daughter learned about him, then I don't think she would have stayed in the city. I think she would have wanted to go up there."

"Up where?"

Elizabeth stabbed a finger at the table as if she were pointing to a map. "To the North Woods. To Isle Philippeaux."

He rubbed a hand over his face. "Anna," he began.

"Elizabeth."

"That island is imaginary."

"It's on maps."

"Maps that no one in the past century has been able to replicate."

"Just because you can't find something doesn't mean that it doesn't exist," Elizabeth snapped, surprising both of them. "Maybe all it means is that you're looking in the wrong place."

Did he hear it, too? Did he recognize Faye's words in her mouth? For a second, an uneasy silence fell between them. Amelia wriggled and yawned. Finally Faye's dad spoke again.

"And you think you know the right place to look?"

Elizabeth found herself nodding. "I can show you."

"You can't just tell me?"

"No," she said. "I need to go with you."

"I thought you said you wanted to stay out of this. Hasn't Faye gotten you into enough trouble already?"

That was the story, wasn't it? Faye had stolen the knives; Faye had guided her into the woods. Elizabeth had been a fool: she'd trusted Faye, and she'd been played. She didn't have time to correct the record right now.

"It's too late," she said instead. "You were right: I'm already in it." She stared him down, startled by her own boldness, daring him to contradict her. "We all are. That's why we should be there."

Sirens wailed in the distance. She turned her face to what she thought might be north. A lighthouse, a castle, a promise, a friend. She wanted to believe that Faye needed her. That she still had time to do something right.

Faye

When did Faye start to suspect that something was wrong? It wasn't in class, when she watched the professor pace back and forth before the lectern with his hair as wild as his eyes and his face blazing with intelligence, raving about legends and mysteries in a way that made sense, she felt, only to her. It wasn't in his home, where she was distracted by the twins whose tiny fists and ample thighs reminded her so much of Amelia at that age that she was always on the verge of giving up and going home to her. Every night that she spent in that narrow brass bed in that wood-paneled attic, she watched the stars rotate across the skylight and she dreamed of gathering her daughter in her arms again.

No; if she had suspected something earlier, she would not have gone north with him. Or maybe she would have. She was still driven by her instinct, her gut, even though history had taught her not to trust herself. What other compass was there?

It was not until she and Leonard were already two hours north of the city, crossing the plush carpets of the glass and granite mansion gleaming on the lakeshore in Duluth, that she found herself growing wary of him. What, exactly, did he expect from her? They had already seen the maple desk and dresser in the bedroom, the gilded portraits gracing the stairwell, the clawed feet of the porcelain tub in the bathroom, and the stained-glass leaves that glimmered at the far end of the butler's pantry. She was standing in a green-tiled breakfast room that felt more like an arboretum, brushing her fingertips across ferns that were taller than she was, when he joined her at the window and asked her if she sensed something.

"Like what?" she asked.

"Like him," he said. "Everyone thinks that the murder of the mining heiress here was planned and executed by a member of the family. But *you* don't think that, do you?"

She was studying the acorns carved into the high backs of the chairs and the roses painted on the teacups. Someone had arranged them prettily around the table, as if in preparation for a party. If she placed her palm against the teapot, perhaps she'd find it warm. "I didn't even know there was a murder here," she said.

He leaned in. "But now that you *do* know, what do you think? How did it happen?"

"I don't know," she said. The cups and saucers were glistening, listening. "Couldn't you ask the tour guide?"

He made a dismissive gesture with his chin that she'd come to recognize. "He's only going to give the party line. He isn't interested, like we are, in the truth."

Then he placed a hand on her shoulder, and despite everything, it made her feel powerful. Anointed. Like a mage or a seer. "Come on, Faye," he said. "I'm sure you sense something. Wasn't he here? Wasn't he part of it?"

He made her feel like a child again, a student again. She suddenly wanted desperately to supply the answer he was looking for. He was the one adult in the world who still believed that she was worth something.

Tonight, he'd told her, they'd stay at a cottage just up the road. After that, they'd nudge farther north.

"It's possible," she said, testing the syllables on her tongue as they came to her. A crow swooped overhead and cast a long, speedy shadow across the lawn. "He might have been here."

Jack

Jack hadn't been on a plane in over a decade. As the ground fell away beneath him and the flight attendant jammed a beverage cart through the narrow aisle, he tried to remember the last time he'd heard that clatter of bottles and wheels. It must have been the wedding on the West Coast. A little town along the Pacific, an hour north of San Francisco. A second cousin's third marriage, maybe, or a colleague's kid. He couldn't remember. But if he closed his eyes and rested his head against the back of his seat, he could see the white tent staked against the water. The pop of corks on the dock. The stars spinning in cobalt water, the glitter of a city in the fog across the bay. Neither of them had been to California before. At the reception Sylvia tipped toward him with her glass of liquid gold and asked him what he'd do if an earthquake opened up right there beneath them. If the world ended, if the highways crumbled and the planes were grounded—where would he go? What supplies would he grab? How would he get home?

Something about her that evening: the tendrils of hair curling over her ears, the flush of color across her collarbone, the glimmer of her earrings, her hair, her dress. He wanted to tell her that sometimes her face was so familiar to him that he mistook it for his own. He wanted to tell her what a relief it had been when she'd walked into his office that day. What a weight had been lifted when he saw her and understood that he wasn't alone anymore. He blames the click of the bride's heels on the dance floor, or the sappy song of the first dance. He was overcome by the enchantment of it all. That's why he said, like the romantic sap he used to be: "Don't worry about the earthquakes, Syl. There's nothing we can't survive together."

He and the girls tumbled out of the rental car sometime after midnight. The cloak of black sky above them was fastened with stars. One yellow window floated above a darkened yard. He studied the mailbox, double-checked the address against the one he'd scrawled on the inside of his wrist as Rosie dictated the numbers to him over the phone a few hours earlier.

"Can we go any faster?" Anna asked. Amelia's limbs slithered over her shoulders and bumped against her hips. "She's heavy."

He slammed the car door shut and led the way to the front door. Before he could lift a fist to knock, the door swung open, and Rosie was standing before him, the hallway light streaming past her, her face obscured. They'd never been all that close, Rosie and Jack. They'd never been at ease around each other. But there on her concrete stoop, with his duffel balanced on the iron railing, Rosie lurched into his arms, and he felt a blast of heat coursing from his shoulders to his feet. *Oh, right*, he remembered. *This is what family feels like.*

They held each other. Awkwardly, self-consciously. She started to speak and he loosened his embrace. When he leaned back, he saw that she was staring over his shoulder at Anna waiting with Amelia in her arms.

"Is that..." she began. Her face was ashen.

He didn't know for sure what she was asking. *Is that Faye's partner in crime? Is that Faye's daughter? Is that the reason why Faye took off?* So he just said: "Yes."

Then Anna introduced herself to Rosie by a different name, and Jack remembered that she'd tried to tell him about it on the plane. So this time he did his best to brand it on his brain. *Elizabeth, Eliza-*

beth, Elizabeth. Of course. None of them were the same as they had been.

In the living room, he found a tall woman in scrubs. "This is Leila," came Rosie's voice from behind him. "My wife."

"Nice to meet you, Jack," the woman said, approaching him with a half smile. "I've heard so much about you."

He took the offered hand but failed to hide his surprise. "Nice to meet you," he echoed. And then, releasing Leila and glancing at Rosie: "Sylvia didn't say that you had gotten married."

"Sylvia didn't know."

"You didn't tell her?"

"She made it clear she didn't want to hear from me."

"I don't think that's true." This was not the first time he'd reflected on how similar they were in their stubbornness. He could imagine Sylvia's reaction when she'd learned of Rosie's news: the quick stab of betrayal, the ache of isolation. "Congratulations," he said.

Leila's gaze had fallen on Amelia. The little girl was awake now, her head resting on Elizabeth's shoulder, and her hands tucked beneath her cheek.

"And this," murmured Leila, gliding toward them, "must be Amelia. May I?"

Before anyone had a chance to answer, she lifted the girl into her arms. Amelia permitted herself to be transferred and sagged against Leila's chest. Elizabeth rolled her shoulders and stretched her back, shaking off her burden.

"Come on," Rosie said, her voice tighter than it had been. "Let's sit."

He and Elizabeth sank into a pair of navy-blue armchairs while Rosie and Leila arranged themselves with Amelia on the couch across from them. Behind them hung nine framed watercolor paintings of songbirds, arranged in a three-by-three square. Amelia tilted back her head and pointed up at them, and he heard Leila murmuring their names.

Then, a memory that hadn't surfaced in years: the trips to the library with Faye so that she could gather bird-watching books and recordings of their calls. The sound of trilling and whistling from behind the closed door of her room as she practiced mimicking the robin, the jay, the chickadee, the loon. The sight of her kneeling on a chair at the kitchen table, filling an empty soda bottle with sunflower seeds and then the shine of her face as she turned it toward him, asking if he would hold the ladder for her please so that she could hang it from the maple tree.

When he tuned back in to the conversation, Rosie was describing their visit to the professor's wife. "She knew that he'd gone up north," she was saying. "But she didn't know exactly where."

"We think she went all the way up to the border," Jack said. "To a place called—" He paused and looked toward Elizabeth.

"Grand Portage," she said.

"The township?" Rosie asked. "Or the reservation?"

"Isn't the one located inside the other?"

Rosie nodded. "The land belongs to the Chippewa Band," she said. "I've worked on some projects with staff at the community center up there. The reservation isn't huge, but it runs about eighteen miles along the shoreline. Do you have a specific destination in mind?"

"Elizabeth does," Jack said.

He'd packed a bag for him and Amelia, and then he'd driven them all to campus. He'd waited, the engine idling outside the dormitory, while she dashed up to her room to gather her things. When she'd returned to the car and shown him a child's map, he'd shaken his head. "I thought they'd confiscated that," he said. She'd scoffed and refolded it reverently, tenderly, as if it were made of gold or silk. "You really think we didn't have a backup copy, just in case?"

Rosie was staring at Elizabeth. "The last time Faye involved you in her schemes," she said, "you wound up in jail."

"Ro," Leila murmured. "I don't think that's—"

"Relevant? Of course it is."

Elizabeth had drawn her water bottle from her bag. At Rosie's words, she froze with it suspended before her. "That's not the whole story," she said.

"Isn't it?"

"No."

Rosie sighed and pressed her index finger to the space between her eyebrows. "I'm sorry," she said. "It's late, and I'm exhausted. We all are. I don't want to—there isn't any point in dredging up the past. I know that we all love her. But for too long, we've been burdened by her crime. Isn't it time to move forward? If Faye doesn't want to be found, then why are you all trying so hard to find her?"

Elizabeth's expression darkened. She parted her lips, and then pursed them again. Jack could feel her casting about the unfamiliar house for words.

"You don't understand," she finally said. "It wasn't Faye's fault. The whole thing was my idea."

The room filled with an unearthly silence. Jack strained to hear the hum of a refrigerator or the rush of traffic in the distance. Nothing.

The glance Elizabeth threw at him was apologetic, knowing, adult. "That's what I wanted to tell Mrs. Vogel on the phone," she said. "It's why I came to the house. You've spent all these years blaming Faye, but you should have been blaming me."

Her confession shook something loose inside him. He could hear his blood pulsing through his ears. Outside, a siren wailed. Voices rose and fell as a group of young people strolled down the sidewalk in front of the house. Leila brushed Amelia's hair away from her forehead, and Rosie leaned forward. Jack remembered how Anna used to creep into their house so silently that he often didn't know that she was there. To Sylvia and to him, she spoke in whispers. But then Faye would enter the room, and she would grow two or three inches taller. Her speech would grow bolder, her stories more elaborate. She'd come alive.

His head was throbbing. All the ways that Sylvia had tried to make Faye's best friend feel at home: The family movie nights. The birthday gifts. She ate pancakes with them, picked apples with them, rode roller coasters with them. They had unlatched their lives and ushered her in.

Rosie was the first to speak. "I don't understand."

"I was the one who introduced Faye to the Kingman," Elizabeth insisted with a flash of adolescent irritation. "I was the one who found him online. Faye was always telling me stories, you know? I wanted to give her one in return. But he was different from the other stories. The more we talked about him, the more real he became."

"Does Amelia have pajamas in one of those bags?" Leila interrupted, rising abruptly. "A stuffed animal? A toothbrush? I'm going to put her to bed in the other room."

Jack reached down and handed over the duffel bag. "Here. Thanks, Leila."

Elizabeth waited until Amelia had been swept out the door before she said, chastened: "I'm sorry."

"What did you mean when you said that the Kingman became real to you?" Rosie asked. "Real *how?*"

Elizabeth raised one shoulder and let it drop. "Like, we started to see him when we went down to the river. Always in the distance. And we started to feel what he was feeling: a kind of separateness. A—" She struggled to find the right word. "A longing, even if we didn't know what it was a longing for. And through him, we felt what it was like up there, with the mosses and the birds and the frozen waterfalls. Faye really wanted to see those. The waterfalls, stopped in time."

"Stop," muttered Jack. "Please."

Rosie's question cleaved the air between them. "Did Faye wield the knife?"

"Yes, but—"

"Then she was responsible. You both were. There's nothing more to say about it." She flicked her fingers through the air as if to dismiss the entire conversation. "Look. Faye could've said no. The fact that you were the first one to bring up the monster doesn't make her totally innocent, just like it doesn't make you totally guilty. The crime only happened because *both* of you believed it could."

Elizabeth gripped the armrests of her chair. "What do you mean?"

Rosie reached for a tray on the coffee table in front of her and poured a cup of tea from a pot Jack hadn't noticed. She leaned back on the sofa and wrapped her hands around the mug, warming them. From another room of the house, he heard the rush of water into a tub and the sound of Leila's laughter.

"There've been cases like yours before," Rosie said. "*Folie à deux*. That's French for 'the madness of two.' Or three, or four. It's the clinical term for when a delusion is passed or shared between minds." She set down the mug and gestured toward the windows. "If one person imagines a figure lurking out there on the lawn, he's probably crazy. But if two people imagine a figure lurking on that lawn—it's something else entirely. The more voices that lay claim to a fiction, the more likely it seems to be real."

Jack was struck, suddenly, by the strangeness of being in this unfamiliar house, this unfamiliar chair. Wasn't there a fiction, too, in his relationship with Rosie? An illusion, the bond that they agreed to believe in and act upon, the way that drivers agree not to cross the center line into oncoming traffic? There wasn't actually anything connecting them anymore—and perhaps there never had been. Love, happiness, purpose, Jack found himself thinking bitterly. Everything we think, we feel. At some level, maybe all of it is make-believe.

"What I'm saying is that you needed more than one mind to commit that crime." Rosie shrugged as if the facts were boring, as if the case was textbook. At the end of the hallway, footsteps ascended a stairwell. "Neither one of you could've done it alone."

Elizabeth reclined into the puddle of orange light that spilled from the lamp behind her, looking twenty pounds lighter. Although the windows were closed, a strong wind was whistling so keenly through Jack that he couldn't hear what Rosie said next even though he saw her face screwed tightly in concern. The longer he sat in that chair, the harder the ground thundered beneath him. He was light-headed, dizzy, as if something had swooped beneath him and lifted him up and was soaring away with him into the dark.

Sylvia

I dreamed of my daughter. Who else? I was swimming in sky-blue water. I was caught in a riptide. Was I on the beach where I'd grown up? I didn't think so, for when I swallowed a mouthful of water, I didn't taste salt; and when I cast a desperate glance toward shore, my gaze caught on a line of indifferent pine trees. There were no wild grasses; no bungalows. The rocky shore might have been dusted with snow. Or was that sunlight? I slapped my arms against the waves and chopped my feet through the water, but I couldn't make myself move. I gulped for air while ghostly fish drifted beneath me, and Faye watched coolly from the beach.

The first time I dreamed someone into existence was after my mother passed away. I dreamed her into my room, and suddenly she was there: her white blouse rumpled, her fingers heavy with rings, her glasses dangling from a braided cord around her neck. When I hugged her, I sank into her chest. My cheek was warm against her shoulder, my nostrils filled with rose perfume. The experience was so corporeal that when I woke to find her gone again, a fresh wave of grief ripped through me. It was an hour at least until my sobs abated. Jack tightened his arms around me and told me to breathe deeply. From downstairs, the sounds of Faye attempting to make breakfast for us: the bread popping out of the toaster, the lid of the peanut butter jar twisting open, the slice of a knife through ripe bananas on a plate.

I woke to the sound of an orchestra tuning. Beneath the discord of strings and wind came the high-pitched bark of a dog. I didn't know where I was, and as my eyes adjusted to the dark, it took me a minute to recognize the ominous mouth of the pipe stove, the whiskers of an upside-down broom in the corner, the jagged back of a rocking chair. I swung my feet to the floor with the intention of pouring a glass of water, but while I was rummaging in the black cabinet for a cup or a mug, I noticed that the stripes of sky between the trees were glowing.

He also said something about the northern lights, Emma had told us. *I lost the signal at Split Rock.*

I set the glass on the counter, dragged a blanket from an arm of the sofa, and encased myself in plaid and tassels. Then I slid into my shoes, opened the door, and stepped out onto the porch. I shuffled down the steps to the pine-needled path and began to make my way to the lakeshore. My limbs and thoughts were sluggish. It took all my concentration to set one foot in front of the other. As the pebbled beach drew closer to me, the peacock-colored light over the water vibrated more intensely, more brightly, until I finally cleared the trees.

When Faye was growing up, I used to think a lot about the future. I used to watch her at two, three, four years old and imagine what she'd be like at twelve. Fourteen. Sixteen. How would she move? What would her voice sound like? What kinds of things would catch her attention, and hold it? I see now that I was trying to project an image of Faye into the darkness like a film onto a blank screen. Most of the time, we stumble into the future as blindly as I stumbled through that thicket, straining to see what lies ahead. But once I had Faye, it felt like someone had handed me a light.

Maybe that's why I felt her presence on that viridian shoreline; maybe it's why I was suddenly so certain of her proximity. The sky over the horizon pulsed with emerald beams of light, and black clouds wisped swiftly, smoothly, overhead. I scanned the tree line for flashlights, the water for boats, and the gemstone rays ahead of me for familiar silhouettes and shadows. I strained to hear the sound of her breathing, her voice. I whirled in circles, my gaze spinning outward, my legs growing weaker, the sky sizzling with color and possibility. I can't tell you if minutes passed, or hours, or days—only that by the time I wobbled to a stop, the lights had dimmed and I was struggling to make sense of the winged figure that had landed on the stack of driftwood just in front of me.

No, not wings, I decided as I staggered a little closer. A cloak, a crown. I picked up my pace before he vanished. A wooden face, a whittled heart. *At last.*

But then, after another crunching step across the sand and stones: not a cloak, but a hooded black anorak. Not a crown, but a wild nest of hair. The figure wasn't faceless—merely expressionless, colorless, and raw; its eyes closed in a manner that was masklike, deathlike, practically serene. A chill crept through the blanket and began to worm its way toward my bones. The orchestra recommenced its tuning. Was I awake or dreaming?

"Professor Wolff," I breathed.

His eyes snapped open, but he didn't turn his head. He kept his gaze fixed on the aquamarine wash above the horizon, but I could tell that he was listening.

"I'm Faye's mother," I said. "I need to know—" But my thoughts splintered, falling away from one another like pearls on a broken string. They splashed to the sand and rolled underneath the driftwood, shimmering in the dark.

"Please," I said. "I know that she was with you. That you're the last person to have seen her. Where did you take her? Where is she now?"

At this, his cracked lips parted. The words, when they emerged, sounded like they'd been dragged across the forest floor. His tone was rich with silt and mystery.

"What are you afraid of, Mrs. Vogel?" The thread of his voice knotted around my wrists, my ankles. His words bound me to the shore. "Are you convinced that history repeats itself? Do you believe your daughter will always be what she has been?"

In the half-light oozing across the surface of the water, in the ruffled shadows of the pine boughs, his long limbs shifted and multiplied. When he finally turned his face toward mine, his eyes gleamed moon yellow and wild. Was I hallucinating?

Then the thud of the judge's gavel reverberated between my ears. I saw Faye's face, murky behind Plexiglas. "I'm her *mother*," I said.

The beach was filling up with cold blue light. His gaze scoured my face. "I know," he said. His tone turned probing. "But what does that mean?"

On a distant bridge, traffic ebbed and flowed like ocean waves. Had Faye been on this beach with him? Where was she right now? I peered over my shoulder toward the cabin and saw a light in the window that I didn't remember turning on. At the edge of the woods, something glinted on the path.

"Do you have any idea what it feels like to create something?" the professor queried. His tone was soft as a snow shower, and eerily serene.

I turned back. "Yes," I croaked.

His laughter rattled against the trees, the stars. His voice gained strength. "I'm not talking about a child. Most people make children without even trying." The words were silken, hypnotic. Was I talking to myself? "No," he continued, after the slightest of pauses. "I'm talking about creating something that *lasts*."

I recalled the ancient writers of my English classes: the poets who'd believed that their writing would make them immortal. But Leonard Wolff read my mind.

"No, not books, either," he said. "Anybody can throw a handful of words at the Internet and call himself a writer. What I'm talking about—it runs deeper, looms larger, than any of that. I'm talking about creating something *real*."

Faye's warm palm slipping into mine at a crosswalk; her hair billowing behind her as she darted toward the creek. Her downy cheeks, her fevered skin. I looked up as if to catch a glimpse of her dazzling phantom skating over the stained-glass surface of the lake.

Somehow I managed to find my voice again. "That's what a child is."

He laughed again, more melodically this time. "Come now," he said. "You should know better than anyone that a child is nothing but a squirming bundle of your own expectations, your own fears and dreams. No one tells you that about parenthood, do they? When you hold your child for the first time in the delivery room, those kindly nurses stare into your face because they expect to see some kind of revelation there. But they don't tell you about the terrifying weight of the infant you cradle against your chest. No one warns you about how your children will stare at you, how they'll strain to hear your voice, dissect your every move. How they'll drink you in, suck you dry. Tabula rasa."

I shook my head. "No. That's not how—"

"And yet you also fear that you will lose them. Fail them. That's why monsters exist, do they not? To rationalize the accidents and illnesses that snatch children from their parents? Monsters carry the blame for tragedies beyond our control. They provide a way to explain the inexplicable; they're the manifestation of our own fears, our desires. They are the shapes we have given to grief and terror in order to contain them, wrestle with them, and banish them away." The professor peered at me, his skin peridot and shimmering. "You have spent years blaming yourself for what happened to your family. Why not lift that burden from your shoulders, Mrs. Vogel? Why not lay it at the feet of the one who deserves it?" When he tilted creakily toward me, I took two unconscious steps back. "Why don't you allow yourself to blame the Kingman instead?"

"To blame—"

"*The Kingman*," he repeated. He raised an arm and the jacket turned back into a cloak. "You can do it right now," he insisted. "He's standing right here."

I blinked, and looked, and looked again. What is the difference between memory and hallucination? Between vision and dream, truth and fiction? Who is to say that, as I gazed past the jumble of driftwood before me, the sticks and logs like arms and legs, I did not catch a glimpse of my daughter gleaming in the distance?

"Hey!" I shouted. To her, to him, to the lake, to the lights. "Stop!"

I was bone-tired; the world was swimming. But I took off after her anyway, wheeling along the water's edge. The stars trembled overhead and the lights buried themselves beneath the horizon. As the darkness engulfed me, did I see flickers of gold in my peripheral vision? Did I hear, as I turned, footsteps cracking over sea glass? The water whispering like voices? Did I feel before me the aching, looming presence of an entire world unseen? Yes. Yes, *yes*. After all, I am my daughter's mother. I know the kind of potion that runs through her veins. I've seen the way her blood glitters and glows when it catches the light.

I lurched, pendulous and dazed, through the boulders. I thrashed up a slick bank. There was a yank on my ankle and a stab of fear in my gut. I kicked my leg wildly, trying to free my foot of whatever had ensnared it. Then the tumble of limbs into a sodden heap. I lost my balance and, half a second later, my consciousness.

Leila's voice in my ears, Jack's hand on my waist. *Are you happy that you had your daughter?*

Then: a surge of love and of anger. What kind of question is *that*?

A curtain tumbled down. I dreamed that my daughter lifted me from the lake. Her narrow face mirrored mine, and her cold fingers pushed the dripping hair from my forehead. Her touch: confident, but not gentle. She carried me like a child, as I had carried my mother to and from her hospice bed in her final days.

In my dream, Faye grinned as she bore my body aloft through a twinkling city, her impossibly long arms wrapped two, three times around me. Trees waved their branches as if we were friends, and trunks leaned backward to make space for us. The dead leaves conspired, and I strained to understand them.

"Faye," I murmured. "What are they saying?"

Then darkness fell like a magician's cloak, and I had to fight to keep my eyes open. I was convinced that I was closer now than I'd ever been. I was certain that if I peered fiercely enough, wanted it badly enough, I would see a glimmer of what Faye had claimed to see: the magic, the possibility, the vast reaches of the imagination; the edges of the world splitting open to reveal something more.

Faye

The motel was constructed in the shape of a C, and Faye and Leonard had taken rooms on opposite sides of the parking lot. This meant that when she looked through the oval window at the top of her door, she could see across the pavement to his door, and to one of his windows, which was—as she had not expected it to be—dark, even though the sun had set and the sky was dusky and the world inside and outside the rooms was cool and blue. He had not said that he'd be going somewhere. And so she left her room and crossed the lot and passed the parking spot where his car should have been but wasn't. And she tried his door, which was—she had not expected this, either—unlocked. And so she entered it, and crossed the stiff carpeting toward the rolling suitcase he'd left beside the desk because she knew that's where he carried all his papers. And she heaved the suitcase onto the bed and unzipped it and opened it.

Here were the typewritten pages Faye had expected to find: the passages about the missing Egyptian boys, and the pilot's child, and the kids in Hamelin who followed the Pied Piper to the Children's Crusade or something like it. And here were the handwritten pages she'd seen him scrawling because he'd insisted she sit beside him while he drafted them over the past few days. These she was more interested in: the one about the Duluth mansion, and the one about the haunted quilt shop in Castle Danger, and the northern lights above Knife River, and even a few sentences about this very motel, squatting on the highway's edge directly across from the water. As soon as they'd arrived, he'd led her over the road to the black-rock beach and the mangled remains of a cottage that had once graced the shoreline there. Time had turned it into a heap of splintered boards with a rotting roof and broken windows gaping like mouths. He circled it, round and round and round, as if it were a wounded animal and he was a whole pack of wolves. She wanted to tell him to stop, to leave it alone. He asked her if she felt the monster had been there, and she didn't say, *Of course I do*, even though she knew by now that this was the most efficient way to get him back to his desk, back to his work, so that even if she had to sit with him while he wrote, she could read or daydream. Instead she asked, a little plaintively, if they could get something to eat; and when he replied that she sounded like a child, something rent inside her.

"I never was a child," she said. "My childhood was stolen from me. That's why I'm here."

He scrutinized her face as if he'd never seen it before. "What do you mean?"

"I have to make sure it never happens again." She flung her hand toward the water rolling in from the horizon, toward the cabin crumbling on the shore. "Why would I have come all this way, if not to destroy the Kingman?"

"You think he needs to be destroyed?"

"I intend to leave this world with fewer monsters than I found in it." She tilted her head and took two steps backward, toward the road. "Don't you?"

If he had answered her, if he had not stared at her as though he was recalculating, perhaps she would not be standing over his rumpled bedcover in the gloom, rummaging through the pages of his manuscript, running out of time, looking for something she was too afraid to name.

Sylvia

When someone rapped at the cabin door, I was lying in bed again, feeling just as tired as I had the night before. I extricated myself from the sheets and opened the door to find the woman from the rental office standing against a rectangle of daylight. My hand shot up to my face to shield my eyes.

"Where's my daughter?" I asked.

"Your daughter?" The woman's face pinched shut. "I told you yesterday—you're the only one here."

My head was swimming again. The fresh water, the pines. The snow-dusted sand, colors swirled like milk and caramel. My throat was scraped raw, as if I'd been shouting. "But my daughter," I repeated. "She's the one who brought me back. Where did she go?"

The woman frowned. "I came to tell you that there's coffee and pastries in my office and you're welcome to some. Also, someone called looking for you. Not a daughter," she added quickly. "It was a man's voice. I don't remember the name. But I wrote it down, so I can tell you, if you want to walk over there with me."

"I need a minute," I said. I closed the door and returned to bed. I was still there, sifting through the snippets of my memory to determine what I had seen and what I had dreamed, when it opened again. Perhaps that was why, when Jack materialized, I didn't believe that he was really there. Suddenly he was filling up the doorway, silent as a shadow, his black eyes burning holes into my skin. His face drooped; his hair was matted around his ears. He crossed the room in four quick strides and was leaning over the bed before I could prop myself up on the pillow.

"Hey," he hummed, warm and low. At the sound of his voice, the smoky scent of his aftershave, my heart lit up. "Are you all right?"

"Where's Amelia?" I managed.

"Don't worry. She's with your sister and her wife."

He dragged a chair from the kitchenette to the side of the bed and eased himself into it. My body listed like a sinking ship, straining to close the distance between us, and I fought the urge to lay my hand on his knee. *He left you*, I reminded myself, as I'd been reminding myself over and over again for years. Every time I'd lifted the receiver because I'd longed to hear his voice, every time I'd woken in the night craving the crush of his body on mine, I'd repeated the same words. *He left you. And you wanted him gone.*

So why couldn't I bridge the divide between my head and my heart? Why, when Jack was sitting so close to me that I could hear him breathing and see the light etching lines in his skin, couldn't I turn away from him? Why, instead, did I imagine him sliding into this cramped metal bed beside me, touching my cheeks and my breasts, running weathered hands over my belly, my thighs? Why couldn't I stop thinking about his tongue in my mouth? Would I honestly spend the rest of my life wishing he would kiss me?

He was watching me with an expression as focused and fierce as Faye's. He'd always had a gift for reading my mind. He probably knew that I was remembering the sticky leather of his office chair and the look on his face when he'd first stepped through that door and found me there. *Recognition*, he'd told me much later, his tongue at my ear, his lips in my hair, his white coat crumpled on the floor of my bedroom. *That's what it was. I'd never seen you before, but I knew you.*

"Do you ever wonder where we'd be right now if we'd never met that day?" I whispered. "Do you think that we would have been happier?"

The intensity of Jack's expression didn't change. Outside, the waves rushed toward the rocks. "It wouldn't have changed anything, Syl," he murmured. "We would've met some other way. I would've come into your shop, looking for a book. I would've bought you a drink if I'd seen you at the other end of a bar. We would've accidentally knocked our carts together in the produce aisle, or encountered one another in a parking lot. You see what I'm saying?"

All those other versions of ourselves, wandering through other realities, crisscrossing ours. Did I believe it? The truth was that my obsession with the paths our lives could have taken, the decisions we might not have made, the outcomes we could have changed—it was meaningless. All that mattered was the fact that Jack and I were here now, boxed up in this strange pine cabin together, struggling to find our way out.

"Some things," Jack said, so quietly that I had to lean closer to hear him, "are meant to be."

Fated. From the Latin *fatum:* that which has been spoken. By whom, by what?

He extended his arm and rested his fingers on my wrist. The jolt of electricity left me frazzled, my face hot and my eyes full of sparks. By the time the smoke cleared and my words returned to me, we weren't alone in the room anymore.

Jack cleared his throat. His hand slid away from the bed as Faye's best friend stepped forward.

"You're awake," Elizabeth said. "The owner said you might be—"

"She seemed worried about you," Jack said.

Elizabeth perched on the edge of the sofa. The blanket beside her was arranged as neatly as it had been, except for the fragments of dead leaves in the folds. Or had those been there before?

"Were you—" Elizabeth began. She cut herself off, as if thinking better of her question, and glanced at Jack.

The expression that he turned toward me was quizzical and

mild. "Sylvia," he asked, "did you happen to go outside last night? Down to the water?"

The windows glared; the curtains twirled. The grains of sand dusting the floor between the door and the bed could have come from their shoes instead of mine. A puff of air gusted through the heating vents, and together we shivered.

"I don't know," I said. My hands were crosshatched with a hundred tiny cuts. "It's possible."

I went to see Brittany a few days after the crime. Almost nobody knows that. The lawyers had instructed Jack and me not to communicate with either Anna's or Brittany's family. But I'd seen interviews with the nurses on the news, and I'd woken chilled from nightmares in which Faye was the girl on the ground, battling her captors in the bone-dry crunch of last year's leaves. I'd even watched a televised interview with Brittany's father, when he'd appeared on the local morning show before a city of viewers still reeling from the idea of the crime. His tone had been steely, his gaze puffy but cool.

I'd been able to scuttle through the hospital unnoticed, unchecked, but when I reached Brittany's door, her father was standing outside it, his head bent toward the woman beside him. At the sight of me, the color drained from his face. His friend sucked her breath between her teeth. It was she who spoke first.

"What the fuck do you want?" the friend demanded, moving forward to shield Brittany's father from me. "Don't you have any fucking sense of decency? Of *shame*?"

I tried to focus on Brittany's father. "I'm sorry," I said, my voice breaking. I cleared my throat and tried again. "I know that I can't change anything. But I wanted you to know how sorry I am."

"You're damn right that doesn't change anything," snapped the friend. She snatched the father's arm and tugged him a few steps away from me. "Get the fuck out of here."

"I was hoping to see—" I couldn't bring myself to say Brittany's name. "I wanted to tell her—"

"You're not going anywhere *near* her," the friend spat.

"Amy," Brittany's father murmured. "It's all right."

"But—"

"It's all right."

The father's head was buzzed, his face ravaged. He stepped away from the door so that I could peer in the tiny window. A long table on the far side of the room was crammed full of vases, the colorful heads of carnations and daisies quivering beneath an air duct. Hundreds of get-well cards were taped to the walls around the bed. Brittany was buried in a cloud of white blankets, her eyes closed, her lips parted.

"She's sedated," her father said. "She's been having trouble sleeping."

I remained silent, each of his words a puncture wound. I could feel his eyes on me, probing my face for answers that I didn't possess. I wondered what he saw there; wondered at all the ways that he, like Jack, found me wanting.

"They say that she'll pull through," he said. "Thank God. She'll be able to finish high school. Go on to college."

The reporters had written about Brittany's plans to become an astronomer. At various times, Faye had wanted to be a zookeeper, a librarian, or a children's book writer—but none of the journalists seemed interested in that. "I know," I said. "I'm sorry."

The man peered at me strangely, as if I'd responded in a foreign language. "You don't need to be sorry about Brittany. She'll be fine," he said. "If you're sorry for anyone, let it be for your daughter. There won't be any high school for her. No college. No career."

For a long moment Brittany's father continued to study me. "The truth is," he said, his tone deepening, "that *I'm* the one who should be comforting *you*."

I don't remember what I replied, if anything. I know that I

skulked away. But when I recall that moment now, I find myself yearning to know if he ever forgave us. How long does it take for a person to be free of her crime?

Elizabeth offered to fetch coffee and pastries from the rental office. While she was gone, I quickly dressed and pushed a comb through my hair. Jack lit a fire in the pipe stove, so that by the time Elizabeth returned and the three of us had arranged ourselves among the assortment of mismatched furniture, the cabin was mellowing with woodsmoke and heat. We cupped our mugs between our hands and waited to see who would speak first.

It was Jack, finally, who cleared his throat. "Elizabeth has a map," he said.

I blinked. "I thought they confiscated that."

"She's got another one. She says she knows— Well." He turned to her. "Maybe you should explain it."

Elizabeth kept her gaze on her lap. "I told Mr. Vogel that I think I know where Faye might be. I wanted to come up here with him to help you find her."

"Why didn't you tell me before? When I came to see you?"

"Because I didn't know about the new crimes until later, after I called you," she said. "Until then, I didn't know that the Kingman was back."

Jack sat up straighter. "You don't mean 'back.' Something that wasn't real in the first place can't actually come *back*."

The headlines tacked up in the closet. The copycat crimes. Elizabeth slowly raised her head until her eyes met mine. Was she aware of the carved face I sometimes saw in the mirror behind me, or the pine boughs that seized me in dreams?

The fire crackled. "If Faye was trying to reach the Kingman, she would have been aiming for Isle Philippeaux," Elizabeth said.

"I've said it a thousand times," Jack muttered. His tone was exhausted. "The island isn't real."

For a few minutes I stared hard into the flames, struggling to keep the old resentments from rising in me, trying to come up with a way to make him understand.

"Jack," I said suddenly. I leaned toward him, feeling my face warming. "Remember your grandmother?"

Evelyn had been ancient for years already when I'd met Jack. I'd grown to know her mostly through stories and photographs, since, at ninety-six years old, she no longer spoke logically or coherently. When Jack and I visited her nursing home, she told us that rabbits hopped through her room at night and that she'd seen penguins belly flopping in the pond beyond the parking lot. She believed that strange teenagers used her bathtub while she was sleeping and that she was always tired because the mechanic on the floor beneath her made such a racket every morning that it woke her well before dawn.

"But there isn't a mechanic beneath her," I'd overheard Jack lamenting to his father once.

"You can tell her that until you're blue in the face," his father had replied. "But you'll never be able to make her believe you. The best thing to do is to apologize for the noise and ask her if she'd like to take a nap."

"Enter into the delusion?" Jack had asked.

"Enter into the delusion," his father had confirmed.

But when I reminded him of this, Jack only shook his head harder. "That's totally different," he said. "It's one thing to pacify a nonagenarian by nodding when she says that her bedroom smells like motor oil. It's nowhere near as dangerous as telling a person that a mythical monster is real. Come on, Sylvia. You know this."

"I do," I said. "But we're not telling anyone that the Kingman is real. We're just saying—if someone *did* believe that he was real, where would she go? What would she do?"

"To Isle Philippeaux," repeated Elizabeth with surprising serenity. She took a bite of her Danish and chewed.

"But why would she want to get to him, anyway? Even if she knows about the new crimes—even if she thinks he's on the move again, in the world again. If you were her, after everything that's happened, wouldn't you try to keep your distance?"

Elizabeth swallowed. "Because of Amelia," she said. "Because the Kingman knows how to make children disappear. Because she's terrified of losing her daughter."

I remembered waking in the night to find Amelia at the window. Her face wan, her sweaty hair plastered to her forehead. I remembered wondering what she'd seen. Was it possible that Faye had wondered, too?

But Jack was shaking his head again. "How much could Faye have worried about her daughter when she just *left* her without a second thought?"

Elizabeth had been about to take another bite of her pastry, but at Jack's question, she returned the Danish to her plate, wiped her fingers on her jeans, and looked worried. "Well," she said. "I think—I think she may have had second thoughts."

Something snapped in the fireplace. Perhaps a centipede in one of the logs, blackened and popped. "What makes you say that?" I asked.

Elizabeth spun her gaze toward the window, the walls, the fireplace, the door. She looked everywhere but at us. "She called Amelia," she said. "About twice a week. She didn't say anything to me, just asked me to hand over the phone. And Amelia didn't say anything, either. She just pressed the phone to her face, listening and sometimes nodding."

"And you didn't ask Faye—"

"I tried, but she'd only say she didn't want me to get involved this time. When she still wasn't back, at the end of the summer, I told her I couldn't take Amelia back to the dorms with me and asked her what I should do." Finally Elizabeth glanced at me. "That's when she said that we'd have to figure out a way to get her to you."

The heat of the cabin was suddenly smothering. "You mean—the car? The grocery store?"

"All her idea." Elizabeth shrugged. "I'm sorry I didn't tell you before, but..."

She didn't need to finish her sentence. After tracking Faye across state lines, after talking with Emma, with Steph, with Nhia and Chue—somehow, for the first time in years, I was beginning to know my daughter. I could imagine her breath in Elizabeth's ear, her cold hand on her forearm, the way she would have lingered on the word *secret*.

Jack rose to check on the pipe stove. When he jabbed at the logs with an iron poker, sparks poured out of them. "So we're going north?" he asked. "To an island that doesn't exist?"

Elizabeth frowned, squinting into the distance as if into the past. "We figured that the reason people can't locate it anymore is because it doesn't stay in the same place," she said. "You know—like rivers, or continents. Over time, the island moves."

"Then how did you plan to find it?" I asked.

"We were going to climb up as high as we could and look for it," she replied. She leaned over, unzipped her backpack, and withdrew a crumpled piece of notebook paper. When she laid it flat on the end table beside her, I saw a green peak lifting out of a colored-pencil woods. Elizabeth tapped the top of it, her finger dropping into the curlicues of indigo clouds. "Mount Josephine," she said. "It's only two hours north."

As Elizabeth surveyed her childhood map, as Jack paced and growled, I tried to hold the image in my mind: a mossy island, heavy with boulders and bristling with pines, drifting in and out of the pewter bays along the coastline, winking within and behind tendrils of fog. It would threaten ships and beckon children who were searching for something fantastical and safe; something that only they could find.

Faye didn't confront Leonard until they'd reached Grand Portage. First she had to wrap her mind around what she'd seen in that suitcase of papers. Then she had to figure out what exactly she should say to him. But when they rounded a curve in the road and passed a sign for the reservation and caught their first glimpse of Mount Josephine—he raised his hand from the wheel and pointed it out—the words spilled from her without warning.

"I know what you did."

She should have said something else; something more specific. He glanced over at her with amusement.

"Excuse me?"

She tried again. It was harder than she thought to say what she needed to. Through the windshield, the road bucked forward and the clouds descended. "I found the picture of the Kingman. The first one that ever appeared online."

She remembered the first time she and Anna had encountered it: the black-and-white shot of the vintage carousel illuminated at dusk. In the foreground were five children riding five horses. The children had serious expressions and old-fashioned haircuts. The horses' eyes looked like they were rolling back, and their teeth were bared. Perhaps they were supposed to be whinnying for joy; instead, they appeared terrified. On the center of the carousel, behind the horses, were rows of mirrors. You had to look very closely, past the children, to see the black-cloaked, faceless figure standing in the mirror right behind them.

Leonard tensed. She saw his knuckles go whiter on the wheel. But the car kept moving. "So?" he asked, his voice studiedly casual. "It's part of my research."

She shook her head. "The photo I found didn't have the Kingman in it yet. It was just the kids on the carousel. But paper-clipped to it was a sketch of the monster as he looked in the mirror. You—" She was still struggling to make sense of it, and so she couldn't tell if the words were true until she uttered them. "It was never a picture of the Kingman. You pasted him into it. Then you posted it on the Internet and claimed that someone had discovered it."

She'd found other things, too: the parts of his manuscript that were lifted directly from his conversations with her; clippings of news reports or photocopied passages from textbooks that he had borrowed and transformed and inserted his monster into. Ever since she'd read them, those paragraphs had been looping ceaselessly through her mind.

"You aren't *studying* him," she declared. Her voice was gaining strength. "You're *inventing* him. You made the whole thing up."

What she couldn't articulate was the realization that had sliced through her rib cage as she riffled through the papers on that motel room floor: that if the Kingman had never been real, then the only monster in those woods had been her. Now, sitting stiffly in the passenger seat with her gaze fastened on the windshield, she was knotting up everything inside herself to keep her tears from falling.

She had expected him to deny it. When he tilted his head and grinned at her, his expression roguish, his teeth sharp, something slashed through her soul and deserted her.

"You're a smart kid," he said.

Then his expression changed again. A cloud slid away from his brow, and his features were suddenly dazzling, radiant.

Yet the journey out of Egypt was plagued by troubles that felt nearly biblical: camels were struck dead without warning, food and water supplies vanished overnight, and iridescent desert beetles ate entire tents, robes, and blankets. Then, during the Mediterranean passage, seven different men threw themselves overboard. Witnesses said that right before they jumped, they went mad. Each of them claimed to see a figure, glittering as black as obsidian . . .

"You're a fraud," she said. She was making him angry now, but she didn't care. "There is no history, no ancient origins, no mythology. There's only you. Writing fiction."

So he played his pipe and led the rats away to the river, where they all drowned. When the townspeople refused to pay him, he played his pipe and led the children away to a mountain, which swallowed them up forever . . .

If a person commits a crime that is founded on a fiction, can that crime be counted as a kind of fiction, too?

"Turn the car around," she said. "We have to go back."

He pressed on the gas, and the car leapt forward. "But we're so close now."

"Close to *what*? Didn't you hear what I said? I know what you've done; I know it's all make-believe. And I'm going to tell everyone."

"That would destroy my career," he murmured. The car purred and slowed as he swung the wheel and guided it gently toward a gas station. "How about we finish our journey before you ruin me? That feels only fair."

"Our journey is finished already, there's nothing more to—"

"Faye." He tsk-tsked at her. "After everything I've taught you, everything you've been through—are you telling me that you still don't see how stories work?"

*In the heavy gray light before dawn, Lindbergh would climb into
his plane and fly low over his property. His engine would roar as
he looped around and around New Jersey in ever-widening circles.
He was pursuing shadows, said his friends . . .*

"You must have known you couldn't keep it up forever," Faye
said. "You saw what had happened to us. You knew the kind of
devastation it caused. So why would you do it?"

He shook his head so slowly that it took her a second to realize that he was moving it at all. "That's easy," he said. "I wanted to
understand why people believe in things. To accomplish that, I had
to come up with something that they could believe in."

*Or was the source of the disappearance something more mysteri-
ous, nefarious? Searches for the lost colonists have yielded only two
significant clues: first, the word PHILIPPEAUX carved into a fence
post near the main entrance of town, and, second, a collection of
twenty-three large gray stones, each sporting the same crude etching
of a faceless man with a crown of knives . . .*

"You're convinced that I don't understand what you've been
through," Leonard continued. "You think that I used you. And
that might be true. However"—he eased the car to a stop at the
pump—"I know how you felt when you figured it out. I can imagine the devastation, the betrayal, as you asked yourself the question
that I've asked myself a thousand times or more: *What if this is all
there is?*"

*"My brother wouldn't desert me before we had discovered the object
of our quest, before we had found and named the monstrous shadow
of our childhood, the mirthless, flickering figure who haunted our
nightmares and our daydreams for decades. Don't you see, Ludwig?
We had gone in search of stories when we were actually in search
of him . . ."*

———————

While he was filling the gas tank, she turned on her phone to find it had no service. So she told him that she needed to use the restroom, and she hurried inside, past the giant refrigerators and the aisles of chips and popcorn, to search for a landline. When she couldn't find a pay phone, she traced her steps back toward the door, to the front counter, and asked the cashier if she could make a call from the phone hanging on the wall behind him.

"It's kind of an emergency," she said.

Through the windows, she could see Leonard cleaning off the windshield, replacing the squeegee in its soapy bucket, and blowing on his hands to warm them. It was growing colder.

It felt strange to dial her own number, her home number, which she had not called in years. But it was stranger still to listen to the endless ringing and imagine the bell knelling through the kitchen where she'd eaten all her meals, the living room where she'd read all of her stories, the bedroom that she'd tidied before leaving on that final morning. Was her desk the same? Were her books still there? And why wasn't anyone answering?

She let the phone ring for as long as she could before Leonard turned his head and caught her eyes through the glass. How could it be that she was more frightened now than she'd ever been before? She was praying for someone to pick up, anyone to pick up, so that she could tell them that she was sorry she'd been so mistaken, that it turns out the world is not magical or mysterious, that fictions are false and stories are deceiving. Put Amelia on the phone, she planned to say to them, I need to tell her not to worry, not to be afraid, not to bother about the nightmares anymore, because you know what, my little sparrow, you know what? There's no such thing as monsters, after all.

Elizabeth the Good

The hardest part of the journey was finding the trailhead. The drive itself was easy: north along a highway that hugged the lakeshore. A wall of trees in front of them and a wall of trees behind. Elizabeth tried to make herself as small as possible in the back seat while answering the few questions the Vogels asked about her classes, her plans, with the same clipped politeness in which they were posed. She knew that they didn't really want to talk to her. They only wanted to do what she was doing: look out the window at the lakeshore as if they could determine, by the shapes of the trees or the color of the rocks, whether or not Faye had been there. The only time Faye's dad slowed the car was when they passed a charred and splintered cabin smashed right up against the water's edge. "Look at that," he said, and she did, and she imagined Faye circling it, filling it with fantasies and dreams.

The sky swelled above the occasional motel and quilt shop and liquor store. When they finally reached the center of Grand Portage, they passed the trailhead three times before locating it. The crouching clouds didn't help, and a glimmering mist snaked between the tree trunks. If there had ever been trail signs, those had long since been removed. It was Elizabeth who finally spotted it, checking her map against the patch of red-brown grass that they decided to consider a parking lot. It was only when they turned onto the grass, bumping over a low ditch, that they saw the rust-colored car that had been concealed from the road by the pines. Faye's dad said what all three of them were thinking.

"Do you think that's them?"

Faye's mom looked hopeful, and then doubtful. "What are the chances that we happened to arrive here at the exact same time that they did?" she asked.

It wasn't likely, of course; Elizabeth knew that. But to be honest, once she'd caught her first glimpse of Lake Superior earlier that morning, something inside her had clicked into place. As the triangle treetops ticked past her window and the bridges arched elegantly above the car, she'd found herself feeling for the first time in years that an extraordinary thing might be possible. She felt—though she would never say this aloud, given the situation—that she was finally in the right place at the right time. It was she who had led Faye's dad to the cabins in which they'd found Faye's mom, and it was she who had guided them here, too, wasn't it? To this trail through the woods? The air was laden with something she didn't recognize, and she couldn't decide whether the thing she sensed was snow or promise.

She strode away from the car, pointing her face toward the ridge and raising her nose like a bloodhound. The trail was not particularly visible or definable, but something pulled her to the right.

"I think it's this way," she called behind her, and before Faye's parents could catch up to her, she was bounding away from them, crunching across dead leaves and pine needles through a tunnel of silent trees that waited for her like sentinels. *Was she here?* Elizabeth wanted to ask them. *Did she come this way?* She didn't say the words aloud, but when the wind picked up, the trees were nodding.

Fumbling through the woods, she remembered the year before the crime, when she and Faye spent every sleepover whispering about the Kingman until the shadows grew thin and spindly across her ceiling. Faye was in her own bed, and Elizabeth burrowed in the pullout trundle below her. Their voices radiated toward each other, iridescent in the darkness. Although Faye had been the better storyteller, she wanted to hear tales of the Kingman from Elizabeth. So, ever eager to oblige, Elizabeth described a castle concealed in the forest. A spectral island drifting across a vast, textured lake. A cloak and a cape, a crown of jewels, a blank mask where a face should have been. The power to read minds, talk to animals, teleport into homes and lives. In the bed above her, she felt Faye's thrilled shiver. When Faye repeated the stories back to her, she shivered, too.

"Do you think," Faye whispered once, "that he's lonely?"

Deeper into the forest, Elizabeth charged past the rusty carcass of a car and the stone foundation of a crumbling cabin. As she emerged from the tunnel of trees into a tiny clearing, pulling up short to catch her breath and to search for signs of the trail from that point forward, she thought about the silence that ballooned between Faye's parents in the car, and the way Faye's dad had moved through the kitchen as if it was unfamiliar to him, and all the nights that she herself had spent in her dorm room with the desk light illuminating her hands and her pens while strangers' laughter bubbled up from the quad. When she was younger, she used to believe that it was only she who was lonely; everybody else had a person, a place. But now she was beginning to suspect that it was not just her, that adulthood might be just as lonely as childhood, for everybody, and that maybe the monster *was* simply looking for some companionship. Maybe Faye had it right.

Finally she located the sign for the summit, which was staked into the shadows at the base of the trail. She took a couple of deep breaths before crashing through the brown and gold foliage, careening up the rocky hill. She had to scramble over boulders and rotting logs that had fallen across the path. A couple of times she stumbled on a root and caught herself against a gnarled trunk. The higher she climbed, the bigger the rocks became, and the more frequently she glimpsed the lake within the white stripes of birches or framed between the needled teeth of conifers. But she didn't stop just yet, even though the missing island could have been beckoning right there in the distant bay below her if only she knew where to look. She kept going, kept pushing herself higher up the narrowing path and into the thick of the woods, drawn forward by a force that she didn't recognize until suddenly she did, barreling around the final twist of the trail and skidding onto bald rock face that was wrapped in clouds as sheer as tissue paper. There, just a brief jog away from her, standing next to someone at the base of a skeletal metal watchtower, was Faye.

Below Elizabeth stretched an undulating sea of yellow leaves and evergreens. The sky and the lake blurred together and the cold stung her cheeks and made her eyes water, and she had to bend over and place her hands on her knees to catch her breath before she could pull in enough air to call Faye's name. The wind whipped her voice away before it could reach the two figures that were beginning to spider their way up the side of the tower toward a jagged wooden platform at the top.

She remembered, now that she was looking at it, reading about towers like these sprinkled across the North Woods. They'd been originally intended to spot forest fires, but Faye had said that they'd work just as well for finding missing islands. When Elizabeth had admitted that she didn't like heights, Faye had tapped her on the knee with a colored pencil and told her that she'd simply have to be brave.

Elizabeth crossed the flat top of the peak slowly, leaning into the wind, listening to the keening of the latticed steel beams as she approached. The rungs of the ladder that ran up the side were cold to the touch, and the skin of her fingers adhered to them, so that she had to pull her hand back gingerly each time she needed to reach for the next hold. She began to work her way higher, her body retracting and expanding like the centipedes she and Faye used to observe inching across cracked sidewalks. The wind roared and the tower sang and the steps vibrated underfoot, and it was hard not to believe that she would die right there, that her fate had finally come for her, that her day of penance had arrived. *Elizabeth the Good.* She wondered, as she ascended, who would care that she was gone? Clara would be annoyed by the hassle of finding a new roommate. Her aunt and uncle would come to cart away her things. A few former teachers might attend a memorial service.

The only person who would truly feel her absence, she knew, was the person whose startled face she glimpsed as she pushed herself up and over the top of the ladder and went spilling across the platform in a puddle of limbs.

"Lizzy!" Faye cried, her tone wild and sharp with relief. "What are you—why are you—how did you even find me?"

Lizzy. Although this was not a name anyone had ever called Elizabeth before, the sound of it warmed her. She slipped inside the syllables as if into her proper skin and raised herself up and brushed the dirt from her knees. "Are you all right?" she asked.

A pale stranger was hovering behind Faye, his coat cracking in the wind, his gaze pinning Elizabeth in place. She wanted to move across the platform to Faye, but now that she was so far above the ground, she couldn't do anything but grip the railing behind her. If she tried to take a step, she feared, her stomach would heave and her liquid knees would give way.

The stranger rested his fingertips on Faye's shoulder, but Faye seemed determined to ignore him. "Where's Amelia?" she asked.

"With your aunt." The treetops spiked like spearheads. Another blast of cold air hit her face, and she had to close her eyes for a second to shield them. "Everybody's worried."

"Everybody?"

"Yeah. Your parents, obviously, and your aunt—"

"My *parents?*"

"They'll be down there"—with a brief, courageous wave toward the base of the tower before clinging to the railing again—"any minute. They were just a few steps behind me."

Faye's face blazed with unexpected light. Her whole body seemed to gather, then to rise. She strode briskly to the edge of the platform and peered down.

The stranger's arm fell to his side. He hadn't removed his gaze from Elizabeth. "You must be Faye's friend," he said. The wind yanked at his coat, and he rested his hand on the beam behind Faye to steady himself. "The one who was with her when—"

Faye unclasped her gaze from the ground and whirled back to face him. "Stop it, Leonard," she said. And then, to Elizabeth: "Lizzy, he made it all up. There never was a Kingman. Leonard doctored the photographs and wrote the stories and put them online."

Elizabeth stared at Faye, watching the way her black hair whipped and twirled, tracing the features of the girl she'd known beneath the grown-up bones in this adult's face. Her words emerged in visible puffs, and she recalled Faye's desire to see her breath turn into snow.

"What?" Elizabeth said.

"It was all a lie," Faye said, her eyes too large for her head, her expression one that Elizabeth had never seen before. "Everything we talked about, everything we did—it was a *lie.*"

Elizabeth didn't know what to say; she only wanted Faye to stop looking that way. She thought about how far Faye had traveled to track down the Kingman. She imagined how shaken Faye must have been, how hollowed out, when she pulled back the curtain and found only this puny man and his shadow puppets behind it. She could feel the blow to Faye's heart, could feel the blow to her own, the draining of that gorgeous, savage, matchless imagination, and she wished that she'd been there, wished that she could have shielded her friend from despair.

The man stepped closer to Faye. A siren sounded in Elizabeth's mind, urging her to hurry over there, to insert herself between them. Something about this wasn't right. But she couldn't uncurl her other fist from the railing.

"It's not a lie," he said. "It's a story."

Elizabeth felt the sting of something on her face and wondered for a disorienting moment who had thrown sand at her. But Faye and Leonard were staring each other down on the other side of the platform and Faye's parents had not yet appeared between the trees and nobody else was there. When she removed one of her hands slowly, fearfully, to wipe off her cheek, her fingertips came away glistening with ice.

"I may have introduced the Kingman to the world," Leonard said. He nodded toward Elizabeth and moved his fist as if brandishing an imaginary knife. "But you two are the ones who made him real."

Folie à deux. Wasn't that what Faye's aunt had called it? *You needed more than one mind to commit that crime.* Elizabeth didn't think that Faye had needed her to believe. But had she needed Faye?

Faye's voice, when she spoke again, was less certain. "It's just a *story*," she hissed.

Leonard was advancing on her. The weathered boards beneath him groaned in complaint. "What does that matter?" he demanded. All four of their sleeves were beaded with crystals, and the lake was continuing to hurl fistfuls of ice. "You know better than anyone that stories are living, breathing things. They weasel through your skin, your bones; they wriggle through your blood. They hunt you, haunt you. They're a part of you, yes, and also separate from you. It's impossible to articulate the boundaries."

He cocked his head to the side as if listening for something, but there was nothing but the plaintive moaning of the platform boards and the distant thunder of waves on the rocks.

"Stories are hard to get rid of," he concluded, now with both hands on Faye's shoulders. Faye was taller than Elizabeth had realized; she and Leonard were nearly eye to eye. Elizabeth saw her take a step backward, her foot slipping on the ice that was glazing the platform boards. "People are much easier to kill."

If there were ever a time for Elizabeth to release the railing and close the distance between them, it would have been then—when Leonard tightened his grip on Faye's shoulders and began shoving her, herding her, toward the edge of the tower. Faye raised her arms to push him off, and their bodies twisted and writhed in a knot of grappling limbs that Elizabeth could barely distinguish through the sheets of ice that were gusting from the sky. They slid on their four legs from one end of the platform to the other, their faces obscured in the clouds of their breath, their lips contorted, their gazes smoldering with rage or fear or concentration. When they skidded closer to Elizabeth, she swung out one arm and tried to make contact with Faye, but her fingers closed down on icy air. She tried again, with the same result, but the third time they lurched past her, she succeeded in grabbing a sleeve that turned out to be Leonard's, pulling him off-balance just enough for him to loosen his grip on Faye, so that she went spinning toward the railing. She made contact before she had time to fling up an arm to protect herself, and with horror Elizabeth heard the crack of bone against steel. Faye crumpled to the boards and lay there, warm and shimmering, a party dress discarded at the end of a dance.

Elizabeth started to stagger toward her, but Leonard reached her first. It would have been easy for him to tilt her over the side of the tower. Elizabeth pictured Faye's body whistling past the sheer rock face, her eyes wide, her hands and feet trailing behind her. She dropped to her hands and knees to scuttle faster, but the ice burned her palms and cut up her eyes, and so she was forced to stop, and look up through hot tears, as Leonard bent toward Faye and extended his arms. Elizabeth screamed, and the sound went ripping through the pines.

It could have been the scream that startled him, initially, into jerking upright and away. But it was something else that raised him to his full height again, and something else that made his wind-chapped face go suddenly, startlingly blank. Elizabeth had to blink furiously to get the water from her eyes, and even then, she couldn't see clearly through the glaze. She could tell that he was looking at something, but she had no idea what, only that his eyes were fixed on a spot directly above Faye, and that whatever it was had drawn the breath from his lungs because he was gasping, struggling for air, and then he was staggering backward with a hand thrown in front of him as if to ward off—whom? What? Not Faye, certainly, who remained where she had collapsed. And not Elizabeth herself, who was beached across the frosted planks like an ungainly fish on the sand, her chest heaving with exertion and panic, her skin clammy with goose bumps.

She strained to see what it was that had sent him reeling, but the ice was pelting down like tiny silver daggers and the wind was flinging ropes of her hair into her face and her eyes were burning with the cold and it was impossible to be certain of anything, of anyone, in the storm. All she knew was that something was propelling Leonard backward, and that by the time he heard the warning splinter of pine boards, it was too late—they were already splitting and sinking. Because she was peering in the same direction he was, she didn't see the boards give way to a fissure in the platform, to a serrated gap. But she heard the massive crack, and she whipped her head around in time to see his legs vanishing, and then his waist and his torso and his shoulders, and so she also saw the way his neck caught and snapped on one of the barbed planks as he fell, and she saw the way his eyes bulged and his jaw went slack, so that in the last glimpse she had of him, that anyone had of him, his face registered an expression of mingled astonishment and terror. Then the weight of his body jerked his chin free, and she could hear the syncopated thuds as his body struck the crossbeams on his way down.

For a few breaths she remained where she was. Then her name came weakly from the corner and she scuttled, crablike, to the place where Faye had fallen, and she patted at her friend's cold cheeks and raised her limp head into her own lap.

"Faye," she whispered, urgent and insistent. "Come on. We've got to get you down from here."

Faye groaned and curled her lip. "I can't." Her breath was shallower than it should have been. "It hurts too much."

"What hurts?"

Faye only groaned again and closed her eyes. From a hundred feet below them, Elizabeth heard a shout. The wind subsided, and she braved a look down to see two tiny people dashing out from the woods, halting at the base of the tower, and tilting back their heads to peer up.

"Faye, *open your eyes*," she said. "Don't you want to see your parents?"

Faye's eyelids flipped open and a little color splashed her cheeks. "My parents?"

"Right there." Elizabeth pointed as if Faye could see them, too. And then, as if it would be the easiest thing in the world, as if she wouldn't be terrified descending those icy rungs with one arm on the ladder and the other wrapped tightly around the person she loved most in the world: "We've almost made it. All we have to do is climb down."

Sylvia

As we strained toward the end of that trail, the trees grew taller and sparser, the air sparkling with ice, and my legs and lungs seared with the effort of climbing.

"What *is* this?" I asked Jack, turning my palms to the sky. My cheeks and neck prickled with the invisible blades of a million tiny crystals.

"Ice storm," he said. "Whipped up from the lake. Are you all right? Do you want to rest a minute?"

I did, but I couldn't. Black branches glimmered, and our shoes slipped and crunched on the path. The weather was already impeding our progress, slowing us down. We couldn't afford to stop.

"It was strange, wasn't it?" I said between ragged breaths as we shoved past the shrubbery that was overtaking the trail. "All of those things Elizabeth told us?"

The young woman's words were still tolling between my ears. Ever since she'd spoken, my head hadn't stopped ringing. Jack was behind me, so I couldn't see his face.

"Are you thinking about anything in particular?" he asked.

"Yes," I said. I'd been turning it over in my mind, trying to make sense of it, the whole drive up. "The part about how Faye wanted her to bring Amelia to me."

Another twenty or thirty steps. The snap of a twig beneath his boot; an unkindness of ravens lifting like wisps of midnight from the swaying tops of nearby cedars. The sound of the water, always, traveling beside us.

"Why is that strange?"

I halted in the middle of the path and he ran into me. "Whoa!" he said, his hands flying onto my upper arms in an effort to regain his balance. "Sorry, Syl." I could see his breath in the air, feel its heat on my neck.

"If Faye was willing to send Amelia to me," I said, desperate to believe the words as I uttered them, "then she trusted me with her."

It meant that she didn't think I was an incompetent parent, or that I'd failed her. Maybe it meant that she wasn't angry with me, that she didn't blame me. This idea expanded inside my body like a billowing sail, filling my lungs, my head, with air, so that I was surprised, when I tripped across a boulder in the middle of the path, to find that I was still earthbound.

"Of *course* Faye trusted you with her," Jack said. He stopped, and tugged on my arm so that I stopped, too. He narrowed his eyes and studied me for a long, crackling moment before placing his palms on either side of my face and holding it directly in front of his as if to ensure that I wouldn't be distracted, wouldn't be absent, that I had no choice but to hear him. When a creature rustled in the leaves behind me, I couldn't turn. I wouldn't turn. His voice, when he spoke again, was grave. "You're a good mother," he said. Then a quick shake of the head and a twist of the lips that I couldn't decipher. He drove his hands back down his sides, shoving them into pockets as if he didn't trust them. "Now, come on," he said. "We're nearly there."

I turned back toward the summit with tingling limbs, newly aware of Jack's heat and proximity behind me. As we completed the climb, I imagined how it would be to gather my daughter in my arms, how she'd tuck her head into my shoulder, how Jack would stride up to us, too, and widen his arms and fold us both into his chest. All these years, I'd believed that Faye hadn't wanted to hear from me, hadn't wanted to think of me—but if I'd been wrong, then a different kind of future not only was possible but was beginning to take shape, to become real, the higher I climbed and the closer we came to our daughter.

My heart, in other words, was light. And so I wasn't expecting the fresh battery of ice that pelted my face as I rounded the bend and exited the woods, nor the silver mist that slunk around my ankles and snaked up my legs and my torso before clenching my chest. I gaped at the tower rearing out of the murk like an ancient, mechanical beast, and when I shielded my eyes from the ice and glimpsed the snarl of heads and limbs writhing together at the top of the platform, I didn't see my daughter in them. I could only see her monster.

"The Kingman," I murmured. *Of course.*

Another flash of memory: Jack encircling my waist on a New York balcony, the sleet filling up my eyes, the café au lait searing my tongue, the desire for a baby throbbing through my bones.

"What if I were enough for you?" he'd whispered. The hair on my arms rose beneath the crinkly sleeves of my windbreaker. "What if we were enough for each other?"

Enough. From the Old English *genog,* meaning to reach a place together.

We stood there for a minute, swaying on our feet, peering up into the gloom and trying to determine what had caused the high-pitched sound that split the clouds. Then the wind died down and the air cleared, and a bulky creature was making its ponderous way down the steel rungs toward us.

"It's Elizabeth," breathed Jack, beside me. "With Faye."

My blood slushed through my legs when I tried to lift them. There was something wrong with the way they were moving; the way Elizabeth was gripping Faye, the way that Faye's shoulders slumped and her limp, ice-studded hair shrouded her face. I couldn't drag myself closer. I couldn't bring myself to find out. And so I remained frozen to the cold ground beneath my feet while Jack dashed around the side of the tower to meet the girls as they descended. I saw how Elizabeth bore nearly all of Faye's weight, and how my daughter's head tipped back and lolled over her shoulder. I watched Elizabeth pass her to Jack, who leaned her up against the steel beams and pushed her hair from her cheeks and her neck and checked her pulse and pressed his ear to her lips to listen to her breath. He was too far away for me to read his face, to know how to interpret it, and so I didn't know what to think, how to feel, until the three of them shuffled across the peak to reach me. Elizabeth led the way, and Jack followed with Faye in his arms, her eyes closed and jaw slack and her face and hands bloodless and her right arm bent in a way that seemed impossible.

The wind howled harder around me, and Mount Josephine lurched underfoot. The joy I'd felt on the trail evaporated. *Was this it?* I needed to wade toward them, to find out the truth, but my arms were tangled in a diamond-studded net, and my legs were torpid, laden with ice. I felt that I was treading lake water while someone was gripping my feet and dragging me deeper, farther from the shoals.

If Faye was gone, then there was something that I needed to say, something I would tell them if I could only get closer, but the words had deserted me, turned to water and then to glass. I was yanked back twenty-three years to the moment of her birth, and I opened my mouth to say something about that hospital, something about the thirty-hour labor and something about how, when she finally emerged, her skin was faintly blue—like that, like it was now—and she was shrieking like a fury. I wanted to tell them that when the nurses cut the umbilical cord, I *felt* it—the snap in my soul, the severance of my body from hers, the empty chasm of my womb. What I tried to say to them as the distance closed between us, what I thought I was saying, if the syllables spinning around my ears like snow, like sleet, were mine, is that I'd been feeling my child grow away from me for the past twenty-three years, that if Faye had gone from me now, then it was only the most recent departure in a series of departures, that I finally realized what I should have seen coming, that motherhood is simply one loss after another. I wanted to tell them how I thought that parenthood would fill me up, satiate me, but instead? I tried to shake my head, but the motion didn't feel the way it used to. Was I still standing? What was this rock, this moss? What had brought me to my knees? *Listen*, I said then, if I was still speaking, if they could hear me over the wind and the water, *listen* to me. What I'm trying to tell you is that none of this matters. You see? I wanted to laugh savagely, maniacally, at the glaring banality of it. What was today among all other days? *I have been losing her since the minute she was born.*

Jack

The closest hospital was two hours south, so Jack veered toward a local clinic near the water. He drove wildly, erratically, crashing over potholes and sliding up to stoplights on the slippery roadway. Elizabeth sat rigidly in the passenger seat beside him, looking for signs and trying to direct him, while Sylvia propped Faye up in the back seat and murmured to her in a steady flow of syllables in order to keep her awake.

The clouds had lifted a little, but night was falling. The bruised sky throbbed above the trees. The clinic, when they reached it, crouched at the far edge of a dim and empty parking lot with only a handful of its windows glowing orange.

Sylvia paced back and forth across the lobby floor while Faye was being examined. She eyed the nurses' station worriedly and refused to drink the instant coffees that Jack kept pouring for her. He waited for her to walk all the way down to the far end of the hallway before approaching the woman at the front desk. Her hair fell to her shoulders, concealing her face as she read the book she'd propped against the computer keyboard.

"Excuse me," he said. "How do I report—" It took him a minute to find the right word. "An accident? On Mount Josephine?"

She continued studying the page in front of her. "What kind of accident?"

"A fall. From the fire tower. I think—I think there's probably a body in the woods."

That got her to look at him. "Whose body?"

"Just—" Where to begin? "I don't know. I'd never met him. My daughter knew him from—" The woman had closed her book now. "From school. Anyway—usually I'd just call the police, but I know that we're on Native land. Is there a tribal council? Or someone else I should contact?"

"There's a council, yeah. But they don't deal with this kind of thing." She extended a long arm toward the phone on her desk and dragged it toward her. "We contract with the county sheriff. I can call them if you want."

"Please," Jack said with a long exhalation. "Thank you. I'll be right over there."

He turned toward the white plastic chairs set against the wall of the waiting area and sank into the one beneath the single window. On a corner table, a lamp with a cracked ceramic base tossed a half-hearted light across a glossy splay of magazines. After a few minutes, Elizabeth dropped into the chair beside him.

"Are you doing all right?" he asked.

She nodded. They listened to the squish of Sylvia's steps growing fainter.

"Thank God she was awake for the descent," Elizabeth said. "It was only right at the end that she passed out again. How would I have gotten her down?"

"You did great," he said, meaning it.

Her cheeks flushed. "But the professor—" she began. "What do we do about—"

"I'll talk to the sheriff. They'll send someone out tomorrow. So you don't need to worry about that." He patted the back of her hand briefly, distractedly, picturing a body in the woods. A rope around the tower. "You didn't do anything wrong."

An orderly clipped by with a medicine cart, and after the clattering had subsided, Elizabeth said: "Right before it happened— before he fell—I could have sworn—" She shook her head at herself. "I could have sworn that he saw something."

"What do you mean? What kind of thing?"

She shrugged with a kind of performed carelessness. "Something that terrified him."

Jack tried to picture the monster on the platform, but in his mind the Kingman was always wearing the costume of an amateur stage production: a tattered cloak, a cardboard crown, a crudely carved wooden mask that impeded his breathing. None of this was scary to him. And now Elizabeth claimed to have seen the man behind the monster, the wizard behind the curtain. In the car, she'd told Jack and Sylvia what Faye had discovered: how the professor had invented the creature, how he'd fabricated the research. So what remained to be frightened of? To Jack, the Kingman had become—and maybe always had been—a question of psychology, not mythology.

"Why the hell did he do it?" Jack muttered.

Half of Elizabeth's face was cast in shadow. "Maybe he was lonely."

Jack grimaced. "Or maybe he just wanted to see if he could."

Elizabeth fell silent. Jack watched Sylvia pace to the window, peer out into the parking lot, and then return to the hallway. Something in the image spun him back to Boston again, to that November walk to the art museum. The three of them had ambled through the paintings and circled the sculptures. When they'd finally emerged, the sun had sunk behind the buildings. The sky had turned navy blue, and a fistful of snowflakes was falling. As they'd followed Faye's chalk arrows in the direction of the hotel, he'd felt his face warming. His happiness had been such a solid thing that he could almost grasp it in his hand.

"It's not a concussion," the nurse emerged from the examination room to tell them. Sylvia jolted to a halt to listen. "She passed out from the pain of the break. Doesn't help that she's overtired and thin as a rail and probably anemic. We'll know for sure when the blood test comes back. What's her appetite like?" When no one

answered, the nurse continued: "Well, what she needs most is rest
and sustenance. We'll set the arm and discharge her with a hefty
pack of vitamins and a light sleeping aid. After that, you can take
her home."

Jack was feeling faint. "If we were to stay in town for the night,"
he asked, "is there a place you'd recommend? A nearby hotel?"

The nurse cocked his head. "There's a group of cabins about a
mile up the road. They're associated with the clinic, for when families want to be nearby. If you want, I can call the property manager
to see if something is available."

Jack pictured a bed, a blanket, a shower, a fire. "That would be
great."

"If you have the choice of something near the water or something in the woods, what's your preference?"

The conifers uncoiling over the trail; the ice clinging to pine
needles; the stumps and logs that came out of nowhere, hampering
their progress as they stumbled down the ridge toward the car. He
couldn't handle any more trees.

"The water, I guess," he said. "It would be good to see the sky."

Of course the night was ink black by the time they arrived at the
house on the lakeshore, and so there wasn't any sky to see. But the
cabin itself was something peeled from a scenic postcard: painted
log walls, a wraparound porch. Smoke twisted from the chimney
and lights blazed through the windows because the property manager had stopped by before them to warm the place up. In the yard,
they passed the bulky outline of a shed and a weather-worn rowboat tipped up against its siding. They filed through a low door
to find stone floors and paneled wood ceilings, a fireplace and a
kitchenette. Sylvia, who had been holding Faye's good arm as she
helped her out of the car and into the house, guided her to the sofa
and eased her into it, then began pulling blankets out of a basket
beside her and piling them over Faye's thighs until Faye laughed,
weakly, and told her that she was plenty warm.

While Sylvia put a kettle on, Jack and Elizabeth finished explor-
ing. A cramped hallway deposited them in a room with twin beds
and a tidy half bath. Elizabeth dropped her bag on one of the beds
and then followed him up a set of steep stairs leading to a master
suite whose airy ceilings and crisp white walls made the room feel
twice as big as it was. Covering the walls were black-and-white
photographs of the town and its environs when the cabin had
been built a hundred years ago. Elizabeth paused before each one,
squinting at the glass.

The most beautiful space was the sunroom just off the dining
area: a sofa, a writing desk, a standing lamp, and floor-to-ceiling
windows that opened out onto the black mass of water forever rolling in from the horizon. For several minutes Jack stood at those
windows, pretending to peer out into the night when what he
was really watching were the luminous reflections of his wife and
daughter moving through the room behind him.

At the table, they unwrapped the burgers and fries they'd picked
up. When Faye entered the room and sank into a chair, Jack saw
that she'd taken a shower and that someone had braided her hair.
She was wearing a shapeless cardigan and a long cotton skirt.
The gauntness of her face had turned her gray eyes to lakes. He'd
ordered a chocolate milkshake for her, recalling the joy she'd taken
in drive-throughs and soft serve as a child. But as soon as she sat
down at the table, she stood up again, waving away their insistence
that she eat something.

"Is there a phone?" she asked. "I need to check in on Amelia
before I go to bed."

He knew that Sylvia had hundreds of questions to ask. He could
feel them sparking from her like static. But when she tried to speak,
Faye raised a bony, aged hand. She shook her head, her features
whittled and her expression blanched. "I can't," she said. "I'm so
drained. We'll talk in the morning, okay?"

Her skin was splotched with bruises. Her left arm, bulky in a cast, rested awkwardly at her side. But she still looked like her-self; like her many selves. In her face, Jack could see the child she had been. The layers of her life were stacked one over another like striations in a canyon wall.

She must have seen, as he did, the disappointment descend over Sylvia's face, because after she pushed her chair back under the table, she moved to her mother. There she bent down, wrapped a slender arm around Sylvia's shoulder, and rested her head lightly on her neck. Jack saw Sylvia's arms rise to enfold Faye; he saw, over Faye's shoulders, how tightly Sylvia pressed her eyelids shut. He watched Sylvia inhale deeply, slowly. Faye murmured a string of syllables in her mother's ear, but he couldn't make out the words. When Faye drew back, she met Sylvia's eyes. Whatever passed between them then was something that he didn't know how to decipher, but Sylvia's expression was so radiant that it looked as though a light had been turned on inside her.

Then Faye was straightening up and approaching his chair, too, and before she reached him he clattered to his feet so that the embrace, when it came, was solid. As he tightened his arms around his daughter, she whispered something to him, too, and it was only after she'd released him that the words registered as *thank you*.

Her bearing, as she left the room, struck him as regal. She angled into the hallway, rounded the corner, and was gone.

Upstairs, Jack found a telescope stationed at one of the windows. He stood near it for a few minutes, listening to the gentle thunder of the water. He could hear Sylvia turning the tap on and off down-stairs, crumpling paper food containers into the trash bin, carrying drinking glasses from the table to the sink. When a light winked at him from the horizon, he swung the telescope toward him to see what it was. A ship, probably. A freighter of some kind. But when he squinted through the eyepiece and rotated the tube, he couldn't locate it again.

He already knew that he wouldn't return to his mountain cabin. The wind below him throttling the bare branches of dogwood and sassafras. The kestrels hunting among the spruce firs. Winter on the way, bright and stifling.

While the shower was heating up, he peeled off his clothing and dropped the pieces in a heap of mud and pine. His skin was clammy, his torso etched with scratches, his arms and legs aching from bearing Faye down that trail. Once the room was steeped in steam, he pulled back a corner of the shower curtain and eased himself into the tub. For a long minute, he stood as still as he could while the downpour massaged and pummeled his shoulder blades. His limbs felt leaden; his heart cold. He waited like an ice sculpture in the liquid heat, willing the warm water to melt layer after layer until nothing of his old self remained.

Then: a distant knock on the bathroom door, so faint beneath the rush of water that he wasn't certain he'd really heard it. The rattle of a doorknob turning, and two familiar steps.

"Jack?" Sylvia's voice eased into his scrapes, his aches, like a balm. He pressed his palm against the tiled wall to steady himself, to keep his suddenly weak knees from collapsing.

The grinding teeth of a zipper. The shuffle of a sweatshirt tumbling to the bath mat. A second later, the slap of bare feet on tile. He didn't speak, fearing he would say the wrong thing and send her reeling away from him again. Through the steam he could see her shadow on the wall, languid and elongated, stretching an impossibly distended arm toward the shower curtain. In a second, he knew, a row of fingers would appear. She would flex her arm, bend her elbow, and draw the curtain back.

It's possible that he misread Sylvia on the day that he walked into his examination room and found her reading in that reclining chair. The searing blow to his chest that he interpreted as recognition, as love—that could have been, instead, a kind of black premonition.

A warning that he didn't know how to heed. When he saw the glint of a stone on her finger, maybe he should have let her go. When he discovered her fiancé prowling up and down the aisles of the optical shop, he could have pressed her hand politely and said a cordial goodbye. She might have married the other guy. They might have produced five or six children together, each one more doe-eyed and cherubic than the last. She might not have found herself alone in a courtroom with her only child in chains before her and her pigeonhearted husband skulking through the tomb of their house, too gutless to join her.

But when he tried to picture himself releasing her hand, he couldn't do it. The minute her fingers grazed his, he'd been electrified. The spectacles lining the walls had sparkled. At the end of that day, after he'd sent the receptionist home and locked up the shop, he'd floated down the darkened sidewalk and he'd been convinced that everyone he passed could see the change in him. Their faces were illuminated by the light streaming out of his pores.

The water pounded down from the showerhead, and he was battling for breath again. Then she was before him, her flesh veiled in steam, her body older, softer. She closed her eyes as he lifted a soapy hand and passed it over her collarbone, between her breasts, across her navel. He held his breath when she bent to wash the sand and the mud from his shins, his knees, the insides of his thighs. His head was spinning by the time she rose to her feet and slipped her fingers through his hair. *How did we lose each other?* he would have asked her, if she had not closed the distance between them, if he had not wrapped a slick arm around her waist and pulled her to his chest with a groan so low that it hummed through both of their veins.

Her lips were warm against his ear, his cheek, and then her mouth was on his, his tongue flickering against hers, their mouths wet and clumsy and hungry and familiar. As he leaned her gently against the wall of the shower, as he pressed his lips to her skin, he heard her footsteps ringing on their old front porch and he saw the dazzle of celestial lights in the lake and he wondered at how strange it was: all the unfathomable ways in which we show our love for each other in the dark.

Sylvia

Over the years that Faye had been absent from me, I'd begun to think of her as a fiction. But there was once a time when I could cradle her body in one arm. When my muscles burned from the weight of her, when my nipples chafed from her hunger. I slid thermometers under her tongue, pressed damp washcloths to her brow. I wiped up the floor when she vomited. I cleaned her skinned knees and dug splinters from her fingers with a disinfected needle.

Once upon a time she existed in my world not only as a memory but also as a body, as a person built of flesh, blood, and bone. When she embraced me before leaving the table that night, she felt just as I imagined she would. The knobby shoulders. The long limbs, light and strong. The dark mane of her hair knotted and wild, matted with mud and leaves. The smell of mud and sugar in the hollow of her collarbone. The body, now unknowable and strange, that was once a part of mine.

After stepping out of the shower, I wrapped myself in a giant beach towel and descended the stairs to check on her. She was sound asleep beneath a checkered quilt. Elizabeth was dreaming in the bed next to hers. The blinds that I was certain I'd drawn across the windows were open again, and a distant light glimmered along the surface of the lake.

Exhaustion pressed pale blue thumbprints beneath her eyes.

Her braided hair gleamed. I sat down on her bed and set my hand on hers—warily, experimentally. But her breathing didn't change, and her eyelids didn't flutter. When I lifted my hand away, the scrapes on her knuckles skated against my palm.

In the morning, she'd promised. We'd talk about everything in the morning.

I lingered in the room long enough for my eyes to grow accustomed to the darkness. Soon I could discern the outline of the dresser across the room, the wooden chair stiff and expectant in a corner, the faint glow of the brass bed frames. Through the slats in the blinds, I caught a glimpse of a frail moon suspended over the water, and I was tempted, almost, to walk outside and stand on the pebbles at the edge of the shore.

I pulled myself away from my daughter and returned upstairs and padded barefoot across the cold floor to the bed, where the shape of my former husband stirred beneath the comforter. The air was thick and sweet as I slid onto the pillow beside him, and when he rolled over to face me, his eyes shone like pearls underwater.

He eased closer to me and nestled his chin into the space between my neck and shoulder. Something about the weight of him there released a latch in my chest, and suddenly I was breathing easier. For how many years had I been holding my breath?

"I read an essay once," he murmured, still half-asleep, "about a man who was sitting in a café, eating an almond croissant, when his dead wife walked through the door."

How had he known what I was thinking, feeling? Could he sense in my skin the way that I was coming back to life?

"I had to close the book and check the cover to confirm that it was nonfiction," he continued. He rolled onto his back and aimed his words toward the ceiling. "The author turned out to be an immunologist who was making an argument about how we store memories in the physical fibers of our bodies."

Even though it felt like day should be breaking, our room was still dark. Jack lifted his head from the pillow and propped him-self up on his elbow. "Do you remember the day that she was released? I drove down to meet you, and we waited in the park-ing lot until we saw her talking to that police officer through the lobby windows?"

"How could I forget?" The sky had burned with a flame-colored sunset; my whole body had longed to gather my girl in my arms. But when she finally appeared, grown-up and beautiful and mov-ing in a way that was somehow both familiar and strange, I couldn't bring myself to touch her.

"For years, I've wished that I'd hugged her," Jack said. "I don't know why I didn't."

The waves roared in my ears. I was remembering her embrace at the dining table, her sharp chin resting in the scoop of my col-larbone and the bones of her shoulders as delicate, as hollow, as a bird's. I felt, rather than heard, Faye tell me not to worry. Her voice was embedded in my muscles, my limbs. I'd waited so long for that moment, so long to fold her against me, that when it finally hap-pened, it didn't feel real.

"But tonight," I reminded Jack, "you did. You hugged her."

He sank back into his pillow and tugged me closer to him. "That's what I'm saying. The people we love the best are never lost to us, Syl. We store them in our blood, in our lymph nodes, in the marrow of our bones." He pressed his lips to my neck, and my fingers tingled. "We don't always understand how or why certain memories return to us in certain places, at certain times," he whis-pered. "So why should it surprise us if the people we've lost return to us in the hour when we least expect them?"

I remembered the bungalow squatting among the dried sea-grasses. The wind weaving gold strands through the waves. The click of the caseworker's heels and the rumble of her car engine and the cries of the gulls as they pinwheeled overhead. My arms ached, as they always would, with the weight of a missing child.

So I filled my arms with Jack and inhaled the cedar scent of the man I would never stop loving. *Soul mates.* As his heartbeat thudded in time with mine and my body rose and fell with his, I saw us morphing into a single beast with two dark heads and four glistening eyes and more twisting, slithering limbs than anyone could count.

Faye

She knew that Elizabeth was awake without turning her head to look at her. Something in the room had changed: there had been a noise, a scent, a glimmer of metal or teeth. She didn't know exactly what. Then, layered above and beneath the sound of the waves, a high-pitched bark.

Elizabeth's voice wormed through the gloom. "Have you ever heard of *folie à deux?*"

Leonard had mentioned it in his class. "The madness of two," she murmured.

A silence, during which the shadows stretched and shifted on the ceiling above them and a question pulsed between them. It was Elizabeth who finally posed it.

"Were we the ones who made it real?"

Faye didn't answer. Something was gathering at the edges of her consciousness. What was different in the house? What was lurking here that hadn't been before? Why couldn't she put her finger on it, tap it, make it disappear?

She rose from her bed and moved to the window. When she pulled up the shades, a thick stroke of turquoise was singing across the horizon. She could feel the currents in her hair, her fingers. She could see the boat propped up against the sagging shed, its shadow long and rippling and blue. She could see the outline of an island in the distance, ringed with stars. She remembered the cries of her child, startling awake from nightmares in the dark, sweat soaked and inconsolable. Hadn't Faye promised to protect her?

The creak of bedsprings, and then bare feet across the floor behind her. Her best friend's whisper: "How will we know for sure that it's over?"

"We won't," Faye said. "Unless we see for ourselves."

Sylvia

How strange it was to lie beside my husband for the first time in years. My chest moved in time with his and the air between us grew silky with dreams.

That's when it came to me: the memory of the ramshackle church nudging up against the train tracks, its pews in boxes and its stained glass rippled with age. When I had stepped through the open doors, the sun blazing behind me, my veil like a white flame, Jack's gaze fixed gravely, unblinkingly, on mine, everybody in the building had gasped in unison. He was supposed to stand still and wait at the altar for me to reach him. But instead we went sailing toward each other across the ancient floorboards, blown together by an inner wind that cycloned through us both. He met me halfway down the aisle, and I snatched his hand before he could change his mind. Those final steps we took together, our faces glistening in the late-spring heat, our heels ringing through the wood—even now, knowing what I do, I wouldn't give them back for anything.

As I lay among the beveled shadows of that unfamiliar house, I heard different footsteps ringing from a place I could not reach. I wriggled out from underneath the quilt and padded barefoot to the window. On the other side of the glass, the slope down to the water was cloaked in fog, obscuring the tangle of grasses, the narrow stone beach, the ebb and flow of waves. In the distance, twinkling in and out of sight, the glimmer of a ship. I couldn't say exactly what it was I was waiting for as I watched the mist billow over black water like a ghost in the dark. A sign, I guess. A messenger. A silhouette on the shoreline, a phantom island on the move.

Sanity is a matter of borders: inside versus outside, truth versus dream, fact versus fiction. How can a person tell, at any given hour, on any given sleepless night, what side of the line she is on?

I imagined Jack's palm tightening against mine. *They are the shapes we have given to grief and terror.* His words in my ear: "Come back to bed, my love. Your eyes are playing tricks on you."

Mama. My daughter's voice, swirling through my ears like wind through sand. *You're dreaming again.*

I can see why I became obsessed with the idea of changelings. What a relief it would be to learn that your strange child, your violent child, your absent child, wasn't your child at all. What if your true baby—innocent, bright, generous, kind—was waiting in the woods for you to find her and bring her home?

Then again, you can't help but love the one who happens to be in your arms. It is your duty to feed her and bathe her and keep her alive. And after a while, you find yourself falling in love with this mysterious stranger. You find that you can't cut yourself away from her. That no matter what she does, you'll love her until the end of your days.

Are you happy that you had your daughter? Of course it is easier to love someone good than it is to love someone bad. But most of the time, we don't get to choose.

Before I'd joined Jack upstairs the night before, I'd tidied up the kitchen with Elizabeth. She scrubbed the silverware clean while I wiped down the table. The lamplight shone on her face and exposed, once again, the girl that she had been: quiet, awkward, grief-stricken. Before I was consciously aware of the impulse, I'd gathered the young woman in my arms and drawn her to my chest. Here she was in the same house as me, as my daughter, as my husband. Here we were, eating at the same table and sleeping beneath the same roof. The blast of joy that surged through me at this realization, this unexpected resolution, would have knocked me over if I had not been holding her so tightly.

After the first stiffening shock of the embrace, her shoulders eased and her muscles thawed. *How lonely she must have been*, I thought, *all those years after Faye.*

When I let her go, her eyes were damp. She swiped a hand across them and cleared her throat. "I'm sorry," she said.

The ice maker rattled in the freezer. Above our heads, the creak of a few protesting floorboards.

"Should I have been there?" I asked.

She didn't ask me to clarify. Did I mean the stabbing in the park? The years after the detention center? The battle on the fire tower? She simply shrugged and shook her head. "Nobody can be there all the time."

Her words hung in the air even after she'd left the room and gone to bed. They were still echoing in my ears when I picked up the phone to call my sister. She answered after half a ring.

"Sylvie," she said, sounding breathless. "Is everything all right? Faye called to check in, so I figured—"

"We found her."

"Right. I didn't talk to her; Leila answered and passed the phone right to Amelia. How is she?"

"Fine. Asleep now. A broken arm, a few bruises. She's exhausted, but okay."

"Where are you?"

I leaned against the counter, studying my reflection in the darkened window. "We're staying the night in a cabin in Grand Portage. We should be back tomorrow."

My sister hesitated. Then: "You're welcome to stay with us for a while. If you want."

I smiled into the receiver. "Thanks. We might."

For a few beats, neither of us spoke. I pictured my sister in her kitchen, too, the phone pressed against a face that looked a little bit like Faye's and like mine.

"They were up there, you know," Rosie told me. "The guys who made the documentary. They said that they were looking for Isle Philippeaux."

"Did they find anything?"

"I guess they shot a lot of footage in the woods and along the shoreline. They even rented a boat and motored out beyond Isle Royale, looking for the island. But when they returned to their studio and played the tape back, the footage was unusable."

"Unusable how?"

"White and fuzzy. Full of static. They thought about going back and trying again, but they were at the end of the project by then and already over budget."

From the recesses of my mind came the white crackle of investigators' tapes; the snap of a phone line going suddenly, inexplicably dead. I found myself thinking about the crumpled photo I'd found in my wallet while retrieving my driver's license for airport security two days before. It's one that Jack took years ago on the beach by my mother's house, watching me walk with Faye along the sea, snapping the shutter closed just as she reached up and I reached down, so that our fingers touched. We're ambling west, she and I, toward the setting sun, and so it's only our silhouettes that the viewer can see: my head bent toward my daughter, her hair blowing back in the salty breeze, our shadows trailing behind us.

Once I made it through the security line, I dropped onto a bench and studied it while passengers blurred past me, and announcements blared from somewhere overhead. How had I never noticed the other shadow in it before—the one snaking toward our silhouettes? I raised the photograph so close to my face that my eyes crossed. It was only then that I saw the Kingman right there on the coffee-colored sand beside us, waiting just beyond the borders of the frame.

Most of the time, the things we lose are not restored to us. I know this.

But I can't help hoping that when the sun finally rises, when the sky is painted with coral and peach, when the night sinks back into the water and the world reawakens, my daughter will not be gone. I am hoping that when I descend that narrow staircase and cross the cold pine floors to their bedroom, I'll find her fast asleep next to her old friend, their hands tucked beneath their cheeks and the slippery strands of their hair tangled between their fingers. Their coats will still be dangling from the kitchen hooks. The prints of their tennis shoes will not be pressed into the packed dirt path leading down the yard to the shed, the beach, the crosshatched surface of the lake. The boat will not be missing. The monster will not be calling to them, beckoning to them, from a copse of snowcapped cedars while a great gray lake smashes against ice-encrusted boulders and incandescent stones.

Maybe, when I go looking for them, they will still be sleeping. Maybe my footsteps on the floor will wake them and we'll sit at the table drinking coffee and orange juice while the white light slides into the kitchen and the wind whispers through the firs and the house fills with the scent of pine boughs, of pancakes, of stars. Maybe Faye will tell me everything. Maybe, after a while, we'll all walk outside and drive home together, the road rippling like a silver arrow beneath us, pointing us toward something different, something new. Maybe we will finally leave our monsters behind.

It's a vision, it's a hope. It's a fiction, of course. But if I've learned anything from my daughter, it's this: sometimes we can dream things into being.

Acknowledgments

Writing a novel can be a monstrous undertaking. It took me many years to capture this story and pin it to the pages you hold here. I couldn't have it done it alone.

I am grateful to my editor, Caitlin Landuyt, who recognized the potential lurking in an early draft and whose edits and insights helped me bring the story into focus. Laura Langlie, my agent, read revision after revision with patience and insight and good cheer. She never gave up on this project, even when I was ready to give up on it myself.

My work was supported by a travel grant from Augsburg University, where I teach English and creative writing, and also by the wonderful staff of the Jentel Foundation, who awarded me one of their residency spots in a light-filled home surrounded by vast skies and golden hills. Jentel gave me the gift of time, space, and a community of artists whose talent and dedication to their craft continue to inspire me.

I am grateful for the friends and family who, over the years, offered me a critical eye or a sympathetic ear. Several hardy souls were willing to brave the fictional forests with me: Ruth Ann Elias and Christine Schwichtenberg were early, enthusiastic readers; Katie Barthelmes helped brainstorm alternative endings. I am fortunate to count some wonderful writers as my friends: Sarah Myers and Carson Kreitzer, whose talent and warmth kept me going at home and abroad; Eric Rasmussen, whose insights profoundly shaped the early drafts; Bob Cowgill, whose affirmations never failed to lift my spirits; and Leslie Bazzett, whose keen editorial eye made the book sharper, shorter, and stronger.

My father continues to show his steadfast support by keeping me supplied with lattes and breakfast pastries and by saving a whole shelf in his office for my work. My mother reads every word of every draft and comes heroically to my aid when I decide to rewrite the entire ending a week before the deadline.

And to Chris, my partner in adventures both mundane and fantastical: if everything is make-believe, I'm glad I get to make it up with you.